The Hen of the Baskervilles

The Hen of the Baskervilles

A Meg Langslow Mystery

Donna Andrews

Minotaur Books

A Thomas Dunne Book
New York

A THOMAS DUNNE BOOK FOR MINOTAUR BOOKS.
An imprint of St. Martin's Publishing Group.

THE HEN OF THE BASKERVILLES. Copyright © 2013 by Donna Andrews. All rights reserved. Printed in the United States of America. For information, address St. Martin's Press, 175 Fifth Avenue, New York, N.Y. 10010.

www.thomasdunnebooks.com
www.minotaurbooks.com

Library of Congress Cataloging-in-Publication Data

Andrews, Donna.
   The hen of the Baskervilles : a Meg Langslow mystery / Donna Andrews. — First edition.
      p. cm.
   "A Thomas Dunne book."
   ISBN 978-1-250-00751-3 (hardcover)
   ISBN 978-1-250-02299-8 (e-book)
   1. Langslow, Meg (Fictitious character)—Fiction.   2. Murder—Investigation—Fiction.   I. Title.
   PS3551.N4165H48 2013
   813'.54—dc23

                                                      2013009814

Minotaur books may be purchased for educational, business, or promotional use. For information on bulk purchases, please contact Macmillan Corporate and Premium Sales Department at 1-800-221-7945 extension 5442 or write specialmarkets@macmillan.com.

First Edition: July 2013

10 9 8 7 6 5 4 3 2 1

To Sally Fellows,
the perfect reader

Acknowledgments

Thanks, as always, to everyone at St. Martin's/Minotaur, including (but not limited to) Matt Baldacci, Anne Brewer, Hector DeJean, Kymberlee Giacoppe, Lauren Hesse, Andrew Martin, Sarah Melnyk, Matthew Shear, and my editor, Pete Wolverton. And thanks again to the Art Department for yet another fabulous cover.

More thanks to my agent, Ellen Geiger, and the staff at the Frances Goldin Literary Agency for handling the boring (to me) practical stuff so I can focus on writing, and to Dave Barbor at Curtis Brown for taking Meg abroad.

Many thanks to the friends—writers and readers alike—who brainstorm and critique with me, give me good ideas, or help keep me sane while I'm writing: Stuart, Elke, Aidan and Liam Andrews, Renee Brown, Erin Bush, Carla Coupe, Meriah Crawford, Kathy Deligianis, Laura Durham, Suzanne Frisbee, John Gilstrap, Barb Goffman, Peggy Hansen, C. Ellett Logan, David Niemi, Alan Orloff, Valerie Patterson, Shelley Shearer, Art Taylor, Robin Templeton, Dina Willner, and Sandi Wilson. Thanks for all kinds of moral support and practical help to my blog sisters and brother at the Femmes Fatales: Dana Cameron, Charlaine Harris, Dean James, Toni L.P. Kelner, Catriona McPherson, Kris Neri, Hank Phillipi Ryan, Mary Saums, Marcia Talley, and Elaine Viets. And thanks to all the TeaBuds for years of friendship.

Meg's mother's sojourn in the wine pavilion was made easier by Ellen Crosby's expert advice. Anything I got wrong is obviously something I failed to ask her about.

I originally planned to set this book at the official Virginia State Fair, and spent many happy hours there absorbing all the local color. I had no clue that by the time I sat down to write, the fair would be in financial peril and perhaps in danger of disappearing. While Meg and Randall Shiffley probably aren't too keen on having the competition, I am delighted that, at least for the time being, the fair, under its new ownership, is going strong. Long may it continue!

The Hen of the Baskervilles

Chapter 1

I woke up to find three sheep staring pensively down at me.

I stared back, wondering how they'd gotten into Michael's and my bedroom. And whether they'd been there long enough to cause a cleanup nightmare. And why they were staring at my hair, which might be dry and in need of conditioner, but in no way resembled hay. And—

I finally realized that the sheep hadn't invaded my home. In fact, you could argue that I was invading theirs. I was sleeping in a pen in our local fair's sheep and llama exhibition barn. Sleeping solo, without my husband, Michael, at my side and our twin two-a-half-year-olds down the hall. I'd probably awakened because one of the sheep had baaed. I should turn over and get some more sleep before—

"Meg?"

Not coming from the sheep. I sat up and shoved the sleeping bag as far down as it would go. Then I looked around. I didn't see anyone. It was only just starting to get light outside, as I could see through the sides of the barn, which was actually a lot more like a giant carport, all roof and no walls. The sheep were looking over the fence between their pen and the one in which I'd been sleeping. I turned a little farther, and saw that our family's five llamas, in the pen on my other side, were also watching me with the keen interest llamas always took in human behavior.

Maybe I'd imagined the voice.

"Meg?"

I turned all the way round to see a small, meek-looking man standing in the aisle between the rows of pens. He was wearing a green and yellow John Deere baseball cap and a green t-shirt that said KEEP CALM AND JOIN 4-H. Presumably a farmer.

I glanced at my watch. It was 6:33 A.M. This had better be important.

"Can I help you?" I asked aloud.

"Having trouble finding some chickens," he said.

I waited to hear more, but he just stared back at me.

"That could be because this is the sheep barn," I said, in the careful, calm voice and very precise pronunciation that would have revealed to anyone who knew me that I was not happy about being awakened by someone too clueless to read his fair map. "If you're looking for chickens, you should try the chicken tent. You can find it—"

"I know where the chicken tent is." He sounded offended. "I'm the volunteer monitor for it."

"Oh! I'm so sorry." I peered at him as if I needed glasses, though actually my eyesight was still pretty close to twenty–twenty. "I'm not at my best in the morning." Especially not before dawn. "You said you're having trouble finding some chickens? What chickens?" When I'd gone to bed—not all that long ago, actually—the chicken tent had been half full of birds brought in by farmers who were arriving early to the fair.

"Pair of bantam Russian Orloffs," the farmer said. "Owners came in this morning and had a conniption fit when they found them missing. They think they've been stolen. Could just be that they left the cage unlatched or something, but I figured you'd want to know about it."

Suddenly I was very wide awake.

"Have you called the police?" I asked as I scrambled the rest of the way out of my sleeping bag.

"Not yet." He looked sheepish."Wasn't sure if I was supposed to. Tried to find the mayor, but he's not around, so I thought I'd tell you. You're his go-to girl on this fair project, right?"

"Deputy director," I corrected him, managing not to snarl it. "Call the police while I put my shoes on." Except for my shoes and socks, I was already dressed. Given the very public nature of my bedroom stall in the sheep barn, I'd decided to sleep in my clothes.

I listened in on his call while rummaging through my baggage for clean socks and donning them and my tennis shoes.

"Hey, Debbie Ann? Bill Dauber. I'm over at the fair. We got us a chicken thief out here. . . . Uh-huh. Sometime last night. . . . Right."

He hung up and tucked the phone back in his pocket.

"Vern Shiffley's already over here," he reported. "Debbie Ann will have him meet us at the chicken tent."

"Great," I said. "I'd like to be there when he talks to the owners of the missing chickens. What's their name, anyway?"

"Russian Orloffs," Dauber said. "Bantam mahogany Russian Orloffs. They've got black and dark brown feathers—"

"I meant the owners. What's *their* name?"

The farmer looked blank and frowned, as if this were a trick question. My fingers itched to open up my notebook-that-tells-me-when-to-breathe and add an item to the day's to-do list: *Demote Bill Dauber and find a competent head volunteer for the chicken tent.*

"Baskerville, or Bensonville, or something like that," he

said finally. "Hobby farmers, not longtime chicken folks, or I'd know them. Want me to wait for you?"

Probably his subtle way of asking how much longer I'd take to get dressed. I'd have been on my way already if I hadn't been trying to untie a stubborn knot in one shoelace. Served me right for just kicking them off and crawling into my sleeping bag last night.

"No, you go on back," I said. "I'll be right along."

He nodded and dashed out. I finished with my shoe and started to follow. But as I was about to leave the barn, I turned to glance around, wondering how many people had overheard our conversation. If someone really had stolen the missing chickens, it would upset the rest of the exhibitors. Not just the chicken owners, but everyone who'd brought animals.

The pen where I'd been sleeping was in the front right corner of the barn. From it I could look out over the small sea of pens. The aisles running between them—either up and down or across the barn—were empty. About a third of the pens were filled with small clumps of sheep. Here and there, I could spot the taller forms of alpacas or llamas—the latter being the hated rivals against whom our beloved family llamas would be competing here at the fair. Scattered throughout were pens where the animals' owners had set up camp, both to keep watch over their livestock and to save the expense of a hotel room. The few humans I could see were still peacefully curled up in their sleeping bags, cots, or folding recliners.

Dauber hadn't been loud. So with luck, no one else here had heard us, and maybe tongues wouldn't start wagging before I found out what was going on. Through the open sides of the barn, I could see the goat barn to the left of us and the pig barn on the right—downwind, thank goodness, at least for the moment. All peaceful looking. Maybe the problem was confined to the chicken tent. After all, chickens were a lot more portable than sheep, goats, cows, pigs, or horses, and thus a lot easier to steal.

I ducked back into the pen long enough to scribble a quick note to Michael, who was coming in this morning, bringing our sons, Josh and Jamie—we'd decided to give the boys one more peaceful night at home before plunging them into the excitement of the fair. Then, after placing the note very visibly on top of my sleeping bag, I hurried to follow the volunteer.

The animal barns and poultry tents surrounded a large open area where the farm equipment manufacturers had parked their displays of tractors and other large machinery. To my left was a sea of John Deere equipment, all of it painted in the company's distinctive trademark forest green. To the right I could see at least half an acre of the equally distinctive orange of Kubota. Beyond the sea of green I could glimpse a few splashes of Caterpillar yellow. A couple of farmers with towels over their shoulders and shaving kits in their hands were standing in the pathway, calmly discussing the finer points of a piece of Kubota equipment that looked like a cross between a tractor and an overgrown hedgehog. I didn't see anyone else around. I nodded good morning as I passed the mechanical hedge-hog fanciers.

From across the field, I could hear the crowing, honking, and gobbling that meant the occupants of the poultry tents were waking up. But no human shrieks and wails. That was a good sign, wasn't it? I followed the path between the green and orange toward the chicken tent.

Any optimism vanished when I entered the tent. I saw no loose chickens, only chickens safely in cages or in the arms of their owners—more of both fowl and humans already than there had been last night. But the whole tent seemed more like a busy barnyard where a flock of particularly lively chickens was foraging. No, make that where a bunch of foraging chickens had suddenly been frightened by a fox. People dashed up and down the aisles, carrying cages or individual birds. Other people merely darted about aimlessly, gathering in clumps to talk, scattering when anyone new came near, then clumping again nearby.

But they all seemed to steer clear of the far corner of the barn. I could see the tall form of Vern Shiffley, the senior deputy who was in charge of the police presence at the fair. He was talking to someone.

Two someones, as I could see when I finally shoved my way through the agitated flock of chicken owners. Presumably the Baskervilles or Bensonvilles or whatever their names were—the owners of the missing fowl. Both were short and round and rather nondescript. The man was wearing khaki pants and a beige shirt. The woman wore a flower-print dress in shades of beige and pale pink so muted that it looked faded even though I suspected it was brand new. She was holding a small brown and black chicken and stroking it absently.

"Hey, Meg." Vern waved me over. "Meg Langslow's the assistant director of the fair," he said to the couple.

The two turned their eyes toward me without appreciably moving their heads. I almost flinched under their mute, accusing stares.

"I'm so sorry about this," I said. "Vern, what can we do to help?"

"Any chance you could round up some volunteers to help us search for the chickens?" Vern said.

"Absolutely." I pulled out my notebook-that-tells-me-when-to-breathe, as I call my trusty planner and to-do list, and began scribbling some notes on who to enlist. Then I noticed Bill Dauber, the tent volunteer, standing at my elbow. No, he was standing a little behind me, as if he didn't want to be seen.

"Organize a search," I told him, in a low voice.

"Roger!" He dashed off, as if glad to have an excuse to leave.

"They could be miles from here by now," the man said. The woman sniffled and the chicken she was holding squawked and struggled—I deduced that the woman had tightened her grip.

"They could, and we'll be doing what we can to track them down," Vern said. "But whoever did this took the chickens, not the cages. For all we know, it could have been a prank. Maybe someone just set them loose. Or maybe someone did steal them, but it can be hard holding on to one riled up chicken—and this guy was trying to carry two? I'd say there's a good chance one or both will turn up if we do a good search nearby."

I hoped if they did turn up they'd still be alive. Should I have some knowledgeable person check the fried chicken stand to see if any of their supplies were a little too fresh?

"How did they manage to steal the chickens?" I asked aloud.

"We had only two officers patrolling the whole fairground last night," Vern said. "We figured since it was only farmers here at night it wouldn't be a high-crime area. Unfortunately, it would be pretty easy for someone to watch until they knew the pattern of their patrols and then elude them."

"But we had a volunteer who was supposed to be here in the tent all night," I pointed out.

"He was here." The husband of the bantam-owning couple, his voice unexpectedly fierce. "He slept through the whole thing."

"Mr. Dauber had himself a lawn chair over near the tent entrance," Vern said. "Looks like he made himself a mite too comfortable and dozed off. My best guess is that the chicken thief slipped in through the back entrance."

No wonder Dauber had been so eager to leave.

"Your best guess," the man echoed. "Have you done any forensics?"

Vern winced slightly, no doubt wishing himself back to the day when *CSI* and other TV cop shows hadn't made "forensics" a household word.

"You forget, we're just a rural sheriff's department in a small and very cash-poor county." Vern's accent suddenly sounded a lot more country than usual. "We have to call in someone to do forensics, and it's hard to justify it for anything less than a murder."

From the way the wife was looking at him, I suspected she was almost willing to provide the murder.

"What about Horace?" I asked. "He's in town for the fair."

"If you think he'd be willing," Vern said.

I was already dialing his number while Vern turned to the couple to explain.

"Horace Hollinsgsworth, Ms. Langslow's cousin, is a veteran crime scene analyst from York County," he said. "With luck, she can talk him into doing the forensics for us."

Luck was with us. Horace was awake and very eager to be of service, probably because another cousin, Rose Noire, was panicking that she hadn't prepared enough stock to sell in her organic herbal products booth and had recruited him to help.

"Are you sure you don't mind?" I asked.

"If I never tie another little pink ribbon on another little purple flowered bag of stuff that makes me sneeze, I'll die a happy man," Horace said. "Beats me why people pay money for a bunch of dried weeds. But don't tell Rose Noire I said that."

"If she asks, I'll tell her you reluctantly agreed to help out for the good of the fair," I said.

"I'll be right over."

I relayed this good news to Vern.

"That's great!" He turned back to the couple. "Now, folks, I don't want you to touch anything until Mr. Hollingsworth gets here. Do you have someplace else you can keep your other chicken?"

I spotted Mr. Dauber, who was buttonholing people to recruit them for the search and assigned him the additional task of finding a new cage for the forlorn fowl, who seemed in ever-increasing danger of being hugged to death. Given how fast Mr. Dauber scrambled to follow my orders, I deduced he was feeling guilty about his failure to protect the bantams. As well he might. And it probably wasn't a bad idea to put some distance between him and the red-faced, scowling husband of the couple who owned the bantams.

"Before you leave," Vern was saying. "One question occurs to me—have you had your birds microchipped?"

"Microchipped?" the husband repeated. "We—"

He clutched his chest and keeled over.

Chapter 2

"Call 911," I said as I scrambled to the fallen chicken owner's side.

"Is he okay?" Vern already had his cell phone to his ear.

"He has a pulse," I said. "And it seems steady enough. But he's unconscious. And his face is pale and sweaty."

Vern was repeating my words into the phone, presumably to Debbie Ann, the dispatcher. I sat back on my heels, took out my own cell phone, and called my father. Although theoretically semiretired from active medical practice, Dad had agreed to act as volunteer medical officer for the fair. Once the fair opened, we'd have EMTs and an ambulance on site, but this early in the day—well, Dad was always an early riser. Maybe he was here already. And there was nothing Dad enjoyed better than a nice adrenaline-laden medical emergency first thing in the morning.

A capable-looking woman knelt down on the man's other side. She loosened his collar and eased his head into a more comfortable position.

The man's wife hadn't made a sound since he'd collapsed—she just stood there, staring and clutching the chicken. The chicken, though, was making enough noise for both of them, at least until a nearby volunteer in a BACKYARD CHICKEN FARMER t-shirt gently eased the poor bird out of her hands.

"Debbie Ann's sending the ambulance," Vern said. "Let's call your dad."

"I've already got him," I said. "Dad, possible cardiac patient in the chicken tent. Are you here at the—"

"On my way," he said. "I was just over in the first-aid tent, getting ready for the day."

The capable-looking woman was taking the man's pulse with one eye on her watch. The doctor's daughter in me recognized the unmistakable demeanor of a trained medical professional, so I stood back out of her way. It actually wasn't more than a couple of minutes before Dad bustled in, carrying his deceptively old-fashioned–looking doctor's bag, which he'd equipped as a fully functional modern first-aid kit. The local EMTs had occasionally been known to borrow supplies and equipment from him. He waved absently at me and hurried over to the fallen man. After a few moments, he glanced up, gave me a quick thumbs-up, and turned back to his patient.

I let out the breath I hadn't realized I'd been holding and took Vern aside for a quick word.

"Evidently Dad thinks he'll be all right," I said, keeping my voice low. "Does Randall know about this?" Vern's cousin Randall Shiffley, in addition to being the mayor of Caerphilly, was the fair's director.

"Not yet," Vern said. "He just took off to meet some reporter at the front gate and give him a tour of the fair. I figured it was better to wait until they'd finished."

"Good call," I said. "But what if he was planning to bring the reporter here to the chicken tent?"

Vern winced slightly and turned a little pale.

"Yeah, he probably is planning to," he said. "He's that proud of all the rare and unusual chickens people brought.

Can you figure out a way to get the word to him? I should stay here and handle the situation. It'd help if we can just keep the reporter away till the ambulance gets here. Once Mr. and Mrs. B are off to the hospital things should quiet down a bit."

"Good idea," I said. "But find someone who can take care of their remaining chicken while they're gone. Someone they trust."

"Can do."

"By the way, what is their name? We can't keep calling them Mr. and Mrs. B."

Vern looked chagrined.

"I didn't quite catch it," he said. "And they're so touchy right now I didn't like to ask." He spotted something and his face brightened. "Hallelujah! Here's the EMTs."

I stood aside while the EMTs trotted in. Then I left the tent and pulled out my cell phone. Randall's phone went to voice mail.

"Call me as soon as you get this, even if you're still with the reporter," I said.

But I didn't think it was a good idea to wait until he came back. I decided to look for him.

I glanced around, wondering where to start. I saw a flurry of activity outside the produce barn—four people popped out, then two of them went running off in different directions while the other two popped back inside. I headed that way.

Stepping inside reminded me that I needed to grab some breakfast before too long. Should I feel guilty, thinking about my stomach after the events of the morning? I stifled the thought. Dad seemed to think Mr. B was going to be all right. That was good enough for me.

Or maybe my better nature was overcome by all the sights and smells in the produce tent. Right in front of me were long tables covered with apples of every kind—red, yellow, and green; large and small, all sorted and labeled with the cultivar and the name of the grower. Nearby were grapes, pears, and plums. And a little farther back—

I heard a shriek from the back of the tent, followed by loud wailing. It sounded like a child. I knew my own two toddlers were safe at home with Michael, but the sound triggered a familiar stomach-twisting anxiety. People were turning and heading toward it. I scrambled to follow.

At the very back of the tent were the entries in the largest pumpkin contest. There were already twenty contenders on display, with a few more due to show up today. I had to admit they weren't the most attractive pumpkins I'd ever seen. None of them were the vivid orange you looked for in a pumpkin, and they didn't have a typical rounded, wide-ribbed pumpkin shape. They all looked pale, bloated, and slumped. But they were undoubtedly large. The smallest ones looked like overstuffed ottomans, and you probably could have carved small carriages out of the largest few, which one veteran pumpkin aficionado told me probably weighed at least sixteen or seventeen hundred pounds.

It had made me nervous yesterday every time another giant pumpkin came into the barn, hauled on a trailer behind a pair of tractors, with a dozen burly volunteers to lift it into place. I decided then it was a good thing the giant pumpkins weren't cute and rounded—at least they weren't likely to roll onto one of the hapless movers. Most of them looked more likely to collapse inward from their own weight.

But what if one that was more rollable than most had

been hauled in since I'd given up watching the arrivals? One that could roll over onto someone. Like a child. Of course, the child wouldn't still be wailing if he'd been crushed by a giant pumpkin. He'd be screaming in agony if he could make any sound at all. But if he'd seen someone else crushed . . .

When I pushed my way through the crowd at the pumpkin end of the tent, I saw a boy of about nine or ten sitting on the ground in the middle of the remains of a smashed pumpkin. He was crying uncontrollably and had some kind of goop all over him. Almost certainly pumpkin guts. At a guess, he was surrounded by close to sixteen or seventeen hundred pounds of pumpkin guts.

"What happened?" I asked. "Is he hurt?"

I was already pulling out my cell phone to call Dad.

"Th-they smashed my pumpkin," the boy wailed. He waved his arms, and since both of his fists were clutching handfuls of pumpkin debris, seeds and little bits of flesh flew everywhere. A man was stooped beside him, patting him on the back.

"We came in this morning to check on it," the man said. "And we saw this."

He indicated the mountain of pale orange and white debris.

"Wasn't there anyone here in the barn overnight?" I asked. I was pulling out my notebook and flipping to the page where I had a list of all the volunteers with their cell phone numbers.

"Volunteer was at the other end of the barn," someone said. "Didn't see anything."

I definitely needed to have a word with the volunteers, who seemed under the delusion that their job was purely honorary. And was I premature in seeing a pattern in these two events?

I already had my cell phone out, so I called Vern.

"We have an act of vandalism in the produce barn," I reported. "Someone smashed one of the biggest pumpkins."

"I'll be right over," Vern said. "Just seeing our patient off in the ambulance. He's conscious and complaining."

"Good," I said. "About the conscious part, anyway. Oh, and maybe you could send Horace over when he's finished with the bantam forensics," I added, before he hung up.

"Now I'll never w-w-win," the boy was sobbing.

"We don't know that yet," I said. "We need to put all the pieces of this pumpkin in something."

The bystanders gazed at the huge mound of pulp and seeds.

"Like what?" one of them asked. "A swimming pool?"

I was calling my tent volunteer. As I heard the ringing through my phone, a trilling musical noise arose from one of the bystanders. A woman in jeans, wearing a t-shirt with the FFV logo of the Future Farmers of Virginia, reached into her pocket, pulled out her cell phone, and then looked up to meet my eyes as she said "Hello."

"We need some containers for the pumpkin," I told her. "Keep everyone away from it until Vern and Horace are finished. Meanwhile I'll get Randall to deliver some steel drums—I'm sure they have them or can get them over at his construction company. When they arrive, weigh them on whatever you're going to use to weigh the pumpkins, and then get some volunteers to help you load all the pumpkin debris into the drums."

"Will the judges accept a pumpkin in pieces?" she asked. "Or in a bunch of cans?"

"I have no idea," I said. "But before we ask them to consider doing so, we need to save every bit of this poor boy's pumpkin. Before something starts eating it." And another thought hit me. "For that matter, it's also evidence and needs to be collected no matter what the judges decide. So Deputy Vern will be here in a few minutes. He can supervise the collection, and when the police are finished with it, we'll see if we can get the judges to accept it."

"Okay." She sounded glum, and appeared to be studying the size of the pumpkin mound with dismay.

"After all, the kid had to work hard enough to grow it," I said.

"Work hard?" She frowned slightly. "I'd have thought the vine did most of the work."

"Not with a pumpkin this size," I said. "They have to start the seeds indoors early so the seedlings can get big by the time the last frost is over. Then they plant them and hand-pollinate them. And once a likely looking pumpkin sets, they have to go around every day plucking all the other blossoms and fruit so the plant puts all its energy into the one pumpkin. And I gather growing a half-ton pumpkin takes at least half a ton of water and fertilizer. And after all that work for months, this happens."

"Mercy," she said. "I never knew it was that involved. We'll get every speck up; don't you worry."

Vern arrived just then, and I turned the case of the pummeled pumpkin over to him. I needed to find Randall and warn him that we were having a rash of problems.

Okay, two was a small rash. But the day was young.

Chapter 3

I ducked out of the produce tent and strode rapidly through the fair, tossing off hurried greetings to all the friends I met. I finally spotted Randall over near the front gate, shaking hands with a lanky man in khakis and a navy sports jacket.

"There you are!" Randall was in a jovial mood. "We were just talking about you. This fair wouldn't even be happening if not for Meg. Any real work gets done, she's probably done it."

The reporter probably thought Randall was flattering me. Randall and I both knew he was only telling the truth. Not that I particularly blamed Randall, who also had a town and a construction company to run.

The reporter and I shook hands and exchanged names and pleasantries.

"So, getting back to my questions," the reporter said, turning toward Randall. "This isn't just a county fair, then?"

"No, it's a statewide agricultural exposition," Randall said. "This is our second year."

"What inspired it?" the reporter asked.

"The possible demise of the Virginia State Fair," Randall said. "Oh, I know it's not really dead now, but last year when we started planning our first event, the nonprofit that was running the official fair was in bankruptcy, and no one knew if there'd be a fair that fall. And we thought that was a shame, so we organized our own event. And since it wasn't officially the state fair, we decided to call it the 'Un-fair.'"

The reporter chuckled at that, as most people did.

"And you kept on with your plans even after the state fairgrounds and the right to hold the state fair were sold after all?"

"We did," Randall said. "The folks who bought the rights to hold the official Virginia State Fair own a bunch of state fairs and other events. They know how to run a nice fair, I'll give 'em that. I enjoy going there. But they were out of state, and a for-profit company, so last year we weren't sure what their event would look like. We decided there was room for another kind of event, locally run, and with a different focus."

"What kind of focus?" the reporter asked.

"Heritage animals and heirloom crops," Randall said. "For example, in the chicken tent, we probably have twice as many different breeds of chicken as you'll find at most events. Here, let me show you."

Damn.

"I'd wait on that if I were you," I said, trying to sound casual.

"Why?" the reporter asked. I didn't like the slightly sharp tone of his voice.

"Because the chickens have been there all night," I said. "And the farmers are only just trickling in to clean up. You might want to avoid all the livestock barns and tents right now. Everything's supposed to be clean as a whistle—or at least as clean as barnyard animals get—by opening time." I glanced at my watch. "Two hours from now."

"Good point," Randall said. "Let me take you over to the arts and crafts building. No cleanup needed there. Or would you like to get a backstage tour of the event stage?"

He dropped the name of the minor Nashville luminary who would be giving nightly concerts there for the run of the fair. I'd never heard of her, but I wasn't much of a country music fan. Randall, who was, assured me she'd go over big, especially with the over-fifty crowd.

Maybe the reporter was a country fan, since he opted for the backstage tour. He and Randall strolled off. I waited till they were out of sight, then called Randall's cell phone.

I was in luck. This time he answered.

"Don't let on it's me," I said.

"Good to hear from you," he boomed. "I expect you have some news for me?"

"Someone stole two bantams from the chicken tent last night," I said. "And someone smashed one of the contenders for biggest pumpkin. No idea yet if it was the same someone."

There was a pause.

"Good to hear it." His voice was artificially hearty.

"I take it the reporter is listening."

"You're right about that."

"Vern is already working on the case," I said. "And I suspect Chief Burke will be here soon, and my cousin Horace is doing forensics. Normally I'd say it was overkill doing forensics on what will probably turn out to be misdemeanors, but this could really hurt the fair."

"I completely agree with you," Randall said. "Keep up the good work, and call me if you need anything."

"If it's okay with you, I'm going to have your foreman deliver some steel drums to clean up the pumpkin debris," I suggested. "There's at least half a ton of it, and maybe if we save it all, the kid who grew it can still compete in the contest. And Vern asked if we could round up a few volunteers to search for the missing chickens."

"That's a yes," he said. "Catch you later."

I made my call to the Shiffley Construction Company and then took a deep breath. What next? Should I go back and check the progress of picking up the pumpkin debris and calming down the kid? Should I call Dad to see how Mr. and Mrs. B. were doing? Should I perhaps go back to the fair office, where I had a database of all registered entrants in my computer, and figure out what their name really was?

I should probably check in all the other tents and barns to see if there were any more thefts or vandalism. And was it too early to call Michael to find out how the boys' breakfast had gone without me? And—

My phone rang.

"Meg, dear." Mother. "Can you come over to the arts and crafts pavilion?"

"What's up?" I asked.

"We've had an incident," she said. "In the quilt section."

"What kind of incident?"

"You'll see, dear." She hung up.

I swore under my breath. Knowing Mother's penchant for euphemism and understatement, I wasn't sure I wanted to see what she'd call in "incident." After all, she was in the habit of calling the Civil War "the late unpleasantness." I didn't quite break into a run, but I wasted no time getting to the arts and crafts barn.

Chapter 4

I stepped into the arts and crafts barn and looked around. All seemed quiet at first. To my left were the entrants in the various art categories—the walls and a number of freestanding panels were already nearly filled with paintings, drawings, and photographs, while tables housed sculptures, wood carvings, and ceramics. To my right were the food exhibits—jars of pickles, jams, jellies, apple butter, pumpkin butter, and every other kind of nut and fruit butter imaginable. A bank of glass-doored refrigerators stood ready to hold the homemade dairy butters, yogurts, cheeses, and other perishables, most of which hadn't arrived yet. The delectable scent of fresh baked bread was already wafting from the bakery tables, where loaves and rolls had begun to appear in anticipation of this afternoon's bread competitions, junior division—to be followed on subsequent days by the open bread competition; the junior and open cake and cookie events, junior pies, and on Saturday afternoon, the highly contested open pie event. A fair number of people were delivering foods, arranging the foods that were already there, or just strolling up and down, gazing at the tables and sniffing appreciatively. I made a mental note not to bring the boys here unless they'd been well and recently fed, so they'd be less likely to nibble any of the exhibits.

I threaded my way through all the art panels to the

back of the barn, where the entrants in the various fiber arts categories could be found. Now the freestanding panels and tables held examples of knitting, crocheting, tatting, sewing, embroidery, crewelwork, needlepoint, cross-stitch, yarn-making, dyeing, weaving, and, at the back, in a place of honor, the quilt competition. Randall's carpenters had constructed dozens of wooden frames for hanging the entries, and arranged them in aisles, like the bookshelves in a library. A pair of empty frames hung front and center, to be replaced, after the judging, with the grand prize winners in the junior and open categories. I didn't see many people around, so I walked down the center aisle of the display, looking right and left.

In the last side aisle, on the right, I saw a small knot of people, including Mother, gathered around a gaunt, angular woman in faded jeans and a bright turquoise t-shirt. The woman looked ashen, and a couple of tears were slowly making their way down her cheeks. Two of the women were hugging her, one from each side, while Mother was holding both of her hands and patting them as if to soothe her.

"Courage, Rosalie," Mother said. "Here's Meg now. We'll see what can be done about this."

"What's wrong?" I asked. I was glancing around to see if any of the nearby quilts had been damaged. They all looked fine. But we were standing near a big, empty space. Not the only empty space in the room—quilters weren't required to have their entries hung until this afternoon. Still, not a good sign.

"Someone took it." Rosalie's voice was thin and quavering. "My beautiful Baltimore Album quilt."

I pulled out my cell phone and called Vern.

"Vern, we need someone over here ASAP," I said. "Someone has stolen a quilt from the arts and crafts building."

"Dammit," Vern said. "Not another one. I'll be right over. And yes, I'll send Horace when he's finished with everything else."

"And Dad," I added. "We might need Dad."

I saw Mother nodding approvingly.

"He took the Baskervilles down to the hospital," Vern said.

"Baskervilles? That's the chicken people, then?" The name didn't sound right to me.

"Mr. and Mrs. B," Vern said. "Whatever their name is. But Aida's got EMT training. I'll ask her to come over to check out the quilt lady."

"The police are on their way," I told Rosalie, in my softest voice. "Can you tell me what happened?"

"I came in to make sure it was hanging properly," she said. "And to make sure they fixed the lights so it would show well. And it was gone."

She closed her eyes and seemed to shrink slightly, as if she wanted to curl up in a fetal position. The women at her side kept a tight hold.

I glanced around. Rosalie's slot was in the back corner of the barn. The rear entrance was hidden behind the last set of quilt frames, but it was there, and her quilt was about as close to the back door as you could get. Our sneak thief and vandal definitely had a pattern.

"What kind of quilt was it?" I asked Mother.

"A Baltimore Album, as Rosalie said." Mother seemed to think that explained everything. Maybe it did to a quilter. And fortunately, one of the women hovering around her recognized my look of puzzlement and enlightened me.

"Not a quilter, I take it," she said. "Baltimore Album is a particular style of quilt, usually done with a white background and a design, often quite elaborate, appliquéd on. I can show you an example."

She led me a little farther down the aisle and pointed to a quilt. It was beautiful, intricate, and to my untutored eye, looked like a great deal more work than the average quilt.

"Of course Rosalie's was larger—full size, I think—and much, much more complicated. She's won national ribbons."

"It had a pink dogwood theme," Rosalie sobbed from her place near the empty frame.

"I think I remember it," I said. "From my inspection last night."

In fact, I didn't just remember it, I remembered coveting it.

I pulled out my phone and clicked through the pictures on it until I came to several I'd taken last night. One was of the whole quilt, with branches and pink dogwood blossoms twining in a complex pattern, and the other was a close-up that showed how detailed and intricate each of the hundreds of appliquéd blossoms was.

"Is this it?" I asked.

Rosalie glanced up, nodded, and then burst into tears. Okay, apparently our thief shared my taste in quilts.

Vern arrived, bringing with him Aida Butler, the deputy with EMT training. Someone bustled up with a folding wooden chair and sat Rosalie down in it. Aida took Rosalie's pulse while Vern squatted down and took over the hand-patting where Mother had left off.

Mother gripped Rosalie's shoulder and murmured something in her ear. I could see Rosalie sit up straighter and raise her chin, as if to show a brave face to the world.

Mother glided over to join me and the other volunteer.

"I doubt if this would make Rosalie feel any better," I said. "But she's not the only victim." I explained about the chickens and the pumpkins.

"Shocking." Mother shook her head sadly.

The volunteer murmured her agreement. Seeing Mother's tightly pursed lips and narrowed eyes, I indulged in a brief fantasy of finding the thief and turning him over to Mother. Mother and the assembled quilting ladies.

"One thing," I asked. "How much is Rosalie's quilt worth?"

"I have no idea," the volunteer said.

"It's not for sale," Mother added.

"But if she were to sell it, what would the market price be?" I asked. "In the hundreds?"

"In the thousands, I should think," the volunteer said.

"No question," Mother agreed.

"Then when they catch the thief, they can charge him with grand larceny," I said. "Which in Virginia is anything over two hundred dollars. I wasn't sure the chickens and the pumpkin qualified, but the quilt definitely does."

"If you catch him," the volunteer muttered.

"I have a great deal of faith in Chief Burke and his men," Mother said.

"Especially now that this is grand larceny and they can more easily justify the expense of the investigation," I said.

"And once they catch the thief they can really let him have it," the volunteer muttered. From her tone, I suspected she'd approve of making quilt theft a hanging crime.

"There's also the fact that Rosalie's quilt is one of a kind," I said. "He can't dispose of it as easily as a few chickens. Not without getting caught."

"I only hope she took some pictures of it," the quilter said. "To document it. It might help the police find it."

"If she didn't, I did. I was running around with my phone camera last night, taking some local color shots for the Web site. Tell Vern I'm going to e-mail my pictures of the fugitive quilt to Debbie Ann down at the station."

"Good," Mother said. "Now run along. I'll stay here with Rosalie, and I'm sure you have things to do."

Yes, I did.

I sent the photos off. Then I called Randall.

"Are you still with the reporter?" I asked.

"Yes," he said.

"Sorry to interrupt, then, but there's been another theft. This time a valuable quilt. I think we need to warn the exhibitors. And if you ask me, it's no longer practical to keep that reporter from finding out. Too much has happened. We should break the news to him, putting our spin on it, before he hears it from some other source."

"I agree," Randall said. "And I think we should enlist the assistance of the press. Meet me at the fair office."

Chapter 5

The fair office was a large converted trailer that, when it wasn't fair season, served as a mobile field office for any large projects Randall's construction company took on. It had phones, electricity, and an Internet connection—at least most of the time, and when those failed there were always Shiffleys available nearby to get them going again.

I got there first, and by the time Randall and the reporter arrived, I had already printed out a copy of my master exhibitor list. And figured out that owners of the stolen chickens were actually named Bonneville.

"—several officers patrolling the grounds last night," Randall was saying as he entered. "But we're going to double the police presence tonight."

"You think that will help?" the reporter asked.

"Meg is also organizing some of the exhibitors to do voluntary patrols." Randall was offering the reporter one of our folding chairs.

I was? Okay, I guess now I was. Or maybe Vern's suggestion of a few volunteers to hunt for the chickens had morphed into full-fledged patrols. I flipped to the right page in my notebook and scribbled a few more notes on my plan for the volunteer patrols.

"It's a big area to cover," the reporter said.

"It certainly is," Randall agreed. "A hundred and twenty acres."

He indicated the wall where we'd posted a map of the

fair. It was vaguely shield shaped, a little like the state of Ohio. On the southern side, where Ohio bordered Kentucky and West Virginia, were the entrance gates. If you turned left after you came through the gates you'd reach the amphitheater where all the music and other talent performances would take place. To the right was the big show ring where the rodeo events and major animal competitions would be held. The arts and crafts barn, the vendors' barn, and the wine pavilion were all in the center, where Columbus would be.

The exhibitors' campgrounds and parking lots were in the upper left corner—past the amphitheater—while the animal barns, tents, and sheds filled most of the upper right corner—past the show ring. Beyond the agricultural area, in the very upper right area of the map was the Midway. That part was shaded pink instead of green like the rest of the map, because it was across the border in Clay County.

"Fortunately this is the first incident of this kind we've had during the history of the Un-fair," Randall was saying.

"You only started it last year," the reporter pointed out. "Not much of a history."

"No, but our record last year was unblemished," Randall said. "No theft or vandalism at all in the exhibits."

"No crime at all last year?"

"We arrested a few pickpockets and a few people on drunk and disorderly charges," Randall said. "That's about it for last year. And I'm optimistic that our police chief will be able to bring last night's perpetrator to justice."

The reporter nodded. But he wasn't writing down anything about last year's stellar crime-free record. I tried not to glare at his motionless pen.

"Of course you have a pretty small police force," he said.

"We're a pretty small county with a low crime rate," Randall said. "But we're partnering with Clay County on this fair, and can also call on their resources. And both our sheriff and our chief of police have very cordial relationships with all the nearby counties."

Just then the door opened, and Chief Burke peered in.

"Ah—speak of the devil!" Randall stood up to shake the chief's hand. "Here's Chief Burke now. Out of uniform, I see?"

I admit, I was also surprised. The chief was normally a stickler for wearing his neatly pressed khaki uniform on duty. He looked almost strange in khakis and a blue polo shirt.

"When I got the call, I was already on my way here," the chief said. "Bringing my wife's entries to the pickle and dried flower arranging contests."

"Not the pie contest?" I asked. "I thought Minerva's pecan pie was a shoo-in."

"She hasn't baked it yet," the chief said. "Still fussing over the pecans. Got our whole kitchen table covered with pecans, trying to pick out the best ones. And dried flowers all over the dining room table. I had to eat breakfast on the front stoop."

The reporter was tapping his pen on the desk, clearly impatient with these homey details.

"What can you tell me about the incidents here at the fair?" he asked.

"So far, nothing." The chief's voice became all business. "I have my best people working on it. I'm here to supervise the investigation. And we'll be doing everything we can to apprehend the perpetrator and recover what was stolen."

The reporter asked the same question again in a couple

of different ways, and the chief gave him a couple of different variations on the same answer. Sensing he'd gotten as much as he could hope for, the reporter thanked us and left.

"Off to look for someone who will give him a sensational quote," I said.

"And odds are he'll find it," Randall said.

"But not from me." The chief frowned. "Or from any of my officers."

"And not from the Baskervilles," Randall put in.

"Who?" The chief looked puzzled.

"The chicken owners."

"They're named Bonneville," I said. "And last I heard, they were down at the hospital. Mr. Bonneville clutched his chest and keeled over shortly after they discovered the theft."

"Any word on how he's doing?"

I pulled out my phone, called Dad, and hit the speaker button so I wouldn't have to relay what he said.

"How's your patient?" I asked. "Did he really have a heart attack?"

"Mr. Baskerville is going to be fine," Dad said.

"That's nice," I said. "But the people whose chickens were stolen are actually named Bonneville. Please tell me that's who you're treating."

"Are you sure?" Dad asked. "They've been answering to Baskerville down here at the hospital."

"That's because one of them is having something that looks an awful lot like a heart attack and the other is worried out of her mind," I said. "I have their entry form right here. Bonneville."

"If you say so." Dad still sounded unconvinced. "Here,

let me put Mrs. Bask—er, Bonneville on. She can tell you. She wants to ask you about something anyway."

There was a bit of background noise, and then I head a woman say "hello" in an uncertain voice.

"Mrs. Bonneville, this is Meg Langslow, from the fair," I said. "How is your husband?"

"Your father says he'll be fine." She had a soft, Southside Virginia accent. "Thank heaven he didn't have a heart attack. He had— What was that again, Dr. Langslow?"

"A cardiac arrhythmia." Dad's voice was faint but audible in the background. "It sometimes presents with chest pain."

"Cardiac arrhythmia," Mrs. Bonneville repeated. "Your father says we need to run a bunch of tests, and he may need to be on medication, but he should be fine."

"That's great," I said.

"Have you found our chickens yet?"

"Not yet," I said. "But our chief of police has come out to take personal charge of the case. We'll keep you posted."

"I see." She didn't sound happy. And she didn't say good-bye—she just hung up.

"Well, that's a relief," Randall said. "What's the prognosis on the investigation, Chief?"

"Since I only just heard about this myself a few minutes ago, I don't rightly know yet," the chief replied. "Vern's going to drop by and update me when he can break away."

"Meg just told the chicken lady that you were going to take charge of the case yourself," Randall said.

"Once Vern brings me up to speed, I will."

"Maybe we should call him and hurry him along." Did Randall have doubts about his cousin's detective abilities?

"I'm in no rush." The chief sat down in the folding

chair vacated by the reporter and sighed. "Vern's working on it, and he's a good man, and as long as I'm out here I don't have to pick over those blessed pecans."

"I understand Vern put out an APB on the chickens," Randall said.

"First time for that." From the chief's expression, I suspected it might be the *last* time if he had anything to say about it. "Can't say I expect it to be too useful. Putting out an APB on a couple of chickens in a county that must have a few thousand?"

"These were special chickens," Randall said. "Heirloom chickens. Bantam Russian Whatsits."

"Orloffs," I put in.

"That's it," Randall said. "Not a lot of them in the county—they're a rare breed. Should be easy enough to spot if they're running around loose."

" 'Rare,' " the chief echoed. "So do you think they were stolen because they were valuable?" He had taken out his notebook. Vern looked happier at seeing this concrete evidence that the chief was taking charge.

"They're not that valuable in a monetary sense," Randall said. "Vern asked one of the other chicken people. He seemed to think you could buy a pair for fifty or a hundred dollars. Maybe more if they were champion birds, but these weren't."

"Then why steal them?" the chief asked. "Why those chickens in particular?"

"I think it wasn't how valuable they were but where they were," I said. "The stolen chickens, the stolen quilt, and the smashed pumpkin were all three at the back of their respective tents or barns. All three of which have rear exits, even if they're not open to the public."

"Have to, to keep the fire marshal happy," Randall said. "So they weren't specifically after the three things they stole or smashed—just looking to cause trouble?"

"Maybe," I said. "Or maybe they were after one of them, and the easy time they had getting to it inspired them to muddy the waters by going after the other two."

The chief sighed.

"I'm afraid that doesn't make our job any easier," he said. "Not knowing which of the items was the real target."

"Or whether the fair itself was the real target."

We contemplated this for a while.

"Maybe when you figure out the time line of the incidents you'll get a clue," Randall said.

"Doubt it," the chief said.

"And finding the time line's going to be tough," I added. "Because it all happened overnight."

"I thought we had volunteers sleeping in every building that couldn't be locked up tight," Randall said.

"We do," I replied. "And that's just what they were doing. Sleeping."

"Well, that's a clue. Whoever did this must be pretty light on his feet."

The chief glared at him and Randall shrugged apologetically.

"Chief," I said. "Randall told that reporter that we were going to organize some extra patrols staffed by volunteers from among the exhibitors. Unless you have an objection to the idea, I should go and get that started."

The chief has shifted his glare from Randall to the fair map. He continued staring at it for a few moments, then his face softened.

"No way we can adequately cover this whole area with

the personnel I have available," he said. "Try not to recruit any hotheads, and I don't want any of your vigilantes armed."

"Roger." I stopped short of saluting. "I'm going to do my recruiting during a detailed inspection of every single tent and barn where a theft might have taken place. I think we need to warn the exhibitors."

"We already alerted the media," Randall said.

"And now we need to make sure the exhibitors get the straight scoop from us," I said. "Not whatever melodramatic account the newspapers and radios come up with."

Randall and the chief both nodded glumly.

As I was walking away from the fair office, my cell phone rang. Michael.

"The boys and I are over at the sheep barn," he said. "I found your note—what's up?"

I explained, as succinctly as I could, how my morning had gone so far. And how I expected to spend the rest of the morning, and who knows how much of the afternoon.

"I'll keep the boys busy, then," he said. "We came over a little late because they wanted to help Rose Noire. At least I think we helped. I didn't realize Horace really was on a case. I thought he just figured out a way to dodge the potpourri."

"All too real," I said. "Last time I passed by, things were slow over at the pony rides. The boys would love that. And there's a children's concert on the main stage at two."

"I'll make sure someone else is minding the booth at two." Michael and several of his fellow llama aficionados had set up an information booth topped with a large banner proclaiming THE JOY OF LLAMAS! They were determined to have at least one llama and one human on duty at all times to answer any questions from the public, and

Michael, as the booth organizer and local host, would probably be filling in any time they couldn't get coverage. I wasn't sure I'd have been happy to be that tied down, but Michael was enthusiastic. And he planned to keep the boys with him during his shifts—to demonstrate how family-friendly llamas were—so I didn't have to worry about a babysitter and would know exactly where to find the three of them most of the time.

"Good idea," I said. "Actually, I'd make it one thirty, to give you time to walk over to the stage."

"Any chance you'll join us for that?"

"I'll try."

If I hurried and got through all the barns, tents, and pavilions efficiently, I probably could make the concert. Especially if I focused on briefing the volunteers in charge of each building and left it to them to bring all the exhibitors up to speed. At least I hoped I could safely leave it to them. We had to strike a difficult balance, making people aware of the thefts and vandalism without upsetting them so much they'd pack up and leave.

I was a little worried, at first, that the volunteers would overreact. But most of them caught on right away. Recruiting for the patrols actually helped encourage people, and a surprising number of people signed up. I was collecting dozens of names and cell phone numbers to work from.

I even managed to convince Bill Dauber to hand over running the chicken tent to a different volunteer.

"Just until the Bonnevilles either calm down or leave," I said.

He actually looked relieved and hurried off to his new assignment, guarding the far end of the parking lot.

I had finished with all three poultry tents and the pig,

sheep, and cow barns and was briefing the volunteer in charge of the horse barn when I made a depressing discovery.

"I might have another theft for you," one horse breeder said. "Someone stole one of my horse blankets."

"You're sure it couldn't have just been misplaced?" I asked.

He looked at me over his glasses with his lips pursed disapprovingly.

"I have special blankets made for all my horses," he said. "With their names embroidered on them. Costs a pretty penny, and I'm careful about keeping track of them."

"Sorry," I said. "Just asking. So what happened?"

"I got the horses settled into their stalls last night," he said. "With the blankets on, in case it got cool. Sometimes does in September. There was a stable boy on duty here in the barn, but he must have napped. Anyway, I came in this morning and found someone had taken away Mosby's blanket and replaced it with an old quilt."

I felt a slight chill when I heard those words.

"Could you show me?" I asked.

My tone of voice must have satisfied him that I was taking his loss seriously. He led me down the row of stalls. We were in the draft horse section of the barn. Here and there, the enormous heads of Shires, Clydesdales, and Percherons hung out over the stall doors, watching us go by.

The horse owner led me to a stall containing a beautiful gray Percheron. He patted the horse's nose, then opened the stall door and led me in.

"See?" He pointed to the Percheron.

Wrapped around the enormous horse was a quilt. A very familiar-looking quilt. I pulled out my camera and compared the photo I'd taken last night of Rosalie's quilt with the fabric draped over the Percheron's rump. Yes, it was the same quilt. And still beautiful, in spite of all the mud stains. Or were some of them manure stains? Maybe I should hope they were. Since moving to the country, I'd found that manure was one of the easiest stains to treat. But our reddish yellow Virginia clay . . .

I pulled out my cell phone and called the chief.

"We've had another theft," I said. "And I'm afraid I've found the missing quilt."

Chapter 6

Some misguided soul told Rosalie what was going on and she showed up at the barn while Horace was still doing his forensic examination of the scene. She didn't react well to the sight of her poor, mistreated quilt. In fact, she reacted so badly that after a telephone consultation with Dad, Deputy Aida hauled her down to the Caerphilly Hospital to be looked after.

"I doubt if she'll need to be admitted," Aida said in an undertone to me while Mother and the quilting ladies helped Rosalie into the back of the cruiser. "But you know how good your father is with hysterical patients."

"We must do something," one of the quilting ladies said, as they watched Rosalie's departure.

"Let's take the quilt to Daphne," Mother suggested. "At the Caerphilly Cleaners."

"I'm not sure I'd want to entrust the Baltimore Album to a mere dry cleaner," one of the ladies said. Clearly she wasn't from around here.

"Daphne is no mere dry cleaner," Mother said. "She is a fabric conservation genius."

"Yes," I said. "Around here, it's generally accepted that if Daphne can't get it out, God must want you to wear the stain."

"She has some tricks for dealing with that horrible red clay," said a woman I recognized as the head of the Caerphilly Quilting Club. "But let's make sure Horace's forensic testing doesn't involve putting any nasty chemicals on it. When we had that burglary last year, you wouldn't believe how hard it was to get all that fingerprint powder scrubbed away."

"And before you haul the quilt anywhere, remember that it's evidence." I hated to put a damper on the quilt rescue, but I didn't want them to interfere with Horace's forensics. "Someone did steal it, possibly the same someone who still has those missing chickens. Let's make sure the police don't need to keep it."

Horace was quick to assure them that fabric wasn't a very good surface for fingerprints, and he had no need to put any chemicals on the quilt. With the chief's permission, the quilters bore the quilt away to Daphne's. Four of them insisted on helping carry it, each holding one corner of the folded bundle, and their slow pace and solemn faces made them look alarmingly like pallbearers.

"Is that true, or did you just not want to upset the quilters?" I asked Horace as we watched them depart.

"Well, they're doing some really interesting things in Scotland with vacuum metal deposition to get fingerprints off fabric," he said. "But it's still in the early stages yet. And probably impossible to clean off. Still, it would be interesting to try."

He sounded wistful. Lately I'd noticed that Horace often seemed disappointed at the relatively tame forensic challenges small-town police work had to offer.

"Well, we'll all keep our eyes open for some more fiber evidence," I said, patting him on the back. "Evidence that no one cares so much about."

I dropped by the produce tent and sent the pumpkin owner and his father out for lunch at the Un-fair's expense while two Shiffleys from the Shiffley Construction

Company loaded the remains of the pumpkin into the barrels. Eight huge barrels by the time they finished.

"We just going to leave these here?" one Shiffley asked.

"Because this stuff's already starting to stink," the other pointed out.

"Yes, it will rot, and I have no idea if that will increase or decrease the weight," I said. "Can we put the stuff on ice?"

"Would take a lot of ice," the first said. "Cousin of ours has a refrigerated truck. We might be able to borrow that for a few days."

"Fabulous." I left them to handle it.

Time for me to return to my rounds. Luckily there weren't too many more buildings to visit, and I was guardedly optimistic that by now, any other thefts or vandalism would have been discovered and reported.

And no, there weren't any other incidents. By the time I reached the last building, I realized it was getting close to opening time. I stopped by a food stand that was already cooking Italian sausages, one of my favorites. I wolfed one down, and made a mental note to come back and have another when I had the time to really enjoy it. Then I headed for the front gate.

I had a little time left, so I decided to run a personal errand. I strolled into the farmers' market, a huge barn with booths for farmers and craftspeople who wanted to sell their goods as well as enter them into competition.

I threaded my way through aisles where the vendors were scrambling to set out the last of their merchandise before the first customers arrived. Fresh-baked bread, rolls, cookies, and pies. Fruit and vegetable stalls heaped with corn, pumpkins, squash, beets, string beans, apples, pears, peaches, grapes, tomatoes, onions, potatoes, leeks, and who knows how many other fruits and vegetables. Fresh and dried spices. Freshly made jams, jellies, and preserves. Organic meats. Farm-made sausages. Farm-cured bacon and ham. Saltwater taffy. Homemade fudge. I waved in passing to my cousin Rose Noire, who was setting up her stall with organic herbs, potpourris, gourmet herbal vinegars, and essential oils. She was dressed today in a tie-dyed dress that would not have looked out of place at Woodstock, and her frizzy mane was topped with a wreath of dried herbs and flowers. On me it would have looked as if I'd stuck my head into a jar of potpourri, but on her it looked curiously elegant. I stopped for a cup of locally roasted fair-trade coffee, but resisted all the other temptations. I'd save my calories for later, when I came back with the boys in tow.

My destination was a booth decorated with a large sign that said LEAPING GOAT FARM—ARTISAN CHEESES. My friend Molly Riordan had started her creamery business ten years ago, and was finally seeing some success—winning medals at fairs, getting good reviews in foodie magazines, and most important, selling her cheeses as fast as she could make them. Always good to see someone as nice and as hardworking as Molly making good.

But I could see that she was frowning as she arranged a selection of crackers and sample dishes of cheese spread on the counter.

"Why so glum?" I asked. "If it's about the thefts, our police are on the case."

"No," she said. "I don't leave anything valuable here overnight. Just a little preoccupied."

She was smiling now, but in the rather determined way

people smile when they really don't feel like it. And while she hadn't answered my question, maybe this wasn't the time or place to pry.

"I came to get some of my favorite cheeses before you run out," I said. "I brought a list."

"Always the organized one." Her smile became a little more believable. "Yes, I have all these. You might want to double the quantities. Could be your last chance."

"Last chance? No! Why?"

"You heard Brett left me, right?"

I nodded. I suspected I wasn't the only one of her friends who considered this good news, although I couldn't just come out and say so.

"Well, there you have it." She was slicing thin slices of a huntsman-style cheese that made my mouth water and almost distracted me.

"What do you mean, there you have it?" I gave in to temptation and snagged a small slice. "What does Brett have to do with your continuing to make cheese? I thought he never did a lick of work around the farm."

"No," she said. "But his name's on the deed with mine. And he's filed for divorce already, and demanding his half of the farm. I can't afford to buy him out. I could try to give him half the income, although I'm not sure I could live on half of almost nothing, but he won't even consider it."

"Have you pointed out to him that he'll get a lot more in the long run if he waits?" I asked. "And that maybe without the income from the farm, he might have to get an actual job?"

"He doesn't care," she said. "His new girlfriend is supporting him. Paying for his high-powered divorce lawyer, too."

"Do you have a lawyer?" I asked.

She shook her head, and pretended that the cheddar she was slicing took all her concentration.

"You need one." I was already taking out my notebook. "One who's even better than his. Let me talk to Mother."

She looked puzzled.

"I didn't know your mother was a lawyer," she said. "Does she handle divorces?"

"She handles her family," I said. "She's not a lawyer, but we must have several dozen in the family. And most of them are very, very good at what they do, and I'm sure a few of them do divorce. I will explain to Mother that if she wants to continue serving your cheeses at her parties, she will need to find you a lawyer who can take on Brett's lawyer. And do it on terms you can afford."

"Do you really think she can find someone?" Her hand was trembling, and I was relieved to see her put down the cheese knife.

"You've met Mother," I said. "You know what she's like when she takes on a project. So brace yourself. You're about to become a project."

Molly's smile was finally starting to look genuine.

"Thanks," she said. "You have no idea how great that would be."

"I've got to run." I tucked my notebook back into my pocket. "How about if you put my order together—and yes, double it, not because I think you're going out of business but because just looking at your booth makes me realize I was being way too conservative when I made my list. I'll drop back later to pick it up and give you a check. And I can let you know what Mother says."

She nodded, and I could see that above the smile she was blinking rapidly. Fighting back tears. If we'd been alone, I'd have hugged her, but that would probably make the tears spill over, and I knew here in the crowded vendor hall she'd want to hold it together.

"Later," I said, and headed for the exit. I felt curiously more cheerful after learning about Molly's problem, perhaps because unlike the thefts and vandalism, I felt I knew exactly what to do to solve it.

If only all the day's problems would be this easy.

Chapter 7

Outside, I hurried over to the gate and supervised the opening. I was relieved to see that in spite of the overcast weather, a decent number of people were lined up outside, impatiently waiting to buy their tickets for this first day of the Un-fair. Yesterday's weather had been abysmal, mainly because the remnants of a passing hurricane had dumped three inches of water on us. If I weren't involved in the fair, I might have waited out today's chance of thunderstorms, but here were several hundred people eager to come to the fair. Not bad at all for a Thursday, with only a few competitions scheduled and the Midway, with its rides and games, not opening for two more hours.

But just as the gates opened, I found myself wondering if one of those smiling, eager faces belonged to a chicken thief. A pumpkin smasher. A despoiler of exquisite quilts. I stopped myself from scowling—no sense scaring off the paying customers—but I found myself studying the people as they began to trickle in.

The family groups were probably harmless. No petty criminal worth his salt would encumber himself with toddlers already demanding hot dogs and cotton candy, boys begging to be taken on the rides, or girls pleading to go see the horses. But I had to work harder at not frowning when I spotted men, alone or in pairs.

They could have any number of innocent reasons for coming, I reminded myself. They could be farmers, looking to buy or sell livestock or just check out the competition. They could be coming to see the latest tractors and combines on display. They could be craving barbecue or fried chicken or any of the dozens of foodstuffs on sale throughout the fair. They could be here for the entertainment, which ranged from our minor Nashville luminary to Rancid Dread, an inexplicably popular local heavy metal band.

They could even be spies for one of the other counties or private groups trying to field their own entries in the competition to steal the thunder from the newly restored official state fair.

Nothing I could do about spies any more than chicken thieves. I headed back to the arts and crafts barn so I could find Mother and make good on my promise to Molly. I paused just inside the doorway where the building's volunteer monitor was sitting and craned my neck to see if I could spot Mother.

"She's over in the wine pavilion," the volunteer said. "Your mother, I mean, if that's who you're looking for."

I thanked her and began picking my way through the gathering crowds to the wine pavilion. We'd originally planned to have the wine competitions in the same barn as the rest of the food and craft exhibits, but a few weeks before the opening of the fair our registrar had reported, with a note of panic in her voice, that we already had enough wine bottles, pies, quilts, preserves, carvings, paintings, sculptures, sweaters, photographs, and other arts and crafts to fill the barn, and entries were still pouring in. We'd solved that problem by erecting an enormous tent and christening it the "wine pavilion." With the help of the ladies of the Caerphilly Garden Club, Mother had decorated it. One end resembled a Mediterranean villa, with tile, pottery, fountains, iron tables and chairs, well-aged barrels, and vintage riddling racks. Midway through the tent the style made a graceful, nearly seamless transition toward the neoclassical, with red brick, white columns, and Chinese railings, echoing Monticello and evoking Thomas Jefferson, founder and secular patron saint of Virginia's wine industry. And of course, scattered throughout were several tons of potted foliage. The winemakers loved it.

So did Mother. Even though she was theoretically also in charge of the quilt and pie barn, good luck ever finding her there short of a disaster like this morning's quilt theft. She preferred the more elegant company of the winemakers.

"Meg, dear," she said, when I strolled into the tent. "What's wrong? Are the boys all right?"

"They're fine," I said. "Michael will probably bring them by to see you later."

"More unpleasantness, then?"

"No more thefts or vandalism as far as I know," I said. "But a friend of mine has a problem."

I glanced around to make sure no one else was nearby and then relayed Molly's situation to her as succinctly as I could.

"The poor dear!" she exclaimed. "You're right—we simply must do something."

"Shall I tell her to come and talk to you?"

"Good heavens, no," Mother said. "I'll make a few calls and then go over and talk to her. She wouldn't want to come here."

"Why not?" I asked.

"Don't you realize—never mind. You need to see for yourself what the poor girl is up against. Follow me."

Mother swept through the tent, giving the impression that her simple day dress came with an invisible train and possibly a tiara. She exchanged cheerful greetings with most of the arriving winemakers, and even air kisses with some of the women. I followed in her wake, hoping to pass unnoticed and avoid another round of interrogations about fair security.

"Here we are," Mother said, stopping at one of the booths. "Don't mind us, Dorcas," she stage-whispered to the woman behind the counter. "I just wanted Meg to get a good look at her."

"Be my guest," Dorcas murmured. "And if you block my view, all the better."

"Her?" I asked.

"Genette Sedgewick," Mother said. "The Other Woman."

Chapter 8

"Other woman?" I repeated. "Oh! You mean Molly's husband's new—"

"Precisely." Mother didn't point, or even move her head, but she indicated, with her eyes, the booth diagonally across from Dorcas's. Then she and Dorcas and the winemaker from the booth next door began talking in low voices. I turned around, pretending to be waiting for them to finish, and studied the Other Woman's booth.

It was jarringly out of place. Some of the booths were fairly plain. Most echoed either the Mediterranean or the Palladian theme, whichever prevailed at their end of the tent. Or perhaps Mother had anticipated the booths—she had a keen appreciation of good wine, and had probably already seen the different winemakers' booths at other festivals—and visited their vineyards, too. And had designed the wine pavilion to coordinate with them.

Genette's booth was . . . well . . . loud. It was made of chrome with panels of translucent acrylic or opaque plastic in a variety of harsh, garish colors that clashed horribly with each other, like mustard yellow and bubblegum pink, which seemed to be her signature colors. The booth did provide a perfect background for her wine bottles, whose labels featured the same horrible colors in a jagged abstract design. I'd seen better artwork from Josh and Jamie, and they weren't even three yet. The booth had little alcoves here and there, each displaying a single wine bottle with a couple of wineglasses in colors that matched the labels—where on earth would anyone find mustard-yellow wineglasses? Tucked in with the wine bottles and glasses were peculiar decorative elements, like small trays made of rough-cut trapezoids of corrugated sheet metal, little tangles of barbed wire, and angular bouquets of short PVC pipes. Some enormous letters sprawled across the back panel of the booth, probably spelling out the name of her winery, but in such an odd, jagged typeface that I couldn't actually read it. Two rectangular blocks constructed entirely of black metal and industrial steel grating jutted out into the aisles, impeding traffic. The lighting, a combination of neon and bare lightbulbs, didn't help.

"We made her turn off the blinking lights," Dorcas murmured.

"And the music," Mother added, with a shudder.

Genette herself stepped into view. She was talking on a cell phone, and not, apparently, enjoying her conversation. She was pushing forty, but trying her best to look on the sunny side of twenty. Blond, but probably not by nature. On the slender side, but not nearly enough for the short, tight, bright red dress she was wearing. Considering how she was snarling and gesticulating at the phone, I found it astonishing how serene her face was. After a few moments it occurred to me that perhaps she'd had Botox.

I was watching her out of the corner of my eye, trying to prove or disprove this theory, when another, stouter figure sailed into view.

Brett Riordan. Molly's not quite ex-husband.

"Babe!" he cried, as he approached Genette's booth. He had a half-full glass of red wine in one hand. He wrapped the other arm around Genette and pulled her into a prolonged kiss. Prolonged, but with curiously little heat—he didn't seem to be expressing passion so much as marking territory.

For that matter, so did Genette.

I looked away, and glanced around to see how the other denizens of the wine pavilion were reacting. Most of them were also looking away—some of them rather ostentatiously. A few were tittering or rolling their eyes.

Brett and Genette had finished their kiss but were clinging together, giggling and pawing each other. Brett was still handsome in a beefy way, but he'd gained bulk. His jowls were softer now, and his nose and cheeks a lot redder. I didn't think much of Genette, but she could do a lot better than Brett.

Then again, I'd always been immune to his boozy charm.

"They put on quite a show, don't they?" Dorcas murmured.

"Are we supposed to believe that they can't resist each other?" her neighbor added.

I had the feeling that what they couldn't resist was the opportunity to shove their affair in our faces.

Or had my arrival had something to do with it? Brett was no rocket scientist, but he knew who I was. Was he hoping I'd go back and tell Molly what I'd seen? Not a chance.

A pity I couldn't tell him that. But he probably knew I'd never been his biggest fan. Molly and I had become better friends in the last several years, when I no longer had to rack my brain for the right thing to say when she burbled about how wonderful Brett was. I'd been a lot more comfortable sympathizing when she complained about his spendthrift ways, his inability to hold or even get a job, and her growing awareness that he was turning from a happy-go-lucky young man with a fondness for restaurants and parties into a loud middle-aged alcoholic loafer.

But "I told you so" isn't something you can say to friends. I reminded myself that however tempting it would be to criticize Brett to Molly, it wasn't a wise or kind thing to do. What if they got back together again after I'd told Molly exactly how little I thought of him? Or, more likely, what if slamming him, instead of cheering her up, made her feel like an idiot for marrying him in the first place? No, as long as Molly was around, I'd keep my opinions of Brett to myself.

But Molly wasn't around. And Mother was.

"Honestly," I said, rolling my eyes slightly.

Mother shook her head.

"Precisely." She arched her neck and deliberately turned her back on the two of them. "By the way," she went on. "I want you and Randall to know right now that next year I'm imposing rules on the decor. Shopping malls do it, and homeowners' associations, so I don't see why we can't."

"You think the winemakers will stand for that?"

"They're asking if we can't impose them this year," she said. "I don't think that's fair, but next year, we will send out lists of acceptable colors and materials, and any exceptions must be approved by me. Or whoever you appoint to be next year's arts and crafts director."

"Does this mean you're volunteering to be Quilts, Pies, and Wine Czarina again next year?" I said. "Awesome."

"Only if I'm allowed to evict eyesores like that," she said.

"If you can come up with some enforceable rules, we'll enforce them."

Actually, I had no doubt Mother could do it herself.

"Thank you, dear. And you did have that rule against

exhibitors interfering with other booths. I was able to use that to shut down the music."

"I remember you mentioned music," I said. "I gather we're not talking anything tasteful and classical?"

"Sounded like someone killing hogs," the neighbor said.

"People fled the tent when she turned it on," Dorcas added.

"It made the Rancid Dreads' music sound melodious," Mother said. Possibly the first time she'd every used the word "music" to refer to the sounds emitted by our local heavy metal band, so I deduced that Genette's taste in music must be very strange indeed.

Brett and Genette were still pawing each other, obviously aware of the disapproving stares they were getting. Well, a few disapproving stares, and a lot of disapproving backs of heads. Mother raised one eyebrow and sighed.

"Not a big fan of public displays of affection?" Dorcas asked.

"As long as they're tasteful," Mother said. "But there are limits."

"Like when one of the displayers is still married to someone else," I said. "That's Molly Riordan's husband, you know."

"Don't you mean 'ex-husband'?" Dorcas asked. "I thought I heard they were divorced now."

"They will be, eventually, but right now they're only separated," I said.

"The jerk," Dorcas muttered.

"Precisely." Mother's voice dripped with icy disapproval.

"And Mother, before you ask," I went on. "I don't think we can enforce a rule against adultery in the wine pavilion next year, but we can misplace Genette's application for a booth until all the spaces are taken."

"Thank you, dear." Mother was almost purring with satisfaction.

"Great idea," Dorcas said. "Wish you'd known her well enough to do it this year. Of course, I'm hoping she'll get bored with her vineyard by next fall."

"Yeah," her neighbor put in. "She bought it almost three years ago now. It only took her two years to get tired of running that restaurant she bought in Middleburg."

"And before that, three years to give up on being a world-famous fashion designer," Dorcas said. "Wonder what her next hobby will be?"

"She seems to have expensive hobbies," I said. "Where does she get the money?"

"Inherited it, or so I heard," Dorcas said. "Her family must have been really loaded."

"Wasn't her family, from what I heard," the other wine-maker said. "Came from her late husbands—two of them, both with big wallets and weak hearts."

"Sounds plausible," Dorcas said. "However she got her hands on her money, she certainly never seems to have a problem paying for what she wants."

Genette and Brett finally tired of their exhibition. She fussed over his hair, straightened the collar of his shirt, topped off his wineglass, and waved like a housewife in a fifties sitcom as he ambled off.

Then she turned around, scanned her surroundings, and spotted me. Her face twitched slightly, in what I real-ized would have been a frown if her forehead could move. Then she pasted an artificial smile on her face and gestured to me in much the way an impatient diner would summon an errant waiter.

"Uh-oh," Dorcas said. "You've been summoned."

"Don't let her bully you," the other winemaker said.

"Meg will be fine." Mother smiled encouragement at me.

Armed with that vote of confidence, I strolled over to Genette's booth.

Chapter 9

"Finally," she said, as if she'd summoned me hours ago. "I need to talk to someone about getting my music back."

"I can check with our lost and found," I said, pretending to misunderstand her. "Are we talking sheet music or CDs or—"

"I haven't lost my CDs," she said. "But that woman made me stop playing them!"

She was pointing to Mother.

"Yes, she's in charge of the wine pavilion," I said. "And you do realize that we have a rule prohibiting anything that interferes with your neighbors' ability to do business in their booths, right?"

"But music wouldn't interfere," she protested. "It would liven things up around here. I mean, look at this place! It's dead in here."

I looked. Considering that it was barely a quarter to eleven in the morning—not a time of day I, at least, associated with drinking wine—the tent was pretty busy. A fair number of visitors were already strolling up and down the aisles, or stopping to talk to the winemakers. You could hear the occasional pop of a cork or clink of a glass, and the conversations blended into a pleasant hum, occasionally punctuated by laughter.

"Sounds fine to me," I said.

"Maybe for a morgue. Check this out." She turned

around, punched a button, and a tsunami of noise erupted from the two speakers that had been masquerading as ugly occasional tables. It sounded as if someone were torturing half a dozen cats by throwing them onto drums, into trash cans, and through a couple of large plate-glass windows.

"Turn it off," I shouted. "Turn it off!"

But she couldn't have heard me, and wasn't looking my way to see that I had my hands clapped over my ears. She had her eyes closed, and was swaying and twitching spasmodically.

Evidently neither shouting nor miming was going to work. I glanced down and saw power cords snaking down from the speakers and across the open ground in the middle of her booth to disappear under a chrome and Plexiglas panel. I leaned down and gave one cord a hard yank. A power strip slid from under the booth. I hit its off switch and sudden, blessed silence prevailed.

Utter silence. As I stood up again, I glanced around to see that all up and down the tent, people were staring at us with their mouths wide open and their hands protecting their ears.

"What did you have to do that for?" Genette was actually pouting.

"I'm afraid I agree that your music is in violation of the wine pavilion rules," I said.

"And the county's noise ordinances," called a nearby winemaker.

"I want to challenge everyone's conservative perceptions about wine." It might have sounded plausible if she hadn't said it in the whiny voice of a thwarted toddler— a tone that was becoming all too familiar to me lately.

"I want people to stop thinking of wine as something that only staid, middle-aged, affluent people can buy."

A well-dressed middle-aged woman who was in the process of buying several cases of wine at the next booth turned and glared at her briefly.

"That's the whole idea behind my brand identity." She indicated her booth with a sweeping gesture. "I hired an expensive, cutting-edge New York brand management firm to design it, because I wanted something edgy and urban and new! Not all this medieval Jefferson crap." This time she waved vaguely at the rest of the tent. If looks could kill, Mother would already have felled her from across the aisle. "You need to bring wine into the twenty-first century!"

"We'll certainly take your suggestions under advisement," I said. "For next year. But we have neither the time nor the money to change the decor for this year's fair. So we'd appreciate it if you'd try to work within this year's guidelines."

"So what am I supposed to do with the forty-thousand-dollar sound system I had made for my booth?" She pointed to the hulking speakers, now silent but still radiating potential menace.

"They make . . . interesting occasional tables," I said. "But do keep them clear of the aisles—we wouldn't want anyone to damage them."

With that I went back to where Mother and Dorcas were waiting.

"That woman," Mother said, shaking her head.

"If anyone kills her, I expect an alibi," I said.

"If anyone's planning to kill her, tell them to come see me," Dorcas said. "I want to get in on it."

I glanced back at Genette. She was tugging one of her

hideous speakers back behind the booth line, glaring my way as she did. I'd probably made an enemy just now.

I didn't much care.

"Let me know if she causes any trouble," I said.

"I think I can handle any trouble she causes." Mother sniffed slightly.

"Yes, but I can't ban anyone from the fair for misbehavior unless someone tells me about the misbehavior," I said. "So I want to hear chapter and verse."

"Absolutely," Mother said.

I strolled out of the wine pavilion feeling confident that at least one part of the fair was under control.

As I stepped out and looked around, I heard someone call my name. I turned to see a man following me out of the tent.

"Can I help you, Mr.—" I glanced through the tent opening at the booth I thought he'd emerged from. Stapleton Wineries. "Stapleton?"

He didn't correct me. He glanced furtively in several directions, and then took a step closer.

"It's about Genette," he said, in a voice calculated not to carry very far. "You need to keep an eye on her. She's sneaky."

"I will," I said. "Both eyes, and both ears. But don't worry. I think if she turns on the stereo again, someone will notice, and we'll have grounds to confiscate it. And maybe even kick her out."

"I don't mean the stereo." He waved one hand dismissively. "Though I have to admit, even if I were a Glass fan, that would be annoying."

"Glass fan?"

"Philip Glass," he said. "The composer of that music she was trying to destroy your eardrums with. Not my favorite of his compositions, actually. The wife and I have been known to blast that piece out the window on Halloween, to set the mood. No, I mean the pranks."

"Pranks?"

"The chicken thefts. The pumpkin. The quilt. She's behind it all."

"If you have evidence of this—" I began.

"I don't have any evidence, but it stands to reason. She was after the chickens."

"Seems to me she could afford to buy a few chickens," I pointed out.

"She could afford to buy anything she wants," he said. "But what if someone won't sell to her? What if she doubles the price a couple of times and an animal's owner just keeps saying no? It happened to me."

"She stole your chickens?"

"Lemon Millefleur Sablepoots," he said. "Very rare bantam breed. I had a dozen—I was trying to build up a flock. One day she came over to the vineyard for a visit— God knows why; we're not friends. And she tried to buy the Sablepoots. Wouldn't take no for an answer. I finally told her that as soon as I got my flock established, I'd sell her some chicks. Didn't make her happy. She's into instant gratification. Then a week later, someone stole half of my flock. Including the rooster. Bye-bye future chicks."

"And you think she has them?"

"Couple months later, she held a big party, and one of the things she was showing off was a pen full of Sable-poots."

"Yours?"

"No, chicks. A dozen of them, young enough to have hatched from eggs since mine had been stolen. She claimed she bought them somewhere. Real secretive about where, though, and I can't find any reputable breeder who recalls selling to her. I'm almost positive she has another farm somewhere with my Sablepoots stashed on it. And who knows what else. But I can't find it—it's probably out of state. So she's building up a prize-winning flock of Sablepoots with stock she stole from me, and I'm still on the waiting list till another breeder has some chicks. A long list."

"Sounds . . . suspicious," I said. "If she does have another farm where she stashes stolen animals, wouldn't that be a job for law enforcement?"

"Yeah," he said. "And our sheriff back home agrees with me, or at least he doesn't think I'm crazy. But he needs more than just me saying I think she did it. She's rich, and she's got political connections. If he tried to do a search on her assets, it would set off red flags. And if he goes after her and doesn't find anything—well, he likes his job."

"So you think she's expanding to Russian Orloffs?"

"Could be. She had some Dutch Belteds and Red Polls at her winery spread last time I heard. Cows," he added, correctly guessing from my expression that I had no idea what species he was talking about. "And then they disappeared. Did she sell them, or move them somewhere else? Someone should look."

"I wouldn't have taken her for an animal fancier," I said. "I can see her with a spoiled little purse dog, but cows and chickens?"

"Only rare ones. She likes to brag about how rare they are. And she hires people to do the actual work. Usually people who were perfectly happy working for someone else before she offered them double the salary to work for her. I guess it's a hobby."

"Raising animals or acquiring other people's property?"

"Both," he said, with a gruff chuckle. "Whiles away the time while she's waiting for the grapes to grow. For us working vineyard owners, the days are too short, all year long, for all the work we need to get done, but for a hobby owner like her . . ."

He shrugged.

"I understand why you'd be worried," I said. "But I'm not sure what we can do."

"Ask those poor people who lost their Orloffs if she ever tried to buy them," he said. "And that kid whose pumpkin was smashed—his father raises Gloucestershire Old Spots—that's a rare breed of pigs. I haven't heard she was into pigs, but you never know. Ask him. Ask who-ever had her quilt stolen if she raises some kind of rare livestock. Or maybe Genette's looking to expand and the quilt's owner also owns some land that borders on hers."

"Or maybe Genette tried to buy the quilt, in spite of the 'not for sale' sign on it?"

"Yeah. You're catching on."

I was also catching on to the idea that if someone did knock off Genette, I wouldn't be the only one needing an alibi. The chief would need a scorecard to keep all the suspects straight.

And why did the idea of Genette being murdered keep popping into my head? Was it just my way of blowing off a little steam or was I having some kind of premonition?

"Thanks," I said. "Although our chief of police is really the one who should hear about this."

"Maybe you could pass it along," he said. "And I'd be perfectly happy to talk to him myself, as long as we do it someplace where she won't know about it. I don't want to get on her bad side—I live too close for that."

"Is yours one of the farms she's trying to buy out?"

"Not yet," he said. "Right now, there's still two farms be-tween me and her. But that could change. Used to be three farms. Here."

He handed me a business card.

"My cell phone's on it. I'll be around if your police chief wants to talk to me."

With that he nodded and stepped back inside the wine pavilion.

I fingered his card for a few moments. Then I tucked it in my pocket and headed for the fair office. The chief might still be there. I could fill him in on Stapleton's sus-picions and find out if he and Vern had made any prog-ress solving the chicken thefts. And then maybe I could head for the nearby llama exhibit and say good morning to the boys.

When I entered I found the chief and Randall Shiffley sitting on folding chairs. Vern Shiffley was pointing to the map of the fair, and the chief and Randall were studying it.

"Oh, good—Meg's here," Randall said. "Vern's going to update us on the investigation so far."

"For what it's worth," Vern grumbled.

Chapter 10

Apparently Vern had just finished complaining, not for the first time, about his Clay County counterparts.

"Not much we can do about it now," Vern said. "But I say next year we put the Midway on our side of the border. And I don't just mean so we can get all the sales tax revenue. Did I tell you I figured out why they never arrested any pickpockets over there at last year's fair?"

"Let me guess—they just make 'em pay for a pickpocketing license?" Randall suggested.

"No, but you're close," Vern said. "They just beat the pickpocket up a little, empty his pockets, and escort him to the county line."

"I'll have a word with Sheriff Dingle." The chief didn't exactly sound thrilled at the prospect.

"Chief, there's no talking to these people," Vern said. "They're not in the twenty-first century yet. They're still trying to find the seventeenth. If we—"

"I'll have a word with their sheriff." Chief Burke's voice was calm, but I had the feeling this wasn't the first time they'd had this discussion. "He may not agree with me, but I think he's well aware that they need to work with us if they want to retain their small but very lucrative piece of the fair. Have we made any progress on the thefts and vandalism?"

Vern grimaced and shook his head. He had a small notebook in his hand, and he looked down at it and flipped a page.

"Horace couldn't get any usable fingerprints off the pumpkin or the cage the chickens were taken from," he said. "He said there was no use even trying with the quilt. Half the quilters are over at Rosalie's camper, consoling her, and the other half are mutinous because they think she now has an unfair edge in the competition, even if Daphne can't get all the mud off."

"And they could be right, but that's not something we can do anything about," the chief said.

Vern nodded, and went back to his notebook.

"Knowledgeable sources in the produce tent say the kid whose pumpkin was smashed was probably headed for a medal," he went on. "But no one—except the kid—thinks it would have won first prize. Third through sixth, according to my sources. Haven't heard yet whether the judges are going to let him enter those barrels of pumpkin goop we had collected. And things are pretty crazy in the chicken tent. A few of the exhibitors are threatening to go home, but no one really believes they will before the judging. Still, they're all running around like—well, like chickens with their heads cut off. No other thefts or pranks, and no idea if those three are related."

"I heard a theory that might explain it," I said. I pulled out Stapleton's card, handed it to the chief, and relayed what he had told me about Genette.

"You think there's something to this?" the chief asked when I'd finished.

"I have no idea," I said. "People who know her better than I do seem to think so. Of course, they're all people who dislike her. Haven't talked to anyone who likes her, if such a thing exists. But even if Stapleton's wrong, I bet he's not the only one saying stuff like this. There are some serious bad feelings down there in the wine tent. You might want to keep an eye on her."

"Are you worried that she might be up to something, or that the other exhibitors, who think she's up to something, might take matters into their own hands?"

"Either," I said. "Or both. There's also the possibility that someone might be deliberately trying to cause troubles that would be blamed on Genette."

"I don't have the manpower to guard Ms. Sedgewick," the chief said. "We're already stretched thin patrolling a hundred acres of fairgrounds."

"One hundred and twenty, to be exact," Randall said. "With the possibility of expansion if— Sorry, chief. Force of habit."

"Patrolling over a hundred acres of fairgrounds," the chief went on. "Unless we are reasonably sure that Ms. Sedgewick is either dangerous or in danger, I can't justify putting a watch on her, if that's what you mean."

"No," I said. "I just meant keep her in mind as you investigate the chicken theft."

The chief nodded.

"So how are your patrols going?" He was looking at Randall.

Randall looked at me.

"I've got twenty-two volunteers so far," I said. "I'm going to organize them in mixed teams."

"Mixed how?" Randall asked.

"Geographically and by exhibition category," I said. "And before you say I'm overthinking this—if whoever did this is an exhibitor, and I assume they're among the leading suspects, what's to stop him from volunteering for our patrol?" At least that was what serial killers always did in the mystery books and TV shows Dad loved so much. But I didn't mention that, because I'd already figured out that it annoyed the chief when people made television-based assumptions about how his department worked.

"Involving himself in the investigation," the chief said, nodding. "Not uncommon."

"He'd be a fool not to volunteer," Randall added.

"So we don't send two chicken breeders to patrol the chicken tent," I said. "We send a hog man from Tazewell and an apple grower from Gloucester. Different farm specialties; opposite ends of the state."

They both nodded.

"I think we need to concentrate on the east side of the grounds," Randall said. "Particularly the northeast corner where the Midway is."

"Are you suspicious of the Midway people?" the chief asked. "Or Clay County?"

"Yes," Vern said, and we all chuckled.

"Actually, it's because we have that eight-foot chain-link fence around the rest of the perimeter." Randall traced the fairground borders on the map. "South, west, north—all fenced in. But the east side backs up against really dense woods and a lot of swampland. We figured only locals could find their way in from back there, and most of them are already working the fair and don't need to sneak in."

"Next year, I think we need to fence in that side, too," I said. It was an old argument between Randall and me.

"Next year," Randall agreed. "But for now, I say we concentrate our patrols along the east."

"Actually," I said. "I was thinking we'd concentrate on the exhibit tents and barns."

"Because you think the perpetrator is already inside?" the chief asked.

"Maybe," I said. "But whether he's sneaking into the fair or already in, he can't do any damage if he can't get at the exhibits."

"Good point." The chief nodded.

"But I'll set up a few patrols in the northeast corner, too," I added.

"Before I go," the chief said. "Do you have a list of exhibitors?

"Meg can print you a list," Randall said. "She's set up a whole database of 'em. Come on—let's show him."

"I didn't set up the database." I turned on my laptop and opened the file. "It was Rob's contribution to the Un-fair. One of the perks of having a brother who owns a computer game company."

"I thought your brother was supremely nontechnical and only came up with the ideas for the games." The chief was looking over my shoulder at the screen.

"He didn't do it himself. He assigned his best database programmer to work with me on it. And I've got his help desk on speed dial in case we need anything fixed. What information do you want on the exhibitors?"

"What do you have?" The chief reached back and pulled up a folding chair to sit at my elbow.

"What doesn't she have?" Randall said, with a chuckle.

"I'll show you a sample record." I called up the last record I'd viewed. "Here's the people who lost the Russian Orloffs."

"The Baskervilles," Randall said.

"They're not—" I began.

"Mr. Holmes!" Randall declaimed, in a not-very-authentic

British accent. "They were the footprints of a gigantic hen! We are searching for the Hen of the Baskervilles!"

"That would be nice," I said. "But the hen's a bantam, not a giant, and their name is Bonneville. Why does every-one keep calling them Baskerville?"

"Maybe because *The Hound of the Baskervilles* is this month's One City, One Book selection," Randall said. "The name kind of sticks in your mind."

"Getting back to the Bonnevilles." I turned to the chief. "We have their name, address, phone number, Web site if applicable, what events they're entered in, whether they've won anything—we fill that in later—where they heard about the Un-fair if we know, whether we issued them a camping permit—it's free to exhibitors, but we want to control who's there, so they need a permit. Stuff like that."

The chief was peering over his glasses at the screen and nodding his approval.

"Show him the map," Randall said. "I just love the map."

I typed in a command and brought up a map of Virginia, speckled with dots.

"Each dot's an exhibitor," I said. "The dots off in what should be West Virginia are all out-of-state exhibitors. The program is set up so whenever we add an exhibitor to the database, it puts a corresponding dot on the map. We can see where our exhibitors are coming from, and what parts of the state we're not reaching. I can also show you by cat-egory, like just the winemakers, or just the sheep exhibi-tors, or just the people who have entered the pie contest."

As I spoke, I typed in commands and the map changed to show different, smaller configurations of dots.

"Can I get a copy of that?" the chief asked. "Not a paper copy, a copy of the file on your computer."

"It's not on my computer," I said. "It's on the server at Rob's office. I can see if they can give you a copy, or maybe all you'd need is access to the data."

"Access would be excellent," the chief said.

A few minutes later he walked out with a printout of all exhibitors with their cell phone numbers and a star beside those who were staying at the campgrounds. And back at the station, Debbie Ann had a user name and password for the Un-fair database, since in addition to being the dispatcher she was the one person on the force who really liked computers and knew how to use them.

Of course, there was no guarantee our thief and vandal was there in my database. But it was as good a place as any to start.

Randall and I took care of a few fair-related chores—he made a call to harangue his cousin who was supposed to have delivered another batch of portapotties. I turned on my laptop and began sorting the patrol volunteers into unrelated pairs. If I could get the volunteers organized and notified quickly, maybe I'd still have time to join Michael and the boys at the children's concert.

Then my brother, Rob, strolled in.

"I thought you were minding the exhibitors' gate," I said.

"Need your expertise," he replied. "We've got some guy who wants to know what to do with his crackers."

Chapter 11

"Crackers?" I echoed. "I suppose they'd go under baked goods. We don't have a separate cracker competition."

"Maybe they fall under bread," Randall suggested. "What kind of crackers?"

"Florida crackers." Rob perched on the edge of my desk. "And I already tried to give him directions to the food exhibits, and he got all steamed up. Says they're not that kind of crackers and asked if I was a complete idiot."

"A complete idiot?" I said. "I'll take the fifth on that. Hang on a sec."

I opened up a browser, typed a few words into my search engine, and found the information I needed.

"Aha," I said. "Florida Crackers are a heritage breed of cows."

"Cool." Rob was already pulling out his cell phone and punching numbers. "It's okay," he said. "The Crackers are cows. Send him to the cow barn. Right."

"You could have called with that question," I said. "Or—wild and crazy idea—gone to look in his truck."

"I did call, but your phone kept ringing busy," he said. "Needed a break, anyway. And I wanted to get the scoop on the great chicken robbery. Did the thief get the whole flock?"

"Two chickens are missing," I said.

"Is that all?" he asked. "Then why do you have Horace going crazy doing forensics? Are they that valuable?"

"They are to the owners," I said.

"And they're a rare, heritage breed," Randall put in.

"What is with all this heritage and heirloom stuff, anyway?" Rob asked.

Talk about giving Randall the perfect opening to talk about his latest obsession. I tried not to giggle.

"Heirloom crops are ones that are in danger of falling by the wayside because they're not the ones that Big Agriculture finds useful," Randall began. "Same with heritage animal and bird breeds."

And speaking of those breeds, I decided it would be useful to print out a copy of a page I'd bookmarked—the American Livestock Breed Conservancy's list of farm animals and poultry that were a conservation priority. I was tired of being confused when people talked about Sablepoots and Old Spots. And I'd already figured out that the more obscure the animal's breed, the more annoyed its owner would be if you didn't recognize it.

"So what's so special about these heritage animals?" Rob was asking.

"Let me show you one," Randall said.

He strode out the door and disappeared. Rob had to scramble to keep up. I grabbed my printout and followed along for the entertainment value. From the enthusiasm with which he extolled heritage livestock and heirloom seeds, you'd think Randall was a fifth- or sixth-generation farmer. And some of his family were farmers, but a lot more of them were carpenters, plumbers, electricians, mechanics—just about any skilled trade that would get them out from behind a plow. Randall as the champion of the old-fashioned farm was a new role that still amused me.

He led us to a small pen.

"This," he said, "is an American Mammoth Jackstock donkey."

Staring back at us was a large donkey. His coat was black on top, shaded to gray or white on his belly and the inside of his legs, and he had a white nose and pale rings around his eyes. His ears were so large they seemed incongruous, as if someone had stuck a pair of fake bunny ears on a horse. But they were definitely real. One of them swiveled ninety degrees to the right, apparently tracking a sound so faint none of us noticed, and then snapped back to attention facing us.

"I thought donkeys were little," Rob said. "He's the size of a small horse."

"They were bred for size and strength," Randall explained. "By George Washington and other early colonial farmers. You breed one of these donkeys to a saddle mare and you've got yourself a decent-sized riding mule. Breed him to a draft mare and you've got a big, strapping work mule."

"But why go to all that trouble of breeding mules when you've already got horses and donkeys?" Rob asked. "Why not just use them? Plus with horses and donkeys you can always make more little horses and donkeys, but mules are kind of a dead end."

"Mules get the best of both parents," Randall said. "They're more patient and surefooted than a horse, and can carry bigger loads. And they're bigger and stronger than donkeys. And supposedly more intelligent than either horses or donkeys. No offense, Jim-Bob."

He patted the donkey's neck. Jim-Bob took a sideways step closer to Randall and lowered his head slightly, as if to suggest that he wouldn't say no if someone offered to scratch behind his ears. Randall obliged, and Jim-Bob's long face took on a dreamy look.

"And they eat less for their size than horses, which is another big selling point with a small farmer," Randall went on. "A hundred and fifty years ago, your mule was like your tractor and your pickup, all rolled into one. By 1920, there were around five million mules in the U.S., and probably hundreds of thousands of these donkeys that the mule breeders used to produce them. And then along came Henry Ford and the model T."

Jim-Bob pulled his head back. I wondered at first if he was objecting to Randall's mentioning the man whose invention had led to the downfall of his breed. Then Jim-Bob stuck his head forward again at a slightly different angle, so Randall could reach the other ear.

"Poor old guy," Rob said. "I guess with nobody using mules anymore, this guy's out of a job." He stepped forward and began scratching the ear Randall had abandoned. Jim-Bob closed his eyes and sighed with delight.

"Lots of people still use mules."

We glanced around to see a woman with cropped gray hair, blue jeans, and a t-shirt with a picture of a mule and the words MULE PROJECT on it.

"Hey, Betsy," Randall called.

"The Amish use mules." Clearly this was Betsy's favorite topic. "They may use horses for their buggies, but they plow and harvest with mules. And mules are popular for wilderness trekking. In fact, in parts of the world where you can't take a car, people still use mules for daily transportation. The U.S. Army uses them in places like Afghanistan where the terrain's too steep to drive or even land a helicopter."

"Betsy's one of the people trying to keep the American

Jack Mule breed from dying out," Randall added. "What happens if we discover a whole lot of new uses for mules, and can't get top-quality ones?"

"She's protecting the strategic mule reserve," I said. "I like that."

"And I aim to go home with all the mules and donkeys I came with," Betsy said. "You hear me, Randall?"

"Betsy," Randall began. "We're just as sick as anyone about the chicken thefts, and we're tightening up security considerably now. I know you're worried that someone will steal your stock, but we're doing our best to guard the animals—"

"No, I'm not that worried about theft," Betsy said. "My mules and donkeys pretty much guard themselves. Heaven help the poor rustler who goes after them. No, I'm talking about that blond hussy who keeps coming 'round trying to bludgeon me with her checkbook."

"Genette Sedgewick?" I asked.

"That's her. She's been trying to tell me she's a big supporter of the American Mammoth when she can't even tell a mule from a donkey," Betsy went on. "For that matter, she can't tell a jack from a jenny."

"I'm afraid I don't even know what a jack or a jenny is," Rob said.

"Same as stallion and mare in horses," Randall put in.

"Okay, I think I could figure that out, now that I know the terminology," Rob said.

"You're allowed not to know the terminology." Betsy's gruff tone softened a little. "You're not pretending to be an experienced mule and donkey owner." She turned back to Randall. "If that woman comes around here again, I might throw her in the pen with Henry, my orneriest mule, and see which one comes out alive."

Randall glanced over at me.

"You think we could come up with a rule about harassing exhibitors?" he asked.

"I assume by 'we' you mean 'me,'" I said. "I'll work on it. Do you mean for this year or next year?"

"Next year won't help me if she drives me crazy this year," Betsy said.

"It's our fair," Randall said. "I don't see why we can't put out a rule to cover an unforeseen problem. Not the first complaint we've had about her."

I was already scribbling in my notebook.

"I'll draft something," I said. "But frankly, I'm not sure Genette will pay much attention to a rule. Might be a good idea if someone had a talk with her."

"Great idea," Randall said. "You can probably get through to her much better in person."

With that he gave Jim-Bob a parting pat and strode off.

"You walked right into that one," Rob said.

Betsy snickered.

"Much as I would enjoy reading Genette the riot act, I'm afraid she's a hard case," I said. "I'm going to call in expert assistance."

Rob and Betsy looked puzzled.

"After all," I said. "Mother is in charge of the wine pavilion."

"Awesome," Rob said. "Can I watch?"

"Ask Mother."

"By the way," Betsy said. "We haven't seen your grandfather this year. He's been such a supporter of the mule rescue and heritage animals in general. Is he okay?"

She sounded worried—as well she might. Grandfather was well into his nineties, although he was still active as a roving zoologist and gadfly environmentalist, and kept up a travel schedule that would have killed me.

"He's fine," I said. "He'll probably be here by Saturday. He and Caroline Willner from the Wildlife Sanctuary went to Australia with a film crew to do a special on endangered species."

"Lovely!" she said. "So we'll be seeing him on Animal Planet again sometime soon?"

"Along with any number of Bulmer's fruit bats, northern hairy-nosed wombats, and bridled nail-tail wallabies," I said. "And don't ask me what any of those creatures look like—I'm waiting to see the footage."

"Fabulous!" she said. "Give him my best, and tell him we'd love to have him stop by. We've just started a Web site for the Mule Project and I'd love to have a picture of him and Jim-Bob on it."

"I'll definitely tell him." The notion of seeing a photo of my stubborn grandfather appearing on the Mule Project Web site had a curious appeal. "I'll catch you later."

I gave Jim-Bob a friendly pat on the head and then headed for the wine pavilion. Behind me, I could hear that Rob was still intrigued by the mules and donkeys.

"So is it true that they're really stubborn?" he asked.

"They can be," Betsy said. "But mainly because they're better at sticking up for themselves. A horse will let you ride him to exhaustion or into a dangerous situation, but not a mule or a donkey . . ."

Hmm. We'd been thinking of getting ponies for the boys. Would small mules be a safer choice?

As I headed for the wine pavilion, I made a mental note to ask Betsy later. Right now, coping with the evil Genette was more urgent.

Chapter 12

Mother was delighted to see me. She was standing beside a booth at the Mediterranean end of the pavilion, delicately sipping from a glass with a splash of white wine in it, while a woman winemaker watched intently, as if Mother's verdict would make or break her wine's reputation. For all I knew, perhaps it would.

"Meg, dear." She held out a glass. "Do try some of this lovely Chardonnay!"

"Later," I said. "When my taste buds have time to think. Would you like an opportunity to take Genette to task, or shall I do it myself?"

"Ooh," the Chardonnay's maker said. "What's she been up to now?"

"Harassing other exhibitors to sell their livestock to her," I said. "Anyone who feels harassed by another exhibitor should report it to the fair office, and we'll deal with it. Repeat offenders can be banned. Permanently."

Mother smiled.

"Last time I looked she'd stepped out," she said. "I think I'll wander down to that part of the tent. Thank you," she said to the winemaker. "Can you save me a few bottles? In fact, make it a case."

"Absolutely."

Mother sipped the last bit of Chardonnay and sailed off.

"I may be the first to report Genette," the winemaker

said. "If she comes back and badgers me again to buy a copy of our customer list. Not that I'm afraid of losing customers to her—not if they taste her wine. But I shudder to think what kind of marketing she'd do if she ever got my customers' names and addresses. She doesn't exactly run a very classy operation."

"Yeah," I said. "I've seen the labels."

"Oh, I don't mind the labels." She shook her head and chuckled. "Her labels sell a lot of my wine. One look at that monstrosity and anyone with a smidgen of taste wants to run away and find something a bit more elegant."

She pulled something out of her pocket and handed it to me. A wine label. No, actually it was an oversized business card made to look like a wine label on one side. The reverse held her name, address, telephone numbers, e-mail, Web site, and even a small map with directions to her winery.

And the label itself did look rather elegant. There was a white column on either side, with roses growing up the left hand one and grapes on the right. The winery's name was printed in a very traditional typeface. The colors were bright, but not gaudy. Yes, elegant.

"Nice," I said. "May I keep it?"

"Of course." She held up a handful to show that she had plenty more. "Anyway, it's not the labels that drive me crazy. It's how she runs her winery. She tore down a bunch of perfectly lovely, mellow old buildings and put up a bunch of ugly new ones. They look a lot like her booth, actually. Then she put in a helipad. You have no idea what it's like having helicopters swooping back and forth all the time, raising clouds of dust and frightening the horses. And then she caught on to the idea of using her winery as an event space." She rolled her eyes as if this were the last straw.

"Aren't a lot of wineries doing that these days?" I asked.

"Of course," she said. "Sometimes that's the only thing keeping us afloat in the bad years. But it doesn't always set well with the communities we're located in. So most of us do what we can to minimize the negative impact on our neighbors and the environment and have orderly well-run events. Classy events."

"That doesn't sound like Genette's style," I said.

"Every weekend is a nightmare." She was shaking her head and wincing. "Rowdy frat parties and bachelor orgies and wild wedding receptions. Rock bands and fireworks all night. Drunken partyers careening down the roads till all hours. A lot of sirens—police breaking up brawls, ambulances carrying out the casualties."

"Sounds horrible," I said. "Can't the police do anything?"

"They're trying," she said. "But she's got all the money in the world to fight back. It could take years, and all that time she'll be busy turning a peaceful, rural county into a drunken slum. And making it that much harder for the rest of us who are trying to run our businesses responsibly."

She shook her head and turned to go behind the counter of her booth, then turned back to me again.

"And in case no one else has said it," she added, "we appreciate what you and your mother are doing to keep her from ruining the wine pavilion."

With that she turned to serve another customer.

Another name to add to the list of suspects if anything happened to the much-loathed Genette. I walked slowly down the aisle and found Mother in the Jeffersonian end, where she was supervising Michael's attempts to rearrange some vines so they climbed more gracefully up a white-painted trellis, and then hung more elegantly over the tables and chairs in a nearby booth. The boys were sitting at the table, clutching enormous wineglasses in their tiny hands. Jamie was holding up his glass, which was filled with red liquid, and peering through it to see what the world looked like with a rosy tint. Josh had just taken a sip from his glass and was swishing it around in his mouth with a thoughtful look on his face, in a spot-on imitation of what I'd seen adult connoisseurs do.

But what were the boys doing swilling down wine?

"Don't worry," Mother said, following my glance. "It's organic."

The winemaker held up the bottle for me to see— organic grape juice.

"More, please." Josh held out his glass.

"Genette's not there," Mother said. "But I can see her booth from here."

"Good," I said. "We really need to keep an eye on her."

"Why?" Mother forgot about the vines and stepped out into the aisle so she could look at Genette's booth. "What else is she doing now?"

"Nothing that I know of," I said. "But these people really hate her. If I were her, I'd keep my back to the wall and I wouldn't drink any wine I hadn't poured myself. From a freshly opened bottle."

"Shh!" Mother glanced around as if afraid of someone overhearing. "Don't let any of them hear you say that. I can't imagine any of these nice people poisoning someone with their own wine. Or any other nice wine, before you suggest that."

"They could use her wine," I said. "I haven't heard anyone suggest it was particularly nice."

"Nice wine." Jamie said, holding up his glass.

"Find out if any of them make Malmsey," Michael suggested. "That's how the Duke of Clarence was killed in *Richard III*. Drowned in a butt of Malmsey."

"Is Malmsey wine?" I asked. "I always assumed it was beer."

"It's a kind of Madeira," Mother said as she refilled both boys' glasses. "And I'm sure none of them would do that, either. If one of them did decide to kill her, I'm sure they could find lots of perfectly suitable methods that don't involve wine at all. Thank you, Michael; I think that's fine now."

With that she wafted off to the other end of the tent.

"I heard that." It was Dorcas, the winemaker whose booth was so near Genette's. "And she's right. None of us would ever kill someone by poisoning their wine, and we wouldn't kill her in your mother's pavilion."

"I'd use some other kind of poison," suggested the winemaker whose booth Mother and Michael had been improving. "I doubt if there's a vineyard in the state that doesn't have some kind of nasty fungicides lying around. Probably on a back shelf, because the stuff's been outlawed, and we haven't figured out how to dispose of it safely and legally. Why not dust a little on her fried dough?"

"Fried dough now?" Josh suggested.

"Fried dough soon," I said.

"Have some raisins," Dorcas said, offering a bowlful. "Organic," she added to me.

That proved a popular suggestion. Both boys grabbed handfuls and began devouring the raisins.

"Could we kill her with her own speakers?" Dorcas said. "Tie her up, put her in a soundproof room with them, turn up the volume, and see if sound can kill."

"It doesn't." The other winemaker shook his head. "Just

makes you crazy, and she's already that. But yeah, you could use the speakers. Just drop one on her. But not here. Do it at that fair she's putting on next month."

"What fair?" I asked.

"I can't do it at her fair," Dorcas said. "Because there's no way I'm going to her trashy event. Here." She handed me a mustard-yellow flyer. "I only took one because I thought maybe you folks would like to know about it."

The flyer was for something called the "Virginia Agricultural Exposition," "a statewide celebration of the agricultural riches of the Old Dominion." It was hard to read and not very professional looking, which probably meant that she'd used the same so-called cutting edge graphic designer who'd done her wine labels and her booth.

Interesting that at the bottom of the flyer was Brett Riordan's name and contact information. And he was listed as the chairman of the Virginia Agricultural Exposition Committee.

I was willing to bet that the real head of the committee was Genette. And that if there was anyone other than her and Brett on the committee, they were her tame minions.

"What about a corkscrew?" Dorcas was saying. "One of those big old wrought-iron antique ones that nobody uses anymore except to hang on the wall and look pretty."

"If we're talking antique tools, how about a scythe or a sickle?" the other winemaker suggested. "Doing it with a corkscrew is a lot more work."

"Good thing we know they're not serious," Michael said, in an undertone.

"Do we?"

He shrugged.

"It's the ones who aren't venting and getting it out of their systems that I'd be worried about," he said. "Well, now that I've taken care of your mother's chores, the boys and I should be running along. If you need us, we'll be staffing the llama exhibit."

"What about the children's concert?" I asked.

"Already over," he said.

"Over?" I looked at my watch. "Oh, no. Were the boys too disappointed that I didn't make it?"

"Old MacDonald had a farm," Jamie sang.

"The ants go marching one by one." Josh countered.

"They were at first," Michael said over the increasing din of the dueling songs. "But I told them that Mayor Randall had left you in charge of the whole fair. They were very impressed. Now, whenever they want something to be different, they say, 'Mommy fix soon.'"

"Fix now," Jamie corrected.

"So what changes do they want?"

"Free cotton candy," Josh suggested

"And more frequent pig races." Michael gave me a quick kiss and strolled off.

I stared at the flyer again.

"Meg, dear."

Mother had returned.

"She's still not there." I couldn't recall the last time I'd seen Mother so impatient.

"She'll be back," I said. "Meanwhile there's something else I wanted to show you. Have you seen this?" I held up the flyer.

"Virginia Agricultural Exposition," Mother read. "How nice. I've never been that fond of the whole Un-fair name. Whoever thought of this name—"

"Genette," I said.

"—was at least making an effort to come up with an elegant name," Mother said. "Not, of course a successful effort—too pretentious, but . . ."

She shrugged.

"Nice recovery." I handed her the flyer and she studied it. "Nothing that much wrong with the name, but apparently she's going around trying to convince everyone who's here to come to her fair instead."

"Actually, it lists Brett Riordan as the contact person," Mother pointed out.

"But it's being held at her winery, and you can bet it's being done with her money," I said.

"Then she's wasting her money." Another winemaker had come up behind us and was studying the flyer over our shoulders with a slight frown on his face.

"You don't think people will come?" I asked. "There's going to be a competition. Aren't ribbons and medals good advertising?"

"She doesn't actually say who will be judging the competition," the winemaker said. "What if we all show up and she has some flunky judge the competition and award her a lot of the medals?"

"Can she do that?" I asked. "Who judges wine competitions, anyway?" I was looking at Mother. I'd given her free rein to organize all the wine events. I suddenly found myself worried that she'd just recruited a trio of relatives who liked wine.

"Some competitions use judges certified by a group like the American Wine Society," the winemaker said. "They go through a three-year training program, and they'd better know a lot about wine going in."

"That's who we're using, dear," Mother said. "We have three very prestigious nationally known judges."

"An impressive set of judges." The winemaker was nodding his approval.

I reminded myself never to doubt Mother on what she considered the important things in life, like wine, gourmet food, and interior decoration.

"That's why I insisted that we put our judges up at the Caerphilly Inn," Mother said.

"It was the quality of your judges that convinced a lot of us to come," the winemaker said. "We realized you were serious about making this a good event."

I nodded and filed this away to use the next time Randall complained about the expense of the judges' hotel rooms.

"Some events just recruit from the industry, the trade, and the press," the winemaker went on. "People who make wine, sell wine, or write about it. That's okay, too, as long as nobody's judging anything in which they have a financial interest. But absent any information on who's doing the judging, there's nothing to prevent Genette from rigging the contest in her favor. And nobody wants to help her pull off a scam like that."

"You really think she'd do something that obvious?" I asked.

"She already has." He indicated her booth with a nod of his head. "See the banner?"

Strung above her booth was a bubblegum-pink and mustard-yellow banner proclaiming that she was selling "award-winning wines!"

"The only awards we know of that she's won are a couple of fourth-place medals at her county fair," he said. "And that was in categories where there were only four entries. She claims to have won a first place at a competition held by the Shenandoah Oenophilic Society, but none of us have ever heard of it, so we think it's bogus."

Just then Genette walked in.

"She's back," I murmured.

"Excellent," Mother said. "I have decided it would be better to catch her actually committing an infraction. It shouldn't take long."

As we watched, Genette flicked a few specks of dust off her counter, cast a venomous glance at the booth to her left, which was crowded with chattering tasters and customers, and then hastily rearranged her face into a smile when two couples stopped in front of her booth. She sashayed out from behind the counter and began batting her eyes at the two men, to the visible distaste of the two women.

"Getting back to your question," the winemaker said. "No. Do not expect to see a fabulous wine pavilion at the Virginia Agricultural Exposition."

He nodded and returned to his booth, which was not festooned with gaudy banners advertising the awards his winery had won. He did have them listed on relatively small plaques attached to the front of the booth. They filled five of the plaques, and there wasn't much room left on the sixth.

"He makes nice wines," Mother said. "Very nice indeed."

I hoped by now the winemakers had figured out that Mother's "very nice indeed" was equivalent to most people's "fabulous."

"Special occasion wines," she added.

Which meant they were not only fabulously good, but also fabulously priced.

"But that's not why I called you," Mother said. "He's back."

"Who?"

"Remember that man I told you about? The suspicious one?"

Had Mother reported a suspicious person earlier today? I didn't actually remember, but in the wake of the thefts and vandalism, she'd have been in a very small minority if she hadn't reported at least one suspicious person.

"Remind me what he was doing that was suspicious."

"Precisely what he's doing now," Mother said. "Standing over there, staring fixedly at the wine tent."

She led me to the entrance and we stepped outside, as if to have a private conversation.

"Don't stare," she said. "He's right over there beside that bank of trash cans."

"Wearing the navy-blue windbreaker. I see him."

"He's been there on and off all day."

"I'll check him out." I wouldn't have called him suspicious. Morose, maybe. But if he was making the exhibitors nervous, I'd check him out.

"Thank you, dear." Mother strode back into the tent.

I checked my watch and then set off toward the trash cans in a matter-of-fact manner, looking not at them but at the tent beyond them. But I could see the lurker out of the corner of my eye.

Then an enormous overalls-clad figure stepped between me and my target.

"Are you the fair director?" he asked. "I need to talk to you."

Chapter 13

I tried to keep the lurker in view, but the man in overalls was at least six feet six, almost as wide, and completely blocked my view of him.

"I'm the assistant director," I said. "What can I do for you?"

"I just heard about the problems," he said.

"Problems?" As I talked, I shaded my eyes and edged slightly to one side, as if the glare made it uncomfortable to look up at him.

"All these thefts," he said. "I need to make sure my Romeldales are safe."

I found myself wishing, for at least the tenth time since the fair had started, that farmers would at least try to remember that the rest of us weren't necessarily that familiar with all the heritage breeds. Would it kill him to say "Romeldale chickens" or "Romeldale goats" or "Romeldale apples"?

"We're taking every precaution to make sure that all the exhibits are safe," I said. "I've been inspecting all the buildings this morning, and apart from the three initial incidents, we've had no other reports of any kind of theft or vandalism—not so much as a pea in the produce tent."

"My wife's in the craft barn—she spins the fleeces into wool and exhibits the skeins—and she heard about that poor woman whose quilt was vandalized."

Aha. If Romeldales had fleeces, odds were they were sheep.

"We've got extra security there as well. And—are your Romeldales in the main sheep barn?"

He nodded. Sheep, then.

"My husband and I are there ourselves," I said. "We're camping out with our llamas, and helping our next-door neighbor keep an eye on his Lincolns."

To anyone else, I would have said Lincoln sheep, but someone who kept one heritage sheep breed had probably heard of the others—and if he hadn't, he could get a taste of how confused the rest of us were at all the heritage breed name-dropping.

"We're going to have volunteer patrols out tonight, and they'll be organized out of our end of the sheep barn," I went on. "So while I wouldn't brag about it to the cow or pig people, the sheep will get a little bit of extra protection."

He departed, much calmer. But by the time I'd finished reassuring him, the morose man in the blue windbreaker had disappeared.

I turned and headed for the show office, but I ran into Randall halfway there.

"Mother's dealing with Genette," I said. "Have you seen this?"

I handed Randall Shiffley the flyer for the Virginia Agricultural Exposition. He frowned thunderously.

"No," he said. "But I've heard about it. That Brett Riordan fellow has been handing them out to all the exhibitors."

"Do you think it's a threat?" I asked "To the Un-fair, I mean."

He pondered a moment, then shook his head. It wasn't a "no" kind of shake, more like "who knows?"

"Doesn't look like one to me," he said. "But I might be too close to the whole thing. I don't think it's going over that big with the farmers. Riordan doesn't know beans about farming. Someone asked him if the events at his fair were going to be FFV-endorsed and he didn't even know it stood for Future Farmers of Virginia. But I understand he's connected to the wine community. If the winemakers come in big on his event, it could be trouble for us."

"His only connection is that he's dating a winemaker that every other winemaker in the state hates," I said. "So the smart money says the winemakers will be staying away in droves."

"Let's hope it turns out that way."

"I think it will," I said. "Remember how Mother convinced us we needed to get the best possible wine judges and put them up in the Caerphilly Inn?"

"I hope it was worth it," he said.

"It will be." I explained the winemakers' distrust of Genette's intentions, and Mother's decision to recruit nationally known judges.

"How do the official state fair's wine judges measure up to ours?" Randall asked.

"They might be as good, but they can't possibly be better."

"Great," he said. "Well, I'm off to pick up that country singer."

"Now?" I looked at my watch. "I thought she wasn't performing until this evening."

"Taking her over to the college to do a radio interview," Randall said. "Apparently she's a little cranky about being in a town without a Starbucks, and I'm going to see if having the mayor himself as a chauffeur impresses her much. You're in charge."

He ambled off, head swiveling to check out every detail as he passed.

No doubt some emergency would crop up as soon as he left, but in the meantime, I decided to drop by the poultry barns to see how things were going there. Earlier, the mood had been tense and anxious in all three barns, but I was hoping now that the fair had begun and admiring visitors were thronging the tents, things would have calmed down.

And that seemed to be the case in the duck barn. People were feeding and grooming their own ducks, inspecting each other's ducks, and trading bits of duck-related advice and gossip.

"—don't take his word for it—he wouldn't know a Buff Orpington from a Muscovy—"

"—you need to adjust their feed—they need a lot more protein when they're laying—"

"—I always use a broody hen—I just don't think you give the poor ducklings a proper start when you stick the eggs under an incubator—"

"—she's going to let me know when she starts selling some of the ducklings—"

"—sounds as if you need to worm them—"

"—yes, but the eggs are *supposed* to be that color in a Cayuga—"

I had to admit that the variety of ducks in the barn was an eye opener to someone who'd grown up knowing only fuzzy yellow ducklings and fluffy white ducks. There were plenty of ordinary white domestic ducks, but also beige ducks, brown ducks, black ducks, iridescent beetle-green ducks, blue-and-white ducks, and ducks whose color I would have described as "brown tweed," although I doubted that was the official term.

I paused to admire a display of ducklings that was a popular attraction for the children attending the fair. The ducklings seemed to be having a great time, swimming around in a little pool, climbing out, waddling up a long, shallow ramp, and then sliding down a slide to land in the pool again with a plop.

"I should bring my kids to watch this," I said to a woman leading a little girl not much older than Josh and Jamie.

"Only if you want to have them nag you for the next year about getting their own ducklings," she said.

"We could keep them in our tub," the little girl said. "They'd like it in our tub."

The woman rolled her eyes. She had a point. Did I really want to take care of ducks on top of five llamas, two toddlers, two dogs, and a husband?

But they were cute. Maybe I could talk Dad into getting some ducks.

The goose and turkey barn was also—well, not exactly calm. If you stood in the middle of the tent, you could hear a deafening chorus of honking from one end and frenzied gobbling from the other. But the human inhabitants were busy and cheerful, if a little too ready to brag about their charges.

I heard several goose owners asserting that their birds weren't ill-tempered and noisy and didn't produce copious amounts of manure, while nearby other goose fanciers were touting their geese as expert sentinels and extolling the lush state their lawns could achieve when fertilized by geese.

The heritage breed turkey fanciers all seemed inordinately proud of the fact that their birds were all capable of breeding without artificial insemination. Or maybe they were just relieved.

"You mean every single turkey we see in the grocery store is a test-tube turkey?" one visitor was asking. "There must be millions of them!"

"Over two hundred and fifty million last year alone," the heirloom turkey breeder replied. "And every single one of them a turkey-baster turkey, so to speak."

"That seems like a lot of work for something so . . . so . . ."

"So easy for my birds to do without any help whatsoever from me," the farmer said.

The women held out her hand for a flyer on how to order an heirloom turkey for Thanksgiving.

I didn't need a flyer. I had all the turkey breeders' names and addresses in my Un-fair files.

"But how do they do it?" the woman asked.

I decided this wasn't something I wanted to hear about, so I moved on to the chicken tent.

As soon as I stepped inside, I realized that the chicken tent was still seething with tension and anxiety. Maybe it was understandable, since they were the ones who'd actually been hit by the thieves. But I was hoping that seeing the police hard at work on the investigation, together with the news of our patrols, would help.

Alas, no. As I looked around, I could see people walking around with their shoulders hunched tensely. People starting when someone came up behind them. People frowning or snapping at each other. Even the chickens were not cackling and clucking and crowing with the same carefree abandon they'd displayed yesterday, during the setting up, before the cruel abduction of two of their number.

I looked around to find the volunteer in charge of the

tent. The new volunteer, now that Mr. Dauber had been exiled to the far end of the parking lot.

"How's it going?" I asked.

"You have no idea," she said.

"Actually, looking around, maybe I do," I said. "Seems even gloomier than it was this morning. I'd have thought everyone would have calmed down by now."

"I think they would have if not for the Bellinghams," she said.

"The Bellinghams?" Probably yet another heritage breed whose owners would be mortally insulted if I didn't pretend I'd heard of it. I was fishing in my pocket for the list of breeds I'd printed from the American Livestock Breed Conservancy's Web site. "What's wrong with—oh! You mean the people whose Russian Orloff bantams were stolen? They're the Bonnevilles."

"Whatever." She rolled her eyes. "If they'd just go home already, I think the mood would pick up."

"Home? I thought they were down at the hospital."

"They insisted on coming back to the fair," she said. "Against your father's orders. He's still trying to talk them into going back to the hospital for more tests. But they have one chicken left, and they don't trust anyone else to guard it. I gather it was sick with something last night, and Mrs. Bell—Mrs. Bonneville was nursing it back to health in their trailer, or it probably would have been stolen with the others. So unfortunately they're back, at least until after their chicken competes."

"Unfortunately?" Was it just my imagination, or did I detect a distinct note of hostility in her voice. What was going on here? A severe case of "blame the victim" or something else?

"Sorry," she said. "I know I don't sound very sympathetic. It's just that—well, see for yourself."

She led me down the aisles and then stopped, looked around rather furtively, and then indicated something to our right.

In the middle of the bank of wire cages were two cages decorated with giant black bows at least a yard wide, with trailing ends that drooped onto the sawdust floor. Between the two decorated cages, and almost hidden by the bows, was a third cage, in which a small black-and-brown hen was sitting. I recognized the bird Mrs. Bonneville had been holding so tightly this morning.

"Good grief," I muttered.

"Excessive grief if you ask me," the volunteer said. "I know they love their chickens—I love mine. But if I went around the bend every time a fox got one—that'd be crazy."

"Besides, we don't know that they're dead," I said. "Or gone for good. I think the police are seriously pursuing the theory that someone stole them to build up his own flock of Orloffs. Which means the thief would take good care of them, and there's a good chance the chief will catch him and the Bell—the Bonnevilles will get their Orloffs back."

"Yeah, but in the meantime they're determined to make everyone else feel their pain," she said. "If you think the cages are over the top, get a load of that—"

I turned to see what she was pointing at, and saw the diminutive figures of the Bonnevilles walking slowly down the aisle. He was wearing a dark gray suit with a black armband on his right sleeve and was leaning heavily on a cane. She was dressed all in black, complete with a veiled black hat, and was leaning on his arm in a way that seemed ill-advised unless the cane was purely for effect.

"Did they bring those funeral outfits with them, I wonder?"

"Apparently they stopped off to pick up a few things in town," she said. "If you talk to them—"

"I don't plan to if I can help it," I said.

"Don't ask them whether their birds were microchipped." She rolled her eyes again. "No idea why, but the question totally freaks them."

"I saw what happened when Vern Shiffley asked them about that," I said. "I have no intention of causing an encore."

"Did he really have a heart attack?"

"Not according to Dad. Possible cardiac arrhythmia. Or maybe just a panic attack."

"Not the way he tells it." She shook her head. "And before you ask, I have no idea why the idea of microchipping would bring on a coronary. Or a panic attack. Heck, I've been wondering if you're allowed to do it to children. Wouldn't that be nice?"

"I'm waiting till they get a GPS feature, so you can always tell where they are," I said. "Maybe the Bonnevilles decided not to microchip the birds and are mad at themselves."

"Could be," the volunteer said. "Or maybe if their birds are microchipped, they're afraid the thief will find out and destroy them if he thinks he's about to get caught with them. Either way, if you value your sanity, don't bring up microchipping."

"Got it," I said. "I need to run."

"Wish I could," the volunteer grumbled.

I wasn't actually fleeing the tent to avoid the Bonnevilles. An idea had struck me. I hurried over to the fair office, made sure it was empty, and pulled out my cell phone.

Chapter 14

I called Stanley Denton, a private investigator who'd recently relocated to Caerphilly.

"I know, I know," he said, as he answered his phone.

"You know what?" I asked.

"I assume you're nagging me because I haven't shown up yet to support the fair. I promise, I'll be there with bells on soon. Maybe tomorrow, certainly by Saturday. I've been stuck up in Culpeper on a case, but it's all over now but the paperwork."

That's good," I said. "Because Saturday is the pie competition. You need to be here to cheer Muriel on to victory."

Muriel Slattery, who ran the local diner, was a frequent medalist in the pie competition. I wasn't sure if it was only Muriel's pies that had inspired Denton to relocate to Caerphilly or if he also had designs on Muriel herself, but either way, mentioning her and her pies would ensure his attendance.

"So you just called to remind me to come to the fair?" he asked.

"No," I said. "Actually I wanted to see if something is doable before I try to talk Randall into hiring you to do it." I explained about the chicken thefts, and the winemakers' theory that Genette was hiding the stolen animals on some property other than her vineyard.

"It's doable," he said. "Assuming there's anything to find, how long it takes depends on how smart she's been about hiding her ownership. Let me do a little poking around pro bono. If she's stupid, I could find it with a couple of hours of checking online. If she's smart, or has smart lawyers, it could be more trouble than it's worth. Or at least more than I want to do pro bono and more than the county would want to pay for. But we can cross that bridge when we come to it."

"I appreciate it," I said. "And so will Randall when I tell him."

After I hung up I leaned back in my chair and closed my eyes. Just for a second. Would it really hurt if I took just a small nap? Or stole away to the llama booth to see what Michael and the boys were up to? Maybe I could collect the boys and we could all have a nap. Nothing like a nap to improve a person's mood, regardless of age.

My cell phone rang. The front gate needed more change.

Another call. The portapotties were getting low on toilet paper. A reporter from Richmond wanted a press pass. A farmer from Jetersville wanted to know if he was too late to enter his cattle in the competition. Another farmer from Vesuvius wanted directions to the fairgrounds. One of the pickle judges had indigestion and needed an antacid. Someone's prize sow had gone missing from the pig barn, which caused quite a bit of alarm until she turned up in the rodeo ring, where the high school kid who had raised her was about to compete in the teen calf-roping contest.

"Thank goodness we found her," I said, as I watched the pig being led to safety.

"I wasn't too worried," the pig barn volunteer said. "She's only a Chester White. A prize-winning Chester White, of course, but it's a common breed, so I didn't think it could be part of the rash of thefts of heritage breeds."

"It's not a rash. Not here at the fair. Two bantams does not make a rash."

"I didn't mean it that way." He had started backing away.

"Sorry," I said. "I didn't mean to snap at you. It's just that we're a little sensitive about people thinking this is a fair problem. I've heard of several other people who have lost heritage animals from their own farms, long before we even thought of holding our fair."

"True," he said. "Been happening a lot over the last couple of years."

"So it's a problem that followed the heritage breeds to the fair," I said. "I wish we'd known in advance they were such big theft risks, but now that we do know, we've tightened security. We're determined that we won't lose any more animals, and we'll do our best to solve the theft of those two bantams."

The volunteer nodded, but he was frowning, and visibly thinking hard about something.

"You know," he said finally. "You say you wish you'd known they were a theft risk? I don't think most of *us* knew that until we got here and began comparing notes. I've been raising Tamworths for ten years now, and not long ago I started running a few Mulefoots. Most of us— heritage pig breeders, I mean—we're not trying to keep them to ourselves. We want the breeds to come back strong. We get excited if someone we know is a solid pig man—or woman—wants to buy some piglets and start raising our breed. Bigger gene pool's gonna benefit all of us. Someone wants to get started, we do our best to help them. Theft wasn't the big problem. Getting people to take us seriously was. But since I've been here I've been talking to people. Not just Tamworth and Mulefoot people or even Red Wattles and Gloucestershire Old Spot people, but cow and sheep and goat and poultry people. I don't think I've ever talked to so many heritage breed people at one time, and we're all realizing that theft's getting to be a much bigger problem for all of us."

"And here we come along and create the biggest concentration of heritage breed animals the state has ever seen," I said. "Talk about a target for whoever's doing the stealing."

"Yeah, but you also created the biggest concentration of heritage breed *owners* we've ever had in the state," he said. "Got us talking, and talking made us realize we have a problem. And isn't that the first step in dealing with it?"

With that he nodded, and strode off to help a ten- or twelve-year-old girl in a FFV t-shirt who was trying to steer a pig taller than she was into one of the pens in the barn.

Should I report what he'd said to the chief? As I headed back toward the llama booth, hoping to see the boys before they went down for their nap, I kept trying to decide. Then I spotted something: the morose man in the windbreaker—the one Mother had found so suspicious. He was once more standing by the bank of trash cans, shoulders hunched, hands in pockets, staring.

I strolled up and confronted him.

"Is there a reason you're always standing there, staring at the wine pavilion?" I asked.

He blinked and took a step back.

"Just wishing I was in there, showing my wines," he said.

"You didn't register in time to get a booth?"

"Didn't try to get a booth." He was looking down, apparently focused on his attempt to use the toe of one boot to knock dirt off the side of the other. "Lost my vineyard last year."

"I'm sorry," I said.

"Of course, in a way, my vineyard's in the pavilion, even if I'm not," he said. "Genette Sedgewick bought it after I went bust."

Oh, dear.

"Another member of the Genette fan club," I said aloud.

"Ha, ha." It wasn't really a laugh. "I wouldn't have minded so much if it hadn't been her who sent me over the edge in the first place. We had a bad harvest last year, and a lot of us were scrambling to buy grapes so we could keep our production up."

"You can do that?" I asked. "Sell wine made from grapes you didn't grow?"

"Absolutely," he said. "Lots of vineyards do. As long as you don't claim you grew them, you could have a winery without owning a single vine. Anyway, Genette was buying, too. She drove up the price for Virginia grapes so high that a lot of us couldn't afford them. Some people found a way to absorb the hit. Or maybe they're dying, too, just more slowly. I couldn't make enough wine to pay the mortgage."

"Couldn't you buy grapes from someplace else?" I asked. "I hate to sound disloyal, but Virginia's not the only state that grows grapes."

"State law says you can't have more than twenty-five percent out-of-state grapes and still call it a Virginia wine," he said. "I bought as much out-of-state fruit as I could, made as much wine as I could, and sold it all for good prices. I have—had—a good reputation. But it wasn't enough."

I nodded. He went back to kicking mud off his boots.

"So if you don't have a winery, why did you come to the fair?" I asked.

He looked up, frowning.

"I mean, why torture yourself?" I added.

He grimaced.

"I didn't realize it would be this bad." He shook his head. "I thought it would be a good chance to see people, maybe find out if anyone's hiring. I've been mucking out cow barns at my brother-in-law's dairy farm up in Pennsylvania for six months now. Be nice to come back home. Work with grapes, even if they're not my grapes. But every time I try to work up my nerve to walk into that tent . . ."

He shook his head.

"I think I could do it if I didn't know she was in there," he muttered.

"She isn't always," I said. "Stay here and keep your eye on that door." I pointed to the tent door farthest from Genette's booth. "My mother's in charge of the tent. I'll have her step outside and flutter a scarf the next time Genette takes off. Would that help?"

He looked up, a hopeful expression on his face.

"Yeah," he said. "That would help a lot. Thanks."

"By the way, what's your name?"

"Paul Morot. My vineyard was called Fickle Wind Winery."

I nodded as if I recognized the name. Actually, it did sound familiar. If his winery had had a good reputation, odds were Mother had found his wine and served it. Even before we'd put her in charge of the wine pavilion, Mother had become an avid partisan of the Virginia wine industry—possibly because Dad had begun planting grapes and trying to make his own wine. So far Dad hadn't produced any truly spectacular wine—in fact, these days Rose Noire did a rather brisk business turning his failures into exotic herbal vinegars and selling them. But Mother was already looking forward to the day when she could serve Langslow Reserve to dinner guests and remark, with studied casualness, "Oh, yes—James won a medal with this one at the fair."

So if Mother remembered Morot's vineyard, she'd be even more willing to help him infiltrate the tent in Genette's absence.

Although to be honest, I hadn't asked his name so I could help him. Ever since meeting Genette, I'd had the uneasy feeling that something bad was going to happen. I'd have called it a premonition if I believed in them. In spite of all Rose Noire's arguments to the contrary, I remained convinced that a premonition was actually your subconscious adding up facts your conscious hadn't yet noticed, and coming to a conclusion that would turn out to be perfectly rational if you analyzed everything properly.

And if my subconscious thought that bad things were going to happen, I wasn't going to argue with it, because even my conscious self had seen enough to be worried. What if last night's mishaps were only the prelude?

I strode over to the wine pavilion and found Mother.

Chapter 15

"I checked out your lurker," I said. "He's probably harmless." I explained why Morot had been lurking, and as I suspected, Mother was eager to help.

"The poor man," she said. "And yes, you have had his wine. He makes—made—a lovely Chardonnay, very buttery with a hint of apples. I'm sure you remember."

Actually, I wasn't likely to. I liked wine, but when people started describing it as "crisp" or "buttery" or "robust," or having hints of something-or-other, I just didn't get it. To me, wine was good, or bad, or okay, or maybe sometimes even fabulous, but buttery? Hints of apples?

"It was the white wine we served at Josh and Jamie's christening party," Mother added.

"Oh, that," I said. "Yes, that was nice. Very nice indeed. So he made that?"

"I shall definitely do what I can to help that poor man. Do you remember that lovely Merlot of his? The one with those ever-so-slight notes of chocolate and licorice."

"Chocolate and licorice?" I didn't recall ever drinking a wine that tasted even ever so slightly of either flavor, much less both, and the idea sounded perfectly dreadful. Of course, the odds were if I'd had the merlot, I'd have just thought that it tasted like really good red wine. So I opted for tact. "Not really, but I'll take your word for it."

I left the wine pavilion and headed back for the fair office. On the way, as I was passing the sheep barn, I noticed there was a crowd at the small exhibition ring nearby, so I strolled over to see what was up.

When I got closer, I realized that the crowd consisted almost entirely of teenagers. Most of them, boys and girls alike, were in t-shirts and jeans. Some of them were talking to each other or texting on cell phones. Some were flirting or arguing. Many were just standing there, looking down at their boots or sneakers.

What was odd was that every single one of them had his or her back to the show ring. The entire ring was lined three-deep on all four sides with teenagers who were studiously ignoring whatever was in it.

So of course I was dying of curiosity to see what they were ignoring.

The ring was surrounded on three sides by bleachers that provided a couple of rows of rough board seating. A few kids were perched there, but not many, probably because it was a little uncomfortable to sit on the bleachers with your back turned to the ring. I threaded my way through the crowd, saying hello to the occasional kid who knew me. I suppose I could have asked them what was up, but I was reluctant. After all, I was the deputy organizer—I was supposed to know what was going on.

So I when I reached the bleachers I climbed to the top row and peered over all the heads. As I watched, someone opened a gate on the far side and three sheep trotted into the ring.

Three of the nakedest sheep I'd ever seen.

Michael and I had lived across the road from Seth Early's sheep farm for years now, so I knew what sheep looked like at all stages of life, from fully fleeced to newly shorn. But I'd never seen Seth's sheep quite this closely shorn.

These three sheep looked as if they'd been first shorn and then shaved. Their skins were very pale, but with a slight rosy flush to them, and surprisingly wrinkly in places. Like around the neck and at the top of the legs. As they trotted in formation around the ring, I found it fascinating to see how the skin around their legs wrinkled and smoothed in time with their steps. Amazing how long their legs were, and how slender they appeared without the heavy wool to conceal their real size. They looked . . . graceful. Not a word I'd ever previously thought of applying to sheep.

And yet, as these three trotted around the ring, with brisk steps and an alert manner, I kept feeling the impulse to avert my eyes. I wondered if the sheep found the sudden change from fleece to flesh disconcerting or liberating.

And I still hadn't figured out why the teenagers were very deliberately avoiding even so much as a glance at the naked sheep.

I saw Seth Early leaning on the ring near the gate where the sheep had entered. His Border Collie, Lad, was lying at his feet, staring fixedly at the sheep as if he could barely restrain himself from leaping out into the ring to herd them. I climbed down off the bleachers and strolled over to see if Seth could explain what was going on.

As I walked, I saw a few other adults circulating through the teenagers, handing out sheets of paper and pencils, and warning them to "Wait till we give the word."

"And what happens when they get the word?" I asked Seth, when I reached him.

"They turn around and start judging," Seth said.

"So these three sheep are competing for something?" I asked.

"No, the kids are competing. They've been learning how to judge conformation. Now we're seeing who's learned the most."

An older man—one of Randall's uncles, though I couldn't remember which—stood up on a small platform near us and addressed the crowd.

"Okay—we're ready!" he announced. "When I say the word, you have fifteen minutes. Ready! Set! Go!"

The teenagers all turned around and began staring at the sheep, jostling each other for the best positions on the rail, and scribbling on their sheets of paper.

"Those sheep have already been judged by qualified sheep judges," Seth said. "Now it's the kids' turn to rate them. There's twenty teams from FFV clubs all over the state. The team that comes the closest to matching how the adults rated the sheep wins the blue ribbon."

"Is there a reason for shearing the sheep so closely?" I asked. "They look as if they've been shaved."

"They have," Seth said. "I just shaved them. We do that before they go into the ring, so the judges can see the conformation. Go out there, Fred. Keep 'em moving."

One of the nearby adults went through the gate into the ring and followed the sheep around, chivvying them into motion from time to time. Lad whined a bit as if longing to be allowed to do Fred's job.

"Are you making them trot to show off the conformation, or so one side of the ring doesn't get a closer look than the others?"

"A little of both," Seth said. He leaned on the fence and watched with satisfaction as the sheep trotted.

"So I assume these sheep have flaws that the kids should identify?" I asked. "Because giving them perfect sheep to judge wouldn't be much of a test."

He nodded.

"Any idea what's wrong with 'em?" he asked.

I studied the sheep. I'd spent a lot of time gazing at Seth's sheep over the last several years, both when they were peacefully grazing in his pasture across the road and when they turned up in unexpected places on our land or even inside our house. But I was usually studying them to see if they were about to eat parts of my garden or track dung into the house, not to assess them as worthy or unworthy specimens of their breed.

I waited until the adults were collecting the judging sheets before replying to Seth's question.

"If I were giving a ribbon, I'd give it to the medium-sized sheep," I said.

He narrowed his eyes.

"Why?" he asked.

"The biggest one has a slight sway back," I said. "I don't recall that any of your sheep do. And the smallest one looks as if her body is too big. Or maybe her legs are too small. Out of proportion."

"Not bad." He nodded with approval. "Not bad at all. We'll make a shepherd of you yet."

"Alas, that's unlikely," I said. "We're running out of room for the llamas as it is."

"Last time I was over at the sheep barn, one of your boys was begging his daddy for a sheep," Seth countered.

Would it hurt Seth's feelings if I mentioned that Jamie, an inveterate animal lover, was also begging for kittens, chicks, rabbits, turtles, snakes, axolotls, frogs, canaries, pigeons, turkeys, ducks, guinea pigs, hamsters, and "cowsies"?

"By the way—" Seth began. Then he broke off, looked around as if to see if anyone was eavesdropping.

"We seem to have had another prank," he continued, in

a lower voice. "Not a new one—happened last night, like all the rest of 'em, but wasn't reported."

"What was it?" I asked. "And why wasn't it reported?"

"Someone spray-painted rude words on the side of each of the sheep we were originally going to use for this event," Seth said. "They belonged to Mason Shiffley, and you know how prim and proper he can be."

I nodded. Mason Shiffley had been raising Black and Tan Coonhounds for forty years, and still referred to the bitches as "lady dogs."

"We should have Horace take a look at them," I said. "There could be clues. Where are they?"

"Mason was so mortified that he didn't tell anyone," Seth said. "Just hustled them into his truck this morning, took them home, and sheared them. And then drove himself over to the hospital and checked himself in. Seems he had a heart attack."

"Is he going to be okay?"

"They think so. No thanks to whoever graffittied his sheep. Maybe he'd have had it anyway, but you'll never convince me that prank didn't hurry it along."

Then he chuckled, a little sheepishly.

"I know it's rotten to laugh," he said. "But whoever did it painted the words in that glow-in-the-dark neon-pink spray paint. Mason comes out just before dawn to tend the sheep and all he sees are three really bad words glowing in the dark. You ask me, he probably started having the heart attack then and there. He just didn't give in to it until he'd cleaned up the sheep."

"And destroyed potentially useful evidence."

"He may be prim, but he's thrifty. He'd probably have kept the fleeces so he could separate out the wool that's still usable."

"I'll tell the chief." I was already pulling out my cell phone to do so. "Keep this under your hat, will you?"

"Can do," Seth said. "I only found out when Mason and his sheep didn't show up and we had to find some replacement sheep for the contest. No need for everyone to know. Happened last night like all the rest of the pranks. Everyone already knows there was a prankster out last night. No sense upsetting everyone all over again."

I agreed, and so did the chief when I reached him.

The day wore on. The competitions had begun. In the quilt and pie barn, pickle judging gave way to jams, jellies, and preserves. The first round of calf-roping ended and the first of the sheepdog trials began in the rodeo ring. The karaoke competition (country music division) was underway on the stage. The dairy cow judging (youth division) started up in the small ring near the cow barn. I tracked down the volunteers who'd be on patrol tonight and told them when and where to report for their shifts.

In the late afternoon I ran into the Bonnevilles talking animatedly to someone I recognized as a student reporter from the Caerphilly College newspaper. Talking and posing with their remaining bantam hen in their arms while the reporter snapped pictures with his iPhone. I tried to pass by unseen, but the reporter recognized me and flagged me down.

"Meg, any official comment from the fair management on this chicken theft?" he asked.

"We are shocked and saddened by this outrage." I kept my face solemn and frowned slightly. "And you can be sure that the Un-fair will do everything we can to assist law enforcement in bringing those responsible to justice."

The Bonnevilles nodded as if they approved of my

dolorous tone. I stepped over to them and patted them both on the shoulder.

"Courage!" I whispered. Mrs. Bonneville sniffled and lifted her chin bravely. Mr. Bonneville put his arm protectively around her shoulder.

I retreated while the going was good. Unfortunately, the reporter chose to follow me, leaving the Bonnevilles and their hen standing in a small, forlorn clump.

"Seriously," he said. "Do they think the birds are dead? Is that why they're in mourning?"

"You'd have to ask them," I said.

"No thanks." He shuddered. "I already did, and I wasn't sure she'd ever stop crying. And Chief Burke just says 'no comment.'"

I relented.

"The chickens are from a rare heirloom breed," I began.

"Expensive?"

"For chickens, I expect they are," I said. "But you should ask a poultry expert. And as you can tell from the size of the one they're holding, nobody raises them for meat. So there's reason to be optimistic that the thief took them for breeding purposes, and I have every confidence Chief Burke will recover them."

He was tapping on his iPhone—taking notes, I realized, in his generation's replacement for a notepad.

"Thanks," he said. "Not sure my editor will even think this is worth running—unless she decides my photos of the Baskervilles are good for comic relief."

With that he dashed off, before I had a chance to correct him on the names. I glanced back and saw that Mr. and Mrs. Bonneville were walking slowly down the pathway toward the chicken tent, looking like a small funeral procession. If they were trolling for attention, it wasn't working. People were glancing at them out of the corner of their eyes and giving them a wide berth.

I managed a hurried dinner with Michael and the boys and then it was back to dashing up and down the fair, making sure the judges had their forms and their packets of ribbons, nagging them to turn in the names of the winners, reassuring people that there had been no new pranks, and occasionally catching a few moments of a performance or a competition. Knitting, crochet, and embroidery. Pigeons. Sheep-shearing. Barrel races. Hog-calling. The sheer number of events was overwhelming—thank goodness I'd recruited a senior volunteer to wrangle each event space, instead of running them all myself, as I'd originally planned.

At 6:00 P.M., the agricultural part of the fair grew quiet, but by that time the Midway was in full swing, the country singer was giving her first concert, and the first round of a small (but American Kennel Club–approved) dog show was underway. Michael took the boys to the dog show for the first hour, and I managed to join them just before it was time to whisk the boys away to bed—in Rose Noire's tent, since the sheep barn was too close to the tantalizing noise of the Midway.

I breathed a sigh of relief when the country music and canine fans filed out the front gate, except for a few who sauntered over to enjoy the last hour of the Midway.

"Next year we need to find a way to close off the rest of the fair while the Midway is open," I told Randall when I ran into him backstage after the concert. I was making sure all the tech sheds and dressing rooms were locked and he, presumably, was waiting to escort the singer back to the Caerphilly Inn.

"Put it in your notebook for the postmortem," he said.

"And can you also make a note that next year we need to find a main act who's not a total . . . diva?"

I glanced a little anxiously at the door of the largest dressing room, in which I had assumed the country singer was still changing. It wasn't a particularly thick door, nor were the walls all that soundproof.

"Oh, don't worry," Randall said. "She's gone. You can lock that one up, too."

"I thought you were chauffeuring her." I found the right key and secured the dressing room, which was actually a refurbished vintage fifties Airstream trailer.

"She liked the looks of Rob better," Randall said. "So he gets to show her the town nightlife and I get my beauty sleep."

"Caerphilly has nightlife?" I said. "Who knew? Clearly Michael and I are becoming old fogies."

"I didn't think any of the student hangouts would suit," he said. "So I recommended that he take her to the bar at the Caerphilly Inn. More convenient."

"Convenient?"

"I figure another drink and she'll pass out, and he can get a bellhop to help him heave her into bed," Randall said. "If you thought I meant something salacious, don't worry. Unless his eyesight has deteriorated considerably of late, I think his virtue is safe. He's doing this purely to help me out, and if you see him before I do, tell him I appreciate it."

"Will do. See you tomorrow."

Randall nodded and ambled off.

I continued my rounds, making sure all the buildings were locked, and that the early shift patrols were showing up at their posts. Until the Midway closed, they were keeping a close eye on the path that led from it through the main body of the fair to the gate. By ten o'clock, everything was as secure as we could make it.

The bad news was that instead of curling up in my sleeping bag for a well-earned rest I'd be spending the next four hours on patrol. The good news was that since I was in charge of the patrols, I'd assigned Michael to be my partner, so we'd get to spend a little time together—something that hadn't happened much of late, thanks to all the preparation for the fair.

And our beat was the Midway, which was open till eleven tonight, so we'd at least have a few distractions to help keep us awake during the first hour of our patrol.

Chapter 16

"What about the boys?" Michael asked, when I rounded him up to start our shift. "Is Rose Noire okay with them staying at her tent?"

"She's fine with it," I said. "And if we like, we're invited to join her for breakfast. Organic oatmeal and freshly blended fruit smoothies."

"Good luck to her," Michael said. "Last time I heard they were demanding pepperoni pizza and chocolate ice cream for breakfast."

We checked that we had our flashlights and cell phones and strolled over to the Midway. It was at the same end of the fair as the cow barns, but across the split-rail fence that ran along the border between Caerphilly and Clay counties.

I had to wonder about that fence. It hadn't been erected just for the fair—it was an established fence, well weathered except for occasional spots where someone had patched breaks with newer timbers. Most local farmers found plain barbed wire fences sufficient. Was there some agricultural reason for the more elaborate fence here, or was it symptomatic of the longstanding distrust between the denizens of the two counties?

I shoved the thought out of my mind and concentrated on watching the crowds.

"Shall I see if I can win you a life-sized, glow-in-the-dark, lime-green stuffed hippopotamus?" Michael was pointing to the ball toss and flexing his fingers, as if eager to test the skills he'd honed all summer playing fast-pitch softball.

"They're not life-sized, only four feet tall," I said. "And while either of your sons would love a stuffed hippo taller than he is, you know what will happen if you bring one home and expect them to share."

"True." He shuddered slightly, no doubt remembering the particularly savage battle the boys had had a few days earlier when Josh became convinced that we had given Jamie a larger helping of watermelon chunks.

"I could try to win two," he suggested.

"Try later," I said. "When we're off duty."

"Remind me why we're patrolling the Midway," he said, as he dodged a teenager who was too busy talking on her cell phone to watch where she was waving her giant ball of cotton candy.

"Not the whole Midway," I said. "Only this narrow strip along the fence between it and the agricultural areas."

"Shouldn't we also be patrolling that strip of fields between the woods and the barns?"

"We've got a brace of Shiffleys covering that—they're perched in portable hunting blinds up in the trees. If anyone sneaks out of the woods and tries to cross the open pasture, the Shiffleys will see them. You and I are supposed to keep an eye out for signs that some of these apparently innocent Midway visitors are actually plotting something more sinister."

"Like someone trying to smuggle stolen hens onto the Ferris wheel?" Michael suggested. "Or someone with telltale bits of pumpkin rind on his clothes?"

"More like someone taking an undue interest in any part of the fence separating the Midway from the rest of the fair," I said.

"True." Michael studied the fence for a moment. "It would be easy to slip away, hop over the fence, and sneak up on the barns."

"Easy to slip away and hop over, maybe," I said. "Sneaking up on the barns might be a little harder. About an hour ago, Randall Shiffley put some of his uncle Hiram's goats in the pen just over the fence."

"The ornery ones Hiram trained to chase revenuers away from his still back when he used to be a moonshiner?"

"The ornery ones, yes," I said. "But what's this 'used to be' nonsense? Since when did Hiram reform?"

"I thought he gave it up when Randall was elected mayor," Michael said. "You mean he's still at it?"

"He didn't give it up," I said. "Moonshine's become big business these days—arguably another heirloom crop."

"But still illegal."

"Which is why Hiram moved his base of operations across the border to Clay County, where it wouldn't be so much of an embarrassment to Randall if he got arrested."

"Well, that was thoughtful. And having Hiram's goats on the case should make the exhibitors feel better."

"The exhibitors don't know about the goats," I said. "They also don't know that you and I are patrolling the Midway. We're not on the official patrol list. So if you hear anyone complaining about our leaving a gaping hole in our security, don't enlighten them."

"But—oh. You think the prowler's an exhibitor."

"Could be," I said. "If it was just a prank, why haven't the chickens turned up? More likely, someone wanted to sabotage their competitors, and did a little extra mischief to confuse things—and who would care about sabotaging one of the competitors except another competitor?"

"Which means Chief Burke will be taking a close look at all the competing quilters, pumpkin growers, and bantam chicken fanciers?"

"I assume," I said. "Another possibility is that someone wanted the chickens, and sabotaged the quilt and the pumpkin, again to muddy the waters. And anyone that gung ho for poultry—"

"Is probably here, exhibiting," Michael said. "Makes sense. I can think of another possibility, though. What if someone wants our fair to fail? Someone involved with a rival fair?"

"Then if they're smart, they're here, pretending to be having a great time, and studying everything we do for ways to outshine us and sabotage us."

"And if they're stupid, like Brett Riordan, they're here trying to talk up their own fair right under our noses." He shook his head. "Annoying. But yeah, it makes sense that the prowler's probably here. And has probably volunteered to be on patrol."

"If he didn't, he probably made enough of a fuss about security that one of the volunteers would tell him everything he needed to know about the patrols to shut him up."

"But even if the prowler knows about the patrols, he won't know the Midway is covered," Michael said.

"And even if he notices us on patrol, he won't know about the goats," I said. "The goats are our secret weapon."

"So when were you planning to tell me that instead of being a routine patrol we're part of a cleverly set trap?" Michael asked.

I glanced up, but he didn't look upset. More amused.

"Right about now," I said. Michael chuckled at that.

"When you'd had a chance to get a little bored with the routine patrol, but long before the time when the prowler's apt to make his move."

"Good plan," he said. "Okay, from what I've seen so far, I'd say the only exhibitors in any danger from this crowd would be the microbreweries." He frowned at a group of young men who were all sloshing their beer cans as they swaggered toward the ball toss. "Do those kids look old enough to drink?"

"No," I said. "But they never do these days. And the vendors are being very careful about IDs, thanks to the rumor that there are undercover Alcoholic Beverage Control agents in the crowd."

"Lucky for us that rumor's going around." He nodded his approval. "Should help keep a lid on things."

"Yes, I rather thought it might," I said. "That's why I started the rumor."

For the next hour or so we continued our patrol up and down the fence. The crowd thinned out, and then disappeared entirely. Michael and I stopped by the barbecue tent as they were closing and scored half-price pulled pork sandwiches for a late dinner. By the time we'd finished eating and resumed our patrol, the last few Midway vendors and operators were leaving.

We patrolled the long stretch of fence, paying particular attention to the gate, which was the most likely point of entry for a prowler. At first, I was relieved at how peaceful our watch had become, without the flashing lights, the bells and whistles from the games, the patter of the barkers, the screams and laughter from the crowds on the rides.

But before too long my mood changed. The quiet and darkness began to seem less friendly. More . . . ominous?

Was it just my mood? Or was it maybe a little too quiet? Shouldn't there be more natural sounds? More bugs, frogs, owls? More of all the usual noises you'd hear on an early fall night? Was it just the fair chasing them away, or the fair plus our patrols? Or had they sensed something else?

I was glad I'd assigned Michael to be my patrol partner. At six foot four, he could be intimidating even to people who knew how mild mannered he was. I'd seen him stop a fight once just by standing up and clearing his throat.

But still, the night was creepy. The air was so humid it was actually turning foggy. That didn't help, not being able to see more than a few feet in front of me.

Maybe there was nothing to be seen. Maybe the troublemaker was home in his bed, or over in the campground in his sleeping bag, chuckling softly whenever he thought about all of us out here patrolling through the night. Maybe he'd already accomplished everything he wanted to.

I had just about convinced myself that our patrols were useless and I was letting my nerves get to me when Michael broke the silence.

"Creepy out here," he murmured.

"Yeah," I murmured back.

One end of our patrol route was at the edge of the woods, where we could probably have seen the nearest of the treed Shiffleys, even through the fog, if there had been any moon. From there we followed along the split-rail fence until we reached the gate, from which we could peer through the fog to make out the shape of the nearest of the livestock barns. Just beyond the gate, the fence turned into barbed wire and veered off into Clay County. The border between the two counties—and for that matter, the perimeter of the fair—was still defended, though, by a tangle of what I hoped was impenetrable brush. Beyond that were some locked equipment sheds, and beyond them was the start of the eight-foot chain-link fence that encircled most of the fair.

We trudged between these two end points, starting occasionally when a ghostly white goat loomed up out of the fog on the other side of the fence.

We were about halfway between the woods and the gate when a harsh shriek rang out.

"What was that?" I asked.

"A fox, maybe?" Michael suggested. But we were already running toward the noise. Some instinct made me pull out my cell phone to check the time.

"One fourteen," I said to Michael. "In case this turns out to be anything dire."

When we reached the edge of the woods, we found two Shiffleys already there. One of them shifted slightly when he spotted us, and I decided to pretend I hadn't noticed him hiding his rifle behind a nearby tree. The other had climbed over to our side of the fence and was examining what appeared to be a perfectly ordinary patch of pine needle–covered ground.

"What was that?" Michael asked.

"Could be a fox," the kneeling Shiffley said.

"Weren't no fox," the temporarily unarmed one countered. "Maybe someone trying to imitate a fox. And doing a damned bad job of it."

"Sounded pretty good to me," the first one said.

"And to me, too," I said. "But I'm no expert." Though I'd heard plenty of their shrieks since Michael and I had moved to our converted farmhouse some years ago. At first I'd been alarmed, thinking they'd come from an animal or even a child in horrible pain. These days I usually just nodded and said, "The foxes are out tonight."

Why did such a familiar noise unnerve me tonight? Was it just my nerves?

"You can't really tell much from these pine needles." The kneeling Shiffley stood up and brushed off his hands. "Could have been a fox."

"No way," the other said. "If it was a fox—"

He was interrupted by two loud popping noises.

"Gunshot," both Shiffleys said in unison. They began running toward the sound. So did Michael and I, though we weren't keeping pace with the Shiffleys.

I actually wasn't trying too hard to keep up with them.

"Oh, Lord," I heard one of them say. "He's been shot."

"Who?" I asked.

"No idea," the other one said. "Call Randall."

"Call the chief first," the first one countered.

"Isn't Vern here tonight?" the other asked.

"Call 911," Michael said. "I'll go see if I can get some help. Stay together, all of you."

"He's got no pulse," one of the Shiffleys said.

"Sssh," I hissed. "Are those running footsteps? Turn your flashlights on," I added, pulling mine out of my pocket and following my own orders. Michael did the same thing, and the two Shiffleys were silent—one kneeling by the body while the other punched buttons on his cell phone. We all kept quiet for a few moments, scanning our surroundings with the flashlights, but we could only see a few yards into the fog.

"Nothing," the kneeling Shiffley said. "Someone give me some light down here. I need to see if there's anything I can do for him."

I shifted my flashlight beam toward his voice and the

body he was kneeling beside came into focus. Person, not body, I corrected myself, but when I moved the beam up to the head, I realized maybe I'd been right the first time.

"We've got someone shot down here at the fair," the other Shiffley was saying into his cell phone. "At the gate to the Midway."

"It's one nineteen," Michael said. "In case someone asks. Like the chief."

Then he took off again, running, toward the agricultural section.

"No," the Shiffley on the phone was saying. "No idea who he is."

"Oh, damn," I muttered.

"Yeah, I don't think he's going to make it," the Shiffley said.

"It's Brett Riordan," I said.

He was lying on his back in the open gate between the main part of the fair and the Midway, with his head toward us and his feet pointing toward the barns. He was wearing dark pants and a dark hooded jacket with the hood pulled up around his face. His eyes were wide and staring, and there was a bullet hole in his forehead.

Chapter 17

"Shouldn't we be giving him some kind of first aid?" It was the Shiffley who'd called 911.

"Not sure there's anything we can do," the kneeling Shiffley said. "Two shots, one in the head and one in the throat. Either one could kill you, but both?"

The first one shook his head. And then he began telling Debbie Ann what had happened and where we were.

There were trickles of something dark on Brett's forehead—blood, no doubt. I was glad the flashlight leached out the colors so I was seeing it in black and white. I made sure not to let the flashlight beam drift any higher than his forehead, because there was probably an exit wound that would give me nightmares.

Within minutes of our call to 911, a figure appeared out of the fog from the barn side of the fence. Another Shiffley, by the long, loose-knit shape of him. Since the gate was blocked, I climbed over the fence to greet him. When he got close enough I realized it was Vern Shiffley.

"Hey, Vern," the standing Shiffley said.

"We heard two shots and found him dead," the kneeling one said.

"Chief's on his way." Vern pulled out a flashlight, knelt on the other side of the body, and focused the beam on Brett's face.

"What's going on here?" came a voice from the fog on

the Midway side. He had the twang of a local. Another Shiffley?

"Crime scene," Vern snapped. "Stay clear."

"If it's a crime scene, I'll take over."

A figure appeared. Not a Shiffley. He was too short and wide, more the hulking bearlike shape of a high school football player gone sedentary. He wasn't wearing a uniform, but he was flashing a badge.

"We're already on it," Vern said.

"And now I'm here," the new arrival said. "Deputy Plunkett, Clay County Sheriff's Department."

"We were here first." Vern stood up, looming over his counterpart. "Deputy Shiffley, Caerphilly Sheriff's Department."

"Body's in Clay County," Plunkett said.

"Parts of it," Vern said.

"Looks like he was shot in the head," Plunkett said. "And the head's in Clay County."

"Yeah, but his feet are in Caerphilly. Far as I can see, he must have been standing on them when he was shot. In Caerphilly County."

"But he landed in Clay County."

"Only the top half of him," Vern said. "A little less than half, actually. If you draw a line through the gate it would hit him midway between the waist and the shoulders."

"But he was shot in the head," Plunkett said.

"By someone in Caerphilly County, by the look of it."

"How do you figure that?" Plunkett asked.

"Shot's in the middle of his forehead," Vern pointed out.

Plunkett squatted down to look at the body, grunting as he did.

"Shot probably knocked him on his back like that," Vern went on. "Had to have been from our side of the fence."

"He could have staggered and turned around before he went down," Plunkett said. "For that matter, how do I know you didn't turn him over? To check his vitals or give him CPR or some such nonsense."

"We haven't moved him," the other Shiffley said. "He was lying just like this, and we could see it was no use giving CPR."

"So you say." Plunkett crossed his arms and planted his feet as if to suggest he could stand there all night to argue about it.

It was like listening to Jamie and Josh argue. At least with them you could blame it on the terrible twos. I was opening my mouth to say so when another figure appeared out of the fog on the Clay County side. A short, very stout figure that I recognized, after a second or two, as the sheriff of Clay County. Damn.

"What's going on here?" he asked.

"Body in our county—" Plunkett began.

"Partly in your county—" Vern corrected.

"And they're trying to assert jurisdiction," Plunkett went on.

"Well, that's a load of—cow manure." The sheriff glanced at me in time to soften what might otherwise have been a saltier statement. "Plunkett, go get a board or something so we can haul him off."

"Haul him off?" I repeated. "Without having the medical examiner certify his death? Without having a crime scene crew look for evidence? Without doing any of the things you need to do to catch who killed him?"

I stopped short of what I really wanted to say, which was "How stupid are you, anyway?" He probably guessed I was thinking it.

"We do things our own way in Clay County, young lady," the sheriff said. "Don't you worry your pretty little head."

"Over here in Caerphilly County, we do things the right way," I said.

"And most of him's in Caerphilly County," Vern put in.

"Head's in our county," Plunkett said.

"Never mind what county which parts of him are where," I said. "The whole of him's on my fairgrounds, and I'm asserting jurisdiction."

They all blinked and looked at me in surprise. I was a little surprised myself at what I'd just said.

"Your fairgrounds?" the sheriff echoed.

"Jurisdiction?" the Clay County deputy scoffed.

"As assistant director of the Un-fair, I'm ordering you to leave that body alone until Chief Burke gets here and we can work out an appropriate solution to the jurisdictional issues."

"You may be assistant director of the fair, little lady," the sheriff said. "But I don't see how that gives you any jurisdiction over my body."

"I have jurisdiction over the fair," I said. "And while I don't know precisely how long it would take to pack up every single booth and ride on the Midway and move them across the line to Caerphilly—"

"We could manage it in five, six hours, tops." One of the Shiffleys. "Have it done by the time the fair opens if we start now."

"I'm sure it can be done rather easily," I finished. "And if you insist on touching that body or doing anything else before Chief Burke gets here, I'll have it done. And you can say good-bye to all the really big sales tax revenue from the weekend."

The sheriff blinked. I'd only met him a few times before, but I'd figured out rather easily that he hadn't gotten his job with his brains, his charm, or his knowledge of law enforcement techniques. But he was street smart enough to realize I was serious, and afraid I had the power to do it.

"I'm sure once Chief Burke gets here he'll agree with me on this situation," he said, finally.

"We'll ask the chief when he gets here," I said.

"Ask me what?"

We all turned to see Chief Burke standing behind us. For all I knew, he could have been standing there for a while.

"Sheriff here wants to haul the body away," Vern said.

The chief squatted down near the body.

"Has a doctor certified the death?" he asked.

" 'Certified'?" the sheriff said. "No need to certify—it's obvious he's stone-cold dead."

Chief Burke ignored him.

"No, sir," Vern said.

"Has either county's medical examiner inspected the body to give us a preliminary cause of death?" the chief asked.

Vern shook his head.

"Has a forensic team examined the crime scene?"

Vern shook his head again.

"Then moving the body is premature, don't you agree, Sheriff Dingle?"

"We need to get him out of here before a whole lot of people show up to gawk," the sheriff protested.

"I think our officers can handle crowd control," the

chief said. "At least I know mine can. If we each deploy a few officers to set up a perimeter on our respective sides of the fence, we should have no interference from gawkers."

"Fine," the sheriff said. "Go take care of that, Billy."

"Yes, sir." Plunkett answered briskly enough, but he continued to stand at his boss's side.

"And then once you've done all your newfangled things, I'll have my officers take him down to the Clay County Morgue," the sheriff went on.

I stood by for a few minutes, fuming, as Chief Burke and the sheriff carried on the same argument Vern and Plunkett had. And the chief wasn't making any more headway than Vern had. I finally got fed up. Should I play the Midway card again? Actually, I had a better idea.

"Chief," I said, "may I talk to you for just a moment?"

The look he gave me was pure frustration, and I could tell he was counting to ten before telling me, as politely as possible, to stay out of this. Then I saw his expression soften a little. I hoped that meant he realized I was trying to help.

"Yes?" he said. He took a couple of steps away from the sheriff. I walked over to his side. I glanced at the sheriff and plucked the chief by the sleeve to pull him another step or two away.

"Let them have it, Chief," I said in a stage whisper, as if trying not to let anyone else hear.

"I beg your pardon?" He was also stage-whispering. And I could tell he was about a hair's breadth away from a furious bellow.

"The investigation. Let them have it. Remember what happened last time?"

"Last time?" he repeated. He was frowning again, but sounded more puzzled than angry.

"The last time we had a homicide case."

Now he looked purely puzzled.

"The expense!" I said, out of the corner of my mouth. "You know what it did to the county budget. All those expensive tests the state crime lab insisted on running—on our tab. And then the trial! How much did that set the county back? We're still digging ourselves out of that hole."

I shook my head as if still appalled at the price of justice.

"What's this now?" the sheriff asked.

I saw the chief's mouth quirk into a quick smile, and he took a few seconds to put a serious look back on his face before turning to answer the sheriff.

"Ms. Langslow is pointing out that a high-profile murder case can be a substantial drain on a county's resources," the chief said.

"We've had a few murders in our time, little lady," the Sheriff said. "Didn't cost that much."

"Were they local murders?" I said. "Or murders of wealthy, well-known people from outside the county? Did they take place during an event already crawling with reporters? Did you have a trial that lasted weeks and weeks?"

I hoped he wouldn't realize that I was exaggerating both Brett's reputation and the level of press coverage the fair had achieved so far. He blinked a couple of times. Then the deputy whispered something in his ear. The two of them took a few steps away, turned their back on us, and held a truly whispered conversation. Unlike me, they weren't trying to be overheard. Then they turned back to us with wide mud-eating grins on their faces.

"I think we can work this out, Chief," the sheriff said. "Seeing as how Caerphilly is the larger county—not to mention the more ef*flu*ent—I could see my way clear to letting you take the lead on this investigation. On one condition."

"And that would be?" The chief didn't look like a man willing to grant conditions, but just the fact that he answered was progress.

"I'd want you to include a representative from Clay County on your investigationary team," the sheriff said. "I'll assign Deputy Plunkett here to do that."

"Not to interfere, of course." Plunkett gave us an oily smile. "Just to keep what lawyers would call a 'watching brief.' "

The chief hesitated for a few moments, studying Plunkett. I could tell he didn't like the idea. I suspected Plunkett was the sheriff's right-hand man—maybe even the brains of the department. I wouldn't want to bet on him sticking to a watching brief if he saw a way to put one over on Caerphilly. But I decided if it were my case, I'd probably want Plunkett where I could keep an eye on him, not running around by himself. I could almost see the moment when the chief decided the same thing.

"That would be acceptable," he said. "Provided the deputy is willing to stick to being an observer, without interfering in any way with the conduct of our case."

He didn't emphasize the "our," but it was there.

"Long as Plunkett can report back to me about anything he observes that he thinks I'd like to know about." The sheriff looked pleased with himself.

The chief nodded tightly.

"Then we have ourselves a deal," the sheriff said. "If y'all aren't letting me work the case, I'm going to go back to my bed." He turned to Plunkett. "He needs some manpower from us, you help him out, now, you hear?"

Plunkett nodded.

The sheriff turned and ambled away with more speed

and less noise than you'd have expected from someone of his age and size.

Chief Burke watched him as the sheriff slowly disappeared into the fog. He didn't look as happy as I thought he would.

Chapter 18

When Sheriff Dingle was completely out of sight, the chief appeared to rouse himself from thought and turned briskly back to the rest of us.

"Vern," he said. "Get that perimeter going. Coordinate with Deputy Plunkett on the other side of the fence."

"Yes, sir." Vern glanced at Plunkett, then stepped a few paces away and took out his cell phone. Plunkett smirked a bit, but pulled out his cell phone.

"Meg, Michael's gone to fetch your father. Is there any chance that your cousin Horace is in town for the fair?" the chief asked.

"How come her family all get called to the crime scene?" Plunkett asked.

"Dr. Langslow is the local medical examiner." The chief's tone was so even that an outsider like Plunkett probably had no idea how ticked off he was. "And Horace Hollingsworth is a highly experienced crime scene examiner who does forensic work for us under a longstanding arrangement with the York County Sheriff's Department. We are fortunate that his family ties to some of our citizens give us access to a forensic investigator of his caliber."

Plunkett shrugged elaborately and turned back to his cell phone.

"Horace is in town." I was already pulling out my phone. "I'll round him up."

The chief nodded.

"Debbie Ann," he said into his phone. "Call everyone back on duty. With my apologies, but we've got a murder here."

I had reached Horace's voice mail and left a message to call me back as soon as possible.

"I understand the deceased was one of the exhibitors?"

"Yes and no," I said. "His soon-to-be-ex-wife is an exhibitor. Molly Riordan of Leaping Goat Farm in the vendors' barn. And his new girlfriend, Genette Sedgewick, has a booth in the wine pavilion."

"Lordy," he said. "Any idea where either of them would be?"

"Not really," I said. "If I were looking for Genette, I'd start with the Caerphilly Inn. It might be up to her standards."

The chief blinked slightly. The Caerphilly Inn was a five-star hotel, with prices to match.

Just then my cell phone rang.

"Do you realize what time it is?" Horace said, when I answered. Evidently he hadn't really listened to my message.

"Yes, it's one thirty-seven a.m.," I said. "The murder took place sometime between one fourteen and one nineteen."

"Oh," he said. "Where?"

"In the gate between the Midway and the rest of the fair."

"On my way."

I hung up.

"You're sure of that time window?" Evidently the chief had been eavesdropping.

I explained about looking at my watch when we'd heard the fox—if it was a fox—and then Michael announcing the time after we'd found the body. And then the chief took me through an account of the entire evening, which didn't take long, since the sum total of what we'd done was to walk up and down the fence for several hours until we'd heard the shriek.

By the time he'd finished with me, Dad and Horace had arrived and were doing forensic things to Brett's body and the surrounding area. Plunkett returned, presumably from setting up his perimeter guards, and leaned against the fence to watch. The chief turned back to me.

"We need to talk to Mrs. Riordan," the chief said.

"Yeah, you don't have to look far for the culprit on this one," Plunkett said.

"I can't imagine Molly killing anyone," I said.

"Not even her no-good, womanizing, hound dog of a husband?" Plunkett asked.

I winced. Molly would hate it that her marital problems had become such common knowledge.

"If you ask me she has good reason to get rid of him," Plunkett went on.

"And she was getting rid of him, the only sane way," I said. "They're separated and were getting a divorce."

I wanted to keep going and say that she had nothing to gain and everything to lose by killing him, but I had no idea if it was true. Would Brett's death help or hurt Molly's efforts to save her farm? That would depend on who inherited Brett's share.

If he hadn't made a will—and he didn't strike me as the kind of guy who thought about messy things like dying—wouldn't Molly inherit his half of the farm? In which case her financial problems would be solved. As long as she could prove she hadn't killed him.

Then again, they hadn't been getting along well for some time. What if Brett, since the separation or even earlier, when things began going wrong, had made a will with someone other than Molly as his beneficiary? Like his mother, who had never approved of Molly. Or the Brett pack, as Molly called her husband's four brothers, whose ongoing skirmishes with the law and an ever increasing number of debt collectors made it obvious that Brett was, God help us, the responsible one in his family.

Or maybe even the new girlfriend? Genette would probably define herself as Brett's fiancée, but I found myself agreeing with Mother's refusal to apply that term to someone who was dating a married man. But Mother's disapproval wouldn't prevent Genette from causing trouble if she was in Brett's will.

I looked up and saw the chief looking at me with a sympathetic expression, as if he'd read my thoughts and understood how painful they were.

"Right now, we just need to talk to Ms. Riordan." The chief's voice was gentle. "And for that matter, if they're still legally married, we need to notify her of his death. Do you know where she is?"

"Probably in the exhibitors' campground," I said. "I doubt if she has the money to spend on a hotel room, even if there were plenty available." The chief nodded. Caerphilly had only two hotels—the expensive five-star Caerphilly Inn, and the Whispering Pines Cabins, which was still trying to overcome its lurid past as a hot-sheets motel. Both of them, plus every B and B and boardinghouse and spare bedroom in the county, had been booked for this week for months. That was why we'd set up the campgrounds. "But I have no idea if she has an RV or a tent or if she's just sleeping in her car," I added.

"I've got the info from the DMV." Vern pulled out his radio and spoke into it. "Fred? Aida? I want you to check the parking lot for a vehicle. A 1997 Dodge Caravan. Maroon."

He rattled off a license number, listened for a moment, then looked up. "Chief? What should they do when they find it?"

"I want to interview her myself," the chief said.

"Take no action," Vern said into the phone. "Advise me and the chief of your location and sit on the vehicle and its owner."

Vern strode off in the general direction of the campgrounds, presumably to help with the search. Plunkett looked back and forth between him and the chief a few times, then scurried off after Vern.

"Mind if I use your fair office as my temporary headquarters?" the chief asked. "It's pretty close to my crime scene."

"Fine with me," I said. "And I can't imagine Randall would mind. Look—may I go with you when you notify Molly? She'll be terrified if a stranger shows up at her tent or van in the middle of the night. It might help if someone she knows is there."

The chief studied me with narrowed eyes for a few moments. Then he nodded.

"You will be there solely to help us avoid startling Ms. Riordan and to reassure her that we really are the police," he said.

I nodded.

"Okay, then."

We waited a minute or two until another Caerphilly deputy showed up. Then the chief tasked her with supervising the crime scene and we set out for the other end of the fair. We strode in silence, except for the occasional static-filled burst of chatter from the police radio on his belt. I hoped Caerphilly's small but lively criminal community didn't have police radios, because it was pretty clear from the radio traffic that the whole department, plus all the borrowed officers from nearby counties, were converging on the fairgrounds, leaving the sleeping town woefully unprotected.

We arrived at the edge of the informal campground—it had been a cow pasture until Randall began working on the fair project—and stood for a few minutes, gazing over the sea of cars, pickups, vans, RVs, trailers, and tents.

"Whoever did it could just have slipped back here," I said, in an undertone. "If anyone spotted him, he could just say he was on his way back from the bathroom."

I indicated the line of blue plastic portapotties along the edge of the field closest to the fair.

"In fact," I went on. "If I were the killer, I'd make a bee-line for the portapotties. As soon as I'm anywhere near them, I have a legitimate reason for being out and about in the night. And maybe a nice place to dump anything I wouldn't want to be caught with. Like a recently fired handgun."

"Good Lord," the chief said. We both studied the portapotties in silence for a while.

"Horace might still find it at the crime scene," he said. He didn't sound optimistic.

"Maybe you could assign searching the portapotties to some of the borrowed deputies," I suggested.

The chief frowned.

"Like maybe the Clay County ones. Plunkett could supervise."

"I'll take that under advisement." He didn't actually smile, but his frown had disappeared.

The chief's phone beeped.

"Yes?" He listened for a few moments. "On my way. Do you know your way around this campground?" he asked me.

"Pretty well."

"Vern says they're at location Fifteen R," he said. "Can you find that?"

I nodded, and pointed up at the sign above us, which told us we were at location 1-A. Then I set off down the edge of the campground toward row fifteen.

I'd originally suggested having separate sections of the campgrounds—a motorized section for trailers, RVs, and people sleeping in their vans, and another for tents only. Apparently I was the only one who saw any merit to this idea, and the exhibitors had camped according to how far they wanted to be from the road, the bathrooms, or the fair itself, and who they wanted to camp next to, and what space was still left when they showed up. Each aisle we passed was a motley mixture of everything from pup tents to RVs the size of an aircraft carrier. But I had insisted that we put up location signs, to help people find their way back to their campsites.

I craned my neck when we past the third row, where Rose Noire had camped, but as far down as I could see, the tents and campers were all dark. Good. I hoped she and the boys would sleep through all of this.

We set out down the end of the rows. The chief followed a step or two behind me.

"This is Fifteen," I said, as I turned into the row.

Now we were walking by campsites. Thank goodness it was past 2:00 A.M., and most of the exhibitors were presumably fast asleep. Once we waved as we passed some people sitting around the remnants of a campfire. A little farther along, I heard a noise and a flashlight beam suddenly blinded me. Then it snapped off as suddenly as it appeared.

"Sorry, Meg," a woman's voice murmured. "Just being careful."

"No problem," I murmured back. "Good night."

Probably a good thing she had spotted me, not the chief. People were expecting to see patrols, but I didn't think people would find the sight of the chief reassuring. Especially not if he was glowering the way he usually glowered when in pursuit of someone who dared break the peace in his county.

Just past the 15-Q sign, I spotted Vern and another deputy standing in the middle of the roadway. Apparently they were waiting until we got there before closing in on 15-R. As we approached, I could see that Vern had unscrewed the other deputy's flashlight and appeared to be trying to fix it.

"What's wrong with the flashlight?" the chief asked.

"Nothing," Vern said. "But we thought it might be a good idea to look as if we stopped here for a reason. Here you go, Fred."

He handed the flashlight back to Fred, who pointed it at his shoe and flicked the beam on and off again, very quickly.

Vern, meanwhile, was pointing at a campsite occupied by a dark van and a small tent. It was the last occupied campsite in row fifteen, and not far from the fence surrounding the camp. I wondered if Molly had arrived later than most of the campers or if her frame of mind had made her choose an isolated spot.

"That's her van, and the tent seems to be with it," he said quietly. "No idea if she's in there."

"Meg," the chief said. "You want to knock and see if she's there?"

I nodded and stepped over to the tent. The front flap was zipped, though there was a mesh ventilation window. I tried to peer inside, but it was too dark to see anything. And how does one knock on a tent, anyway? I tapped on the tent pole and spoke as softly as I could.

"Molly?" I called. "It's Meg. Are you there?"

After a few moments, I heard the sound of a zipper and the tent flap opened. Molly peered out.

"Meg? What's wrong?"

She looked anxious, but so would I if someone awakened me at 2:00 A.M. in a strange place.

"There's bad news," I said. "I came to help the police find you so they could tell you."

"Bad news?" Molly tugged the zipper all the way open and glanced beyond me to where the police and the two deputies were standing.

I turned and looked back at the chief. He walked over to stand beside me at the tent.

"It's about your husband," he said. "I'm afraid he's dead."

Chapter 19

Molly blinked as if she didn't quite understand.

"Dead?" she repeated. "Did he wreck his car again? That's it, isn't it? He's had two DUIs in the last year but nothing seems to—"

"Molly." I didn't say it very loudly, but it got through to her. She fell silent and looked up at the chief, waiting.

"Your husband was murdered," the chief said.

"Brett?" Molly looked genuinely baffled. "Who would want to kill Brett?"

"That's what we'd like to find out," the chief said. "I'd like to talk to you. Can you come down to the fair office with me?"

"Okay," she said. "Just let me find my shoes and— Wait."

She suddenly looked completely awake for the first time since she'd opened the tent flap.

"You think I did it, don't you?" she said. "I'm the obvious suspect. The abandoned wife. But you're wrong. I couldn't kill Brett. I couldn't even kick him out. He finally left on his own."

"Should she have an attorney?" I asked the chief. I was already pulling out my notebook.

"If she wants to have an attorney present—" the chief began.

"No," she said. "I didn't do it and I have nothing to hide."

"Here," I handed her a sheet of paper from my notebook. What did it say about my friends and family that I'd

144

memorized the name and phone number of a local defense attorney?

"May we search your tent and your van?" the chief asked. "It's routine in a murder investigation."

"Murder?" Molly repeated. "How did he—how was he killed?"

"He was shot," the chief said.

Molly flinched at his words.

"Oh." She closed her eyes and remained perfectly still for a few seconds. Then she opened them up again and set her jaw.

"Okay," she said. "Let's get this over with. Search all you like."

She reached behind her, pulled out a pair of canvas shoes, slipped them on, picked up a small purse, then walked off with the chief.

I glanced over at the two deputies, who were putting on plastic gloves. Plunkett, the Clay County deputy watched them for a few minutes, then shook his head and chuckled.

"You got a spare pair of them things?" he asked.

Vern rolled his eyes, but Fred pulled another pair of gloves out of his pocket.

"I'll go back to the fairgrounds with the chief," I said, and then hurried to catch up to the chief and Molly. It didn't feel like a good night for wandering around alone. The chief didn't say anything when I joined them. In fact, neither of them said anything until we drew near the fair office. We could see that activity was still ongoing over at the site of the murder, and someone had set up a couple of portable floodlights to illuminate the area.

Molly stumbled, and I glanced over to see that she was staring fixedly at the circle of light.

"Is that where . . . ?" she asked.

I nodded.

"Let me open the trailer for you," I said to the chief.

I unlocked the office, stepped in, and flicked on the light switch. We were in luck—the power was working tonight. The overhead fluorescents made the trailer seem stark, industrial, and almost grim. Or maybe that last part was my mood.

"You might want to use my desk," I said.

The chief glanced at the two desks. Mine wasn't exactly empty, but the papers were in neat stacks and the assorted desk tools were grouped in square wooden baskets. Of course, in the few weeks since we'd set up the fair office, I'd actually spent quite some time working here, while Randall seemed to use his desk only as a place to store stuff.

"I make sure it's easy to clear away so we can use it as a table when we have meetings." I was clearing away as I spoke. The papers went into more baskets, and then all the baskets went onto a series of shelves on the wall behind the desk. In a few minutes, the desk was empty except for a desk lamp and a well-filled pencil holder.

The chief nodded his approval and held a chair for Molly.

"Want me to start the coffee machine before I go?" I asked.

"Please," the chief said. "And thank you for your help."

I turned on the machine, threw a packet of coffee in, and added the water.

"All yours," I said as I exited the trailer.

I glanced at my watch. A little past two. My patrol shift was over. Technically, I could go to bed, but I wasn't sure I could sleep.

I pulled out my cell phone and called Michael.

"Over here by the crime scene," he said, without my even asking. "Standing by to help with crowd control if needed. Was that you going into the fair office?"

"Letting the chief in so he can question Molly."

"Damn."

"Yeah."

We fell silent. If I glanced over toward the spotlighted crime scene, I could make out his silhouette. That was strangely comforting. As was the thought that the boys were across the fairgrounds from all of this.

"Early patrols are all off duty," he said after a while. "Couple of them are still hanging around here, trying to rubberneck. The graveyard shift patrols are all making their rounds. Though it's a good thing they're not armed. Or at least I hope they aren't. Most of them are jittery as hell."

"I told them if I caught anyone with a weapon I'd have him arrested," I said. "No guarantee they listened." In fact, I knew at least one of the Shiffleys hadn't, but he'd been discreet, and I wasn't planning to cause trouble for him. Maybe he'd been a better judge of the dangers of his post than I'd been. "Look," I said aloud. "I'm going to stay here for a little while. If the chief lets Molly go, she's going to need someone."

"And if he doesn't let her go?"

"No idea." With that we hung up.

Randall and I had put a small bench just outside the door of the fair office. I took a seat. If the chief came out, I could tell him I was watching the door for him. And I could keep an eye on what was happening at the crime scene without being close enough to see the details. I'd already seen way more of the crime scene than I wanted, and didn't plan to go near the gate again until the EMTs took away Brett's body. I wondered how soon that would be.

And how soon would the chief release the scene? Did I need to talk to Randall about rounding up some workmen to arrange a detour—another gate through the fence to let people into the Midway?

I pulled out my notebook and scribbled it on my to-do list.

After I put the notebook away, I thought of another task. I'd need to make sure someone cleaned up the area around the gate. Bad enough that people would be gawking at it once they heard what had happened there. No way I'd let anyone near it until there was nothing to see but an ordinary wooden gate in an ordinary split-rail fence.

I didn't pull out my notebook to write that down, though. No danger at all I'd forget it.

Maybe a little danger that I'd fall asleep before I got a chance to do anything about it. I suddenly yawned, and realized that I was tired enough to fall asleep sitting up.

I was still awake, though barely, when the two deputies, Vern and Plunkett, came striding toward me.

"Chief in there?" Vern asked.

"With Molly," I said.

"He'll want to see this," Plunkett crowed. "Show her the gun, Vern."

"Gun?"

Vern frowned, but Plunkett didn't seem to notice.

"Found it in the killer's van," Plunkett said.

"Suspect's van," Vern corrected. He was on his phone. "Chief? We found a gun in the back of Ms. Riordan's van. . . . Okay."

Plunkett reached for the door, but Vern caught his arm.

"Chief says wait," Vern said. "He'll be a few minutes."

"Okay," Plunkett looked around, and spotted the activity over at the gate. "Give a yell when he's ready for us. Can't wait to see his face when he sees what we found."

He ambled off toward the floodlights.

" 'What we found.' " Vern didn't sound his normal, easy-going self. "I know we're supposed to make nice, keep peace between the counties, but you want to know what really happened?"

I nodded.

"We were both searching the van. I started at the front end, Plunkett took the back, while Fred worked on the tent. I was still doing the glove compartment when Plunkett announced that he was going to go have a smoke. Didn't seem like he'd had time to do more than glance into the back, so I just worked my way through the whole thing from front to back. Found the gun under the floor mat in the back."

He shook his head in disgust.

" 'Course now he claims he wasn't finished searching—just taking a smoke break. Tried to get up in my face about trespassing in his part of the van. Wouldn't shut up until I promised I wouldn't tell who found the gun—just that *we* found it."

"A promise you're already breaking, apparently."

"Actually, he only made me promise not to tell the chief." Vern rolled his eyes. "Didn't say anything about not telling anyone else. Including someone who might happen to let the truth slip to the chief."

"So you actually want me to pass the word along." I was puzzled. Vern and the chief seemed to have a good working relationship.

"I did promise not to tell him," Vern said. "But I think

he needs to know. 'Cause I think Plunkett has an ulterior motive here. I know this probably sounds crazy, but I think he wants a job in our department."

"I didn't know you were hiring." In fact, given the county's troubled financial state, I'd thought the sheriff's department, like every other department, was tightening its belt and postponing any new hires.

"We will be after the first of the year," Vern said. "Bill's retiring, and Jamal's going back to college full time to get his MBA. Even in these times, that's more downsizing than we need. We'll be hiring."

"Cool," I said. "But if I were looking to get hired by the chief, I think I'd work a little harder on not ticking him off."

"I don't think Plunkett sees it that way. I bet he thinks he's impressing the chief with his initiative. And that if the chief thinks he was the one smart enough to find the murder weapon, he's a shoo-in."

"So you think the gun you found is the murder weapon?"

"It's a twenty-two," he said. "We won't know for certain till they do all the forensics, but I saw the wound, and I'd be surprised if anything bigger than a twenty-two made it. And the gun's been fired recently. I can tell that all by myself, from the smell. Maybe it's a good thing I did find it. It's hard enough to get fingerprints from a gun to begin with, and if Plunkett had found it, he'd have covered up any we could find with his own."

"And fired it, once or twice, just to see if it works," I suggested.

"Don't laugh; he probably would have," Vern said. "Where do they find clowns like him?"

Just then I spotted an ambulance lurching slowly up the dirt road. No flashing lights or siren, but the headlights alone would wake a few people in the barns. Vern followed my glance and shook his head when he saw the ambulance.

"Poor guy," Vern said. "I feel bad."

I looked up, startled. For a moment I thought was saying that he was ill and needed an ambulance, too. But he wasn't clutching his heart or anything, just frowning slightly.

"Bad about what?" I asked.

"The poor guy's lying there dead and we were squabbling over his body like . . . like . . . I don't know what. It was shameful. A man's dead; he should have some dignity."

"We couldn't just let them take over," I said.

"No." Vern's jaw was set hard. "No, you did good, keeping that from happening. They're real slick over there in Clay County at catching poachers and running petty crooks out of town, but they can't solve this. And if your friend didn't do it, I don't want her framed because they're too stupid to investigate. And if she did do it, I don't want her to get off because they screwed up the investigation."

"Understood," I said. "I feel the same way."

We sat in silence for a few moments.

"Maybe it will turn out to be a simple robbery," I suggested.

"Not likely." Vern shook his head. "His wallet was there. With a couple hundred in it, not to mention a whole deck of credit cards. Might be car theft. We didn't find his keys. And the chief put out an APB on his car—a Mazda MX-5 convertible. Bright red. Expensive taste in cars."

I wondered if Genette had bought it for him or if he'd

used money that could have gone to help with Molly's farm.

We sat in silence for a few more moments, then Vern stood up as if coming to a sudden decision.

"Tell the chief I went over to help the EMTs," he said. "Have him call me to let me know if he wants to see the gun or just have me turn it over to Horace."

With that he strode off.

I settled back more comfortably on the bench. After all, I had been entrusted with an official message for the chief. I wasn't just hanging around being nosy. I was being useful.

I'd been asleep for at least half an hour when the chief gently shook me awake.

"Your friend has a request," he said.

Molly was standing beside him. And Deputy Aida.

"Thanks for the lawyer's name," Molly said. "She's meeting me down at the jail. Any chance you could do something about my booth? I don't know when I'll be back to deal with it."

"I can find someone trustworthy to do sales," I said.

"You think anyone will actually want to buy cheese from a murder suspect?" Molly was shaking her head as if she thought she knew the answer. "I was thinking more of just packing it up."

"On the contrary, the notoriety should send sales through the roof," I said. "I'm thinking we should raise prices before the word gets out."

"Yeah, right." Evidently Molly thought I was kidding. "I'll leave it to you, then." She turned to Aida. "I'm ready."

The chief and I watched as they trudged off toward the front gate.

"You should get some sleep," he said.

"So should you," I replied. "Or Minerva will have your head."

He grimaced and nodded.

"I want to stay nearby in case something comes up," he said. "I noticed a cot here in the closet. I thought I'd bunk down on that tonight, if that's okay with you and Randall."

"It's fine with me, and Randall's not here to object," I said. "Be my guest. Vern said to tell you he'll be over there at the crime scene with the gun he found. I'll be in the sheep barn if anyone needs me."

Chapter 20

Morning arrived too soon. Actually, since I'd already seen three hours of morning before going to bed, what arrived too soon was my adorable and way-too-energetic sons.

"Mommy, wake up! Look at the sheeps!" Jamie was crowing.

Josh contented himself with leaning over me, tugging on my shoulder with one hand while eating a particularly juicy mango with the other. Little bits of mango and dollops of the mango juice and mango-flavored drool were raining on my face.

"Josh, can you eat your mango someplace else?" I said, as I sat up and reached for something to wipe my face with. "No, don't lean over Daddy's face while you eat it."

"It's okay." Michael sat up, a little baggy eyed from lack of sleep, but as always just as cheerful with the boys as if he'd gotten his full eight hours. "Josh, can you give Daddy a bite?"

"Look at all the sheeps!" Jamie repeated.

"Just sheep," I said. "Look at all the sheep."

"Yeah!" Jamie said. "Millions and millions of sheeps!"

"I'm sorry." Rose Noire was standing just outside our bedroom pen, with half a dozen bags and totes over her shoulders. "I thought you'd be up by now. It's eight o'clock, and we open at nine today."

"We were up very late," I said.

"But it's okay," Michael said. He got up and began taking

the bags, which no doubt contained all the boys' clothes, diapers, toys, and other gear.

"That's right," she said. "You were on patrol until midnight."

"Till two," I said. "And it wasn't the patrol that did us in. It was the M-U-R-D-E-R."

"Mur—" she began, and then clapped her hand over her mouth. Josh laughed and pointed at her.

"Little ears," I said.

"Right." She was trying not to look shocked. "Who was . . . er . . ."

"Brett Riordan," I said. "And Molly's been arrested for it."

"She couldn't possibly have done it."

"I'm glad you think so," I said. "Because she's still down at the J-A-I-L, and can't sell her cheeses, at least for the first part of today. Can you rearrange your booth to add in a cheese section and keep her sales going?"

"Of course. I'll get Horace and Sammy to help me carry everything over."

"Horace is doing forensics, and Deputy Sammy's probably been up all night helping with the investigation," I said. "I can send Rob over."

"I'll ask your mother to recruit some help," Rose Noire said. "Not that Rob wouldn't do his best, of course, but—"

"Understood," I said.

"You'll be busy," Michael said. "Would you like me and the boys to drop by for lunch? I can bring I-C-E C-R-E-A-M."

"Okay," Rose Noire said. "And—"

"Want ice cream now!" Josh exclaimed.

We all stared at him. He finished the last bit of his mango and held out the pit for one of us to take.

"He's not really learning to spell." I took the mango pit and tucked it into the trash bag. "He just always wants ice cream."

"Let's hope so," Michael said. "Because when they learn to spell, it's really going to hamper adult conversations. More mango, Josh?"

"Mango ice cream," Josh corrected.

"Mango ice cream later," Michael said. "Just mangoes for breakfast."

Josh frowned for a moment, then took the mango slice Rose Noire was holding out.

"Can I have it?" Jamie asked.

Rose Noire held out a second mango slice, but apparently Jamie was coveting sheep. He ignored the fruit. He was pressed against the side of the pen, hugging one of the sheep.

"Those are Mr. Early's sheep," I said.

"Want sheep!" Jamie sounded on the verge of tears. Josh regarded him with curiosity.

"No idea why he's so gung ho for sheep all of a sudden," I said. "It's not as if he doesn't see them all the time."

"Don't worry," Michael told Jamie. "The sheep are coming home with us after the fair." It was only a small lie. Either Seth Early's fences were unusually porous or his sheep had taken lessons from Houdini. Some of them spent more time in our yard than in their own pasture.

"My sheep!" Jamie exclaimed.

"Come on, Bo Peep," Michael said. "Let's go get some breakfast, and then you can lead the llamas to their pen."

Rose Noire scurried off. Michael grabbed a couple of the bags she'd been toting and led the boys off, still trailing bits of mango.

"Dog show at noon," he called over his shoulder. "I

know between the fair and the M-U-R et cetera you'll be busy, but don't miss that."

"Roger," I called back.

"Ms. Langslow?"

I looked over to see a gray-haired man in overalls and a work shirt standing just outside the pen.

"Can I help you?" I asked.

"You're the fair's deputy director, right?"

I nodded, and stood up, trying to look official, in spite of the mango bits.

"I just wanted to know what you were doing about all the chicken thefts."

"*All* the chicken thefts?" I echoed. "We had one report yesterday that two Russian Orloff bantams were stolen during the previous night. I haven't heard of any more chicken thefts—have you?"

"No," he said. "But two stolen is two too many."

"Absolutely," I said. "I know how I'd feel if anyone even tried to steal our llamas." I gestured to the pen where Groucho and the guys were happily watching our conversation. The farmer eyed them and moved a few inches farther away. Maybe he'd heard all the stories about llama spit.

"I heard there were other problems," he said.

I sighed.

"You could say that," I said. "We had a murder last night."

"I heard about that." He didn't sound particularly alarmed. "Over at the Midway, right?"

I nodded.

"Well, what do you expect? Bunch of carnies, and in Clay County at that. But no more animal thefts?"

"Not that I know of."

"But are you sure you'd have heard?" He was looking anxious again.

I pulled out my cell phone and called the police station. I used their regular number, not 911, but I still got Debbie Ann, the dispatcher.

"What's the problem?" she asked.

"No problem," I said. "If I had a problem, I'd call 911. I just wanted to see if you'd heard about other incidents here at the fair last night."

"Other than the murder, you mean?"

"That's right."

"No. No other incidents."

"That's good," I said.

"Not that I'd expect any," Debbie Ann went on. "With the whole fairgrounds swarming with police all night."

"I agree."

"In case you're curious, your friend's lawyer just arrived, and the chief sent a deputy down to Richmond to take the gun to the crime lab. It's not looking good."

I winced. So much for hoping the real culprit, or at least another strong suspect, had turned up while I was asleep.

"Thanks." I hung up. "No other thefts," I said to the farmer.

"Thanks," he said. "I don't want to take any chances with my livestock. I've got Red Wattles."

I admit, I glanced at his neck, which was red and wrinkled but largely wattle-free, before catching on.

"I see," I said. "Red Wattles . . . they're hogs, right? A heritage breed?"

"That's right." Something that could probably be classified as a smile crossed his face. "Sweetest-tempered hogs I've ever raised, and you should taste the bacon."

I tried not to show my reaction. I was no vegetarian and I'd lived in a farm community for years now, but I was still occasionally surprised—and a little put off—by how matter-of-fact some farmers were about eating their livestock. And I had come to feel particularly sorry for pigs. People might keep chickens for the eggs, sheep for wool, and cows for milk, but if anyone had invented a nonlethal job for pigs, I hadn't heard of it.

"Randall says it's a shame so many of the heritage breeds are so neglected," I said aloud.

"And your fair's doing a good job of getting them some attention," the man said. "I aim to win me some medals here this weekend—long as no one steals my hogs."

"We'll do our best to keep them safe."

He nodded, touched one finger to the bill of his cap, and strode off.

I couldn't decide whether to be appalled or relieved at his reaction to the murder. Appalled, I decided, on general principles, but it certainly would be less trouble for the fair if his reaction was typical. Somehow I didn't think it would be.

I leaned back against the side of the pen, then sat up again when one of the sheep snuffled at my hair. I didn't feel rested, but I didn't think there was any way I could go back to sleep. And as Rose Noire had pointed out, the fair would open all too soon.

I heaved myself to my feet and pulled together a few things. A change of clothes, and my toilet kit. It occurred to me that I'd never found time for a shower yesterday, and maybe I should do something about it before things got too busy.

I stepped out of the barn and looked around. To my right, I could just make out that the gate where we'd found

Brett's body was still cordoned off with crime scene tape, with a uniformed deputy guarding it. No rubberneckers as far as I could see. The few people who were out seemed intent on getting somewhere. To one or another of the barns mostly, with a few people scurrying toward the exhibitor bathrooms.

I headed that way myself.

I was still trying to rinse the last bits of soap off myself—why did it seem so much harder in cold water? And why had I let Randall overrule me on the question of installing a hot-water heater for the showers?—when I had to step out of the shower again to answer my phone.

"Meg, dear." Mother. "You might want to drop by the wine pavilion."

She hung up before I could ask why.

Chapter 21

A few minutes later I was clean and dressed but very far from in a good mood.

"What now?" I muttered, as I half strode, half ran toward the wine pavilion. Its red-and-white–striped exterior seemed incongruously cheerful this morning.

Since in addition to not telling me what the problem was, Mother also hadn't told me precisely where it was, I headed for the entrance closest to Genette's booth. Good call. As soon as I walked in, I could see that Genette's booth was in disarray, with half of its contents missing and the other half askew. But before I wasted too much time wondering what kind of misguided burglar would target her booth with so many better vineyards all around her to choose from, Genette stood up behind the chrome and Plexiglas counter. She was holding one of her little decorative tangles of barbed wire in her left hand and staring at it reproachfully, while sucking a small bleeding wound on her right hand.

"This is impossible!" she wailed.

If anyone else in the tent had uttered such a cry of despair, they would have been surrounded instantly with sympathetic ears and helping hands. I glanced around to see that everyone in the nearby booths was studiously busy.

I strolled over to Dorcas's booth.

"We thought someone should know," she said, sotto

voce. "On the one hand, we're all thrilled at the idea of being rid of her. But if she's the killer and is going on the lam . . ."

I pulled out my cell phone and dialed the chief.

"Yes?" He sounded annoyed, but not necessarily at me.

"I wouldn't interrupt you, except I thought you might be interested in the fact that Genette Sedgewick seems to be packing to leave," I said. "The new girlfriend of your murder—"

"I know who she is," he said. "Blast! She's not local, is she?"

"No," I said. "She's from . . . I can't remember where—near Culpeper? Or maybe near Charlottesville? Near something with a 'C'. Not Caerphilly, though, and it's at least an hour away, whatever it is."

"Don't try to detain her. But keep an eye on her till I can get there."

"Roger." I hung up and looked around for something to do that would keep me unobtrusively busy near Genette's booth. Just then she spotted me.

"There you are!" she exclaimed, as if she'd been searching for me for hours. "I need help!"

"Lucky you," Dorcas murmured, as I strolled away from her booth toward Genette's.

"What's wrong?" I asked Genette.

"I need to leave," she said. "And I don't have anyone to help me take down my booth and pack my stuff."

She stood there, blinking slightly, and pouting, but no longer anxious. Instead, her face wore a look I'd seen often enough on the faces of my nieces and nephews, and lately even my own little sons: the trusting yet slightly petulant look of someone who has handed her problems over to the proper authority and expects to have them solved.

And solved now. As I stood there, almost admiring her nerve, I could see her foot was beginning to tap.

"You'd like to hire someone to help you?" I said. "I can ask around and see if—"

" 'Hire someone'?" she echoed. "Don't you have bell-hops who can do that for me?"

"No," I said. "Hotels have bellhops. We have an all-volunteer staff who are already pulling double shifts, thanks to the thefts and the vandalism and the—other unfortunate events."

At the last minute I stopped myself from actually utter-ing the word "murder." After all, however much I might disapprove of her relationship with a man who was still legally married to one of my friends, she had lost some-one very close to her. Or at least someone whose useful-ness she'd miss.

Unless, of course, she'd killed him. In which case, wouldn't she be suffering from guilt and anxiety?

I didn't see any signs.

"This is ridiculous," she snapped. "How am I supposed to get my stuff home?" She threw up her hands in a ges-ture that smacked more of annoyance than despair.

"How did you get it here in the first place?" I was curi-ous to hear how she'd answer.

"Brett handled all that," she said. "And now that he's gotten himself killed, what am I supposed to do?"

Gotten himself killed. Talk about blaming the victim. I was tempted to turn on my heels and leave her to handle her own problem. But I realized that getting her out of the pavilion would have an immense positive effect on the other winemakers' morale. And I could steer the business to Randall's cousin who owned the Shiffley Moving Company.

"As I said, we don't have staff to handle load-ins and load-outs," I said aloud. "That's clearly stated on the exhibitor's contract. Ordinarily, there would be nothing I could do. But given the unusual circumstances, I would be willing to help by seeing if I can find some workmen you can hire to pack for you."

"When can you have them here?"

"I have no idea." I realized my voice was sounding a little testy. And decided I didn't much care. "*If* I can find anyone, I'll let you know when they'll be able to come. You're welcome to make the arrangements yourself if you prefer."

She muttered something. I didn't catch more than a few words, but most of those would have been bleeped out on TV.

"I beg your pardon?" I said.

"That would be satisfactory," she said, with a superficial smile. "At least I haven't already checked out of that wretched hotel."

With that she picked up her purse and an overstuffed black tote and turned to leave.

"Where can I reach you if I find someone willing to do the work?" I called after her.

No answer. I gave chase.

"Heading for the parking lot, I think," I said to Mother as I passed. "Let the chief know."

I caught up with Genette well before she reached the parking lot. She was walking fast—half running, really—but I was an inch or two taller, in better shape, and not hampered by stylish pointy-toed boots with four-inch heels.

"If you want me to contact you if I find some workmen, you need to tell me where," I said.

"I'll be at my hotel," she said.

"Which one?"

"The Caerphilly Inn. Actually, maybe I should give you my cell number. Heaven knows if anyone in that wretched place will bother to take a message."

She rattled off a cell phone number. I pulled out my notebook and managed to jot it down, then scrambled to catch up with her again.

"Let me make sure I've got that right," I said, and repeated the number back.

"Yes, that's it."

Was she deliberately trying to lose me? Under other circumstances, I might have been favorably impressed by her long stride and fast pace, especially given the impractical boots. But since I was trying to do her a favor, I didn't appreciate having to run after her.

"I'll try to negotiate as good a rate as possible," I said, to the back of her head.

"I don't care what it costs. I just want to get out of here."

We were at the edge of the parking lot now.

"One more thing," I began.

"What now?" she snapped. "Why won't you just let me leave in peace?"

"I beg your pardon—I thought I was helping you leave." I realized I had used what my brother, Rob, called my "Mother voice," a tone of icy precision that left most people in no doubt whatsoever that they had committed some unspeakable faux pas. To my surprise, it actually worked on Genette.

"Oh, yes, and I am soooooo grateful." She turned around and favored me with a smile that showed a lot of teeth but never got near her eyes.

"Do the workmen need to have any special skills?" I

asked. "For example, are your electrical and sound systems complicated?"

"I can't imagine they are," she said. "Brett set it up, so it can't be that complicated, and taking it down should be even easier."

"Okay," I said. "Are all the packing materials there or do you have some back at the hotel? And do you want to come back to supervise or just have the workmen do it?"

"It's all there at the booth," she said. "And yes, just have them pack it and send it. Do you think I'd ever want to come back here, after someone tried to kill me?"

"To kill you?" This was news. "When?"

"Last night," she said. "And they got Brett instead, and I need to get out of here before they try again."

"I can understand how you'd be upset about his death," I said. "What makes you think they were trying to kill you and got him instead?"

"He was wearing my hoodie." She yanked her tote open, rummaged in it, and then pulled out a black hoodie with splotches of mustard yellow and bubble-gum pink. She held it up and shook it out to reveal her winery's logo, silk screened on both the front and the back of the hoodie.

"We had them made up for the fair," she said. "We had them on sale, but I guess people didn't realize it because we haven't sold any yet. I was wearing one yesterday at the booth, and I had Brett put one on so he could wear it around and drum up interest. They must have thought he was me."

It wasn't a totally ridiculous idea. I remembered seeing them embrace—she'd been wearing heels, like today, and they'd been eye to eye. Brett was bulkier, but it had been a dark and foggy night. The killer could have been mistaken.

"Why do you think someone would want to kill you?" I asked aloud. Not that I doubted there were people who did. Given enough exposure to Genette, I could become one of them myself. But I was curious to hear her take on the subject.

"All the winemakers and farmers around here hate me," she said. "They're jealous of my success, and they don't want to let someone new into their closed little club. And Brett's ex-wife, of course. She'll never forgive me for taking away her husband."

Actually, I suspected Molly could forgive Genette quite easily, provided she didn't also lose her beloved farm.

"Have you told Chief Burke your concerns?" I asked. "It might help him solve the case."

"Oh, yeah, like a hick town cop's really going to have much luck solving a murder like this."

"He spent over a decade in the Baltimore PD's homicide bureau," I said. "He knows a few things about solving murders. So I suggest you tell him what you told me."

"And just what was that?" The chief had come up behind us.

"She thinks the killer was after her, not Brett," I said. "I'll let her explain it."

I strolled back to the fair at a considerably slower pace, and pulled out my cell phone to call Randall.

"I hear you had quite a time last night," he said.

"You have no idea," I said. "Can the Shiffley Moving Company do a rush job?"

"How rush?"

"Today."

"I could ask my cousins, but it'd cost an arm and a leg. What's the rush?"

"Genette wants to leave. I have no idea if the chief's

going to let her leave town, but there's no reason not to let her pack up her stuff if she wants. And you have no idea how much morale in the wine pavilion will improve if we can get rid of that hideous booth of hers."

"That's different," he said. "I'll have some men over there within the hour."

"And cost is no object; she said so herself," I added.

"That's good, because we jack up the price a bit if we know in advance someone's going to be a pain in the you-know-what."

"And while you're organizing, we either need to get Chief Burke to release the crime scene or we're going to need some carpenters to build another gate to the Midway. Actually, I think we need a new gate in either case, because we don't really want crowds gawking at the old one."

"Damn. Hadn't thought of that, but you're right. I'm on it."

I hung up before I realized that I'd just delegated to Randall for a change. It felt good.

I made it down to the front gate in time to supervise the opening. By nine o'clock, three or four times as many people were waiting as there had been on Thursday, and I could see more cars streaming into the parking lot. Were they coming to see the fair or gawk at the scene of the crime? As long as they paid their admission fees, I didn't much care.

I made the rounds, checking up on the various barns and tents. In the farmers' market, Rose Noire was doing a brisk business in her own potpourri and Molly's cheese. In the arts and crafts pavilion, there was still a gaping hole in the quilt section where Rosalie's Baltimore Album quilt should have been.

"Any news on the quilt?" I asked one of the nearby

quilters. I didn't need to say more than that—we both knew what quilt I meant.

"Daphne's optimistic," she said. "And determined."

I winced. I didn't want to hear "optimistic" and "determined." I wanted to hear that Daphne had already eradicated all the red mud and horse manure stains and the beautiful Baltimore quilt was on its way back to be hung again in a place of honor.

"Where's the owner?" I asked.

"Rosalie? Not here." She sounded as relieved as I felt. "Back at the campground in her trailer. Your father prescribed a sedative, and we've been taking turns sitting with her."

"Good work," I said.

In the wine pavilion, the exhibitors were watching with undisguised delight as a posse of Shiffleys disassembled Genette's booth. I hadn't seen so much toasting and glass clinking since the last time I attended a wedding.

Although one of the winemakers who didn't look quite as cheerful as the rest took me aside.

"Have you seen Paul Morot today?" he asked.

"No," I said. "Why?"

"He was hanging around outside all day yesterday, staring at the tent."

"He was waiting for Genette to leave so he could come in and ask a few people about jobs," I said. "Mother was going to give him a signal when the coast was clear."

"I heard that," he said. "And I'm one of the ones he would have talked to. And if I'd known he was looking, I'd have definitely given him a job. But your mother says he was never there when she went to give the signal. And he didn't come in and talk to anyone—I asked around.

And he's not here today. And not answering his cell phone."

"You're worried something has happened to him?"

The winemaker frowned as if not sure he wanted to say anything.

"Look, Paul has a temper," he said finally. "And he blames Genette for losing his winery."

"She wasn't to blame?"

"Partly to blame," he said. "Paul is a great grape grower and winemaker, but he's a lousy businessman. Not Genette's fault he was in such dire straits that not being able to buy enough Virginia grapes sent him under. But she was the last straw. And she did buy his farm at a fire-sale price. And yesterday, I heard a rumor that she was going to start bottling her wine under the Fickle Wind label. Give herself a fresh start, because no one who has tasted her swill would ever buy it again."

"Can she do that?"

"If she bought the name along with the physical property, yes," he said. "And if Paul heard that rumor, it would have made him crazy."

"Crazy enough to kill Brett to get back at Genette?"

"No." His whole tone changed. "Never. Paul wouldn't do something calculated like that. But Genette seems to think whoever killed Brett was aiming for her. If Paul heard the rumor, and saw what he thought was her—"

He shook his head, once more looking worried and uncertain.

"You think he did it? Or could have done it?"

He closed his eyes and shook his head.

"I don't know," he said. "Not unless he was really mad, and didn't even realize it wasn't Genette he was attacking.

And I hear it was a shooting—that also doesn't sound like Paul. Strangling her or picking up something and whacking her, yes, but going out and buying a gun? No."

"He could have already had the gun," I said. "A lot of farmers do, for protection."

"Usually it's a shotgun for varmints," the winemaker said. "Yeah, it's possible he already had a gun. But I can't imagine why he'd bring it here."

"Unless he was planning to use it," I suggested.

"And that I don't believe he'd do," the winemaker said. "Look, I don't think Paul did it, and I sure as hell hope he has a solid alibi. But your police chief should know about this, right?"

"Right," I said. "Thanks. The chief will probably want to talk to you directly."

"I'll be here." He handed me a business card and went back to his booth. Another winemaker came over to him, glass raised as if toasting. He picked up a glass with a splash of wine in it, clinked glasses with her, and sipped, but his smile was forced.

I waited until I was outside to call the chief with his name, cell phone number, and booth number. And then I went on with my rounds.

At least the Bonnevilles weren't haunting the chicken tent looking like refugees from a goth convention.

"If you ask me, I think they felt a little embarrassed when they realized there'd been a murder, and them making such a fuss about a bunch of birds," one of the chicken farmers said.

"I doubt it," another said. "Dr. Langslow came over and scared them to death about how serious Mr. Baskerville's condition could be."

"Bonneville," I corrected.

"Whatever," she said. "Anyway, they're over at the hospital getting those medical tests done. Should be back this afternoon, looking like a pair of crows."

The mood of the tent had improved considerably in their absence. The chicken owners and sightseers were still darting and clumping about like hens in a barnyard, but now it was a happy sort of frenzy.

For the first time I had a chance to take a good look at the exhibits. And I had to admit that some of the chickens were quite handsome. The Sebright Bantams, for example, with their beautiful plumage, each glossy white feather outlined in black, making them look like walking monochromatic stained-glass windows. The black-and-white Yokohamas, who were pheasant-shaped with sleek, elegant white tails easily as long as their bodies. And the Sumatrans—similarly shaped, though with slightly less extravagant tails, and the most amazing glossy black plumage. Or was I seeing a hint of iridescent beetle green in the black when the light hit the feathers just right?

I was bobbing around in front of a cage of Sumatrans, trying to find an angle at which I could confirm that elusive flash of green, when Michael strolled up with the boys in tow.

"Something wrong with those chickens?" he asked.

"No," I said. "Except that they're insidious. I covet them."

Chapter 22

Josh was making a beeline to the display of newly hatched chicks in the center of the tent, oblivious to everything else. Jamie toddled over and gave my leg a forceful hug before scrambling in his brother's wake. Michael looked at the Sumatrans and then back at me.

"Are you hinting that I should bring you fried chicken for lunch?" he asked. "Or did you have in mind a longer term commitment, and you're coveting those particular chickens? Is it payback time for all the llamas?"

"I am coveting live chickens," I said. "Not necessarily those chickens, although those are among the breeds I am coveting. Clearly I have spent too much time with all these chickens. I keep having visions of walking out the back door in the morning and chucking grain to eager beaks. Peeking into the coop at night to gaze on my sleeping flock. And taking the boys out to the barn with little matching baskets to collect eggs. It's insane."

"Sounds perfectly sane to me." He strolled over a little closer to the chick display and I followed. "We could have chickens. We've got the room. We've even got the coop. Remember when the Shiffleys were working on our yard, either renovating or demolishing all those run down little sheds that the previous owner left behind? We could convert one of the renovated sheds into a coop. In fact, I think one of them originally was a coop. And chickens would be a lot more practical than llamas."

"Only practical if we got ones that are good layers," I said. "Which these aren't. I asked."

"So people keep these for . . . um . . . roasting or whatever?" Michael glanced over at the cages and looked uncomfortable, as if the chickens could tell we were talking about their suitability for human consumption. "Because I'm not sure I'd really like eating something that's been like a pet. I know it's completely citified of me, but . . ."

He shrugged.

"I feel the same way," I said. "And my vision of myself as a chicken farmer does not include going out into the barnyard with a little ax. And in case you're worried about these chickens, don't be—according to the owners, no one eats Sumatrans. They're more feather than meat."

"Then what are they good for?" Michael asked. "I don't mean that in a philosophical sense, because obviously they add beauty to the world, and have the same right to their place in the sun as any other creature, but farmers tend not to keep animals around unless they're either tasty or useful. If Sumatrans aren't tasty, what do people do with them?"

"Show them," I said. "And hold cockfights with them in benighted parts of the world where that's still considered a sport. But here, they are pampered pets and show creatures. Same with those."

I pointed to one of the Yokohamas across the aisle.

"They don't lay eggs at all?" Michael asked.

"No, not that one," a nearby farmer said. "That's a rooster."

"I meant the breed," Michael said. "Do they not lay eggs at all?"

"If they didn't, we'd have a hard time keeping the breed going." The farmer chuckled at his own joke. "But with a heavy layer, like a Rhode Island Red, you get four, five, even six eggs a week. With one of these ornamental birds, you might get one egg, and it'd be small."

A sudden thought struck me.

"I'm not sure we want heavy layers," I said. "I mean, do we really want to live entirely on scrambled eggs and omelets?"

"You'd need a few hundred of these to do that," the farmer said. "You thinking of adding a few chickens to your spread?"

"Only thinking," I said. "But if we did, we probably wouldn't want heavy layers. We'd need chickens that are friendly enough not to peck the boys. And stoic enough that they won't freak every time they see Spike. Chickens who can thrive under free-range conditions, because we're not going to shut them up in a coop all day. And look pretty wandering around the place without a lot of grooming. If they also lay enough eggs to make us more or less self-sufficient in the scrambled egg department, even better. But I don't want to be sneaking around leaving baskets of foundling eggs on people's doorsteps."

"Lot of women sell the eggs for pin money," the farmer suggested.

Pin money?

"Meg's a blacksmith," Michael said. "She doesn't have time to fool with selling eggs. And you probably don't have time to research chickens, either," he added to me. "I'll figure out which ones fit your specifications and you can make the final decision."

Final decision? How had we progressed so fast from me coveting a few ornamental fowl to setting up a free-range chicken flock in the backyard? Had Michael, too, been

coveting chickens? Or was he trying to be very accommo-
dating to my whims to pave the way for new extravagances
in the llama department?

I was turning to follow him and sort this out when my
phone rang.

"Ms. Langslow?" It was the chief. "Any chance you could
drop by the fair office for a couple of minutes?"

I heard Horace's voice in the background.

"It's impossible!" he was shouting. "I'm through with it."

At least I thought it was Horace. But I couldn't remember the last time he'd actually lost his temper.

"Is this about the information I just gave you?" I asked.
"About Paul Morot?"

"No, something else entirely," the chief said. "We could
use some help dealing with a situation."

I was opening my mouth to recite the long list of other
things I ought to be doing when I noticed a stirring in the
crowd. Mr. and Mrs. Bonneville were back, still wearing
their lugubrious black clothing. And they seemed to have
picked up another reporter.

"I'm already on my way," I said. "Let's talk more about
chickens later," I added to Michael. "Don't let the boys
steal any of those chicks. And be careful next door—
there are some equally adorable ducklings."

As I approached the fair office, I noticed with approval
that Randall's workmen had already installed the new gate
to the Midway, about thirty feet farther down the split rail.
All view of the old gate was blocked by a giant billboard
that proclaimed MIDWAY! with a big arrow pointing toward the new gate. The pathway to the new gate cut
through the field where we'd been keeping the cantan-
kerous guard goats. They still occupied the far half of the

field, behind a new stretch of fence, but in the near half I could see that Randall had arranged some exhibits for the tourists to look at on their way to the Midway. The American Jack Donkeys now occupied one part of the field. A stately trio of American Cream draft horses grazed in the middle part. And the workmen had nearly finished setting up the llama demonstration tent in the last part. I could see the spinning wheel and the loom where some of the llama owners demonstrated the use of llama wool, and two of the llamas were already in the pen behind the tent, peering over the fence to watch the workmen.

I made a mental note to compliment Randall on his ideas, and stepped into the fair office.

Inside, Vern was leaning against the wall with his arms folded and an anxious expression on his face, watching Horace pace up and down the narrow open space in the center of the trailer, at a clip that would have given him a good chance of winning a walking race. The chief was sitting at my desk, frowning slightly.

Both of them looked relieved at my arrival.

"What's up?" I asked.

"I can't work with that man around!" Horace's normally genial round face was scowling.

"Why? What's Vern done?" I suspected it wasn't Vern he was mad at, but decided to play dumb.

"Not Vern," Horace snapped. "Plunkett."

"Glad you're not mad at Vern or the chief," I said.

"Actually, I'm afraid he is," the chief said.

"Yeah," Vern said. "'Cause we just told him he had to work with Plunkett. On account of our agreement with Sheriff Dingle."

"Can't we complain to the sheriff?" Horace asked.

The chief shook his head wearily.

"I wouldn't," Vern said.

"He needs to know his deputy is a complete idiot," Horace went on. "How in the world did he get his job?"

"Nepotism," Vern said. "His mother was a Dingle, and the sheriff is his second cousin, once removed. So there's no use complaining about him. Just work around him, and try to keep him from doing too much damage."

"How?" Horace asked. "I must have given him a dozen pairs of gloves, and he keeps taking them off and losing them. Which wouldn't matter if he could keep his hands to himself, but every time I turn around he's picked something up bare-handed and started wandering around with it. I'm not sure I have a single bit of evidence he hasn't contaminated. We'll be lucky if any of it makes it into a trial."

"Yeah, he's an idiot," Vern said. "What do you expect from Clay County? But maybe that's a blessing in disguise."

"A blessing?" Horace spluttered.

"Yeah." Vern glanced over at me. " 'Cause it's sure looking pretty grim for the widow. Time was she'd have walked on killing a low-down cheating skunk like him."

"Time was," the chief said. "But these days 'he needed killing' isn't a valid defense."

"Pity," Vern said. "But that's what I mean by a blessing. Maybe, annoying as he is, Plunkett is accidentally doing us a service."

"Maybe it's not accidental at all," I suggested. "Maybe he's not as stupid as he looks, and he's screwing everything up out of some kind of crazy backwoods chivalry."

"Could be," Vern said, and I could tell he didn't entirely disapprove of the notion.

"I'm not sure Plunkett has the brains to be chivalrous," Horace said. "And intentional or not, what if he's compromising evidence that would clear Ms. Riordan if I actually got to process it before it was contaminated?"

"Either way, her odds of getting off are good," Vern said.

"And after she got off because all the evidence was tainted, what then?" I asked. "She'd probably have to sell her farm to pay her legal fees, and even if she managed to hang on to it, who's going to want to buy cheese from a woman they think killed her husband and got off on a technicality?"

"I don't see why not," Vern said. "It's not like she poisoned him."

"Vern," the chief began.

"I give up," Horace muttered.

"Think how it looks for us," I went on. "For Caerphilly. Nobody will remember that it was a Clay County deputy who screwed up the case. They'll just think we're a bunch of hicks who don't know any better."

I could see that didn't set well with Vern.

"You've got a point there," he said. "Horace, next time you see Plunkett doing anything wrong, you tell me and I'll have it out with him."

Horace nodded glumly.

"Hey, and at least one thing went right," Vern said. "The jerk was too lazy to do much work when we were searching the van. Imagine what would have happened if he'd found the gun. 'Oooh, lookie! A gun! You think it works? Bang!'"

"Yeah, that sounds about right." Horace didn't come right out and laugh, but he smiled and appeared a lot less stressed.

"Look, I get your point," Vern said. "I'll do what I can to keep him out of your hair and away from the evidence."

"And if Plunkett proves completely uncontrollable, I will have a word with Sheriff Dingle," the chief said. "The terms of our agreement oblige us to include a representative from Clay County in our investigation. They do not oblige us to include Deputy Plunkett."

"Thanks," Horace said.

"I'd have done it already," the chief said. "But I'm afraid anyone they would send as a replacement could be even worse."

"So I gather Deputy Plunkett would not be your first pick for any job openings that might come up in the Caerphilly Sheriff's Department," I said.

"He would not." The chief frowned and looked at Vern. "And I surely do hope you're wrong about him wanting to apply."

"He's been asking me about the pay and benefits," Vern said. "They don't get much of either over there. You know, I think maybe that's why he's driving Horace so crazy. He's trying to look like a good candidate for the job."

"He thinks the chief is looking for annoyingness and incompetence?" Horace sounded irate again.

"He probably just thinks he's showing initiative," the chief said.

"Hustle," Vern put in.

"He's an idiot," Horace said. "But are you going to have a job opening coming up? Because—"

"Speak of the devil," I interrupted. From my place by the door I could see through one of the trailer's two windows. And I'd just spotted a familiar hulking form shambling toward the trailer. "Here comes Plunkett."

"Great," Horace muttered.

The door slammed open and Plunkett strolled inside.

"Hey there!" he said.

"Good afternoon," the chief said.

"Afternoon," Vern echoed. I nodded with as cheerful a face as I could muster, and Horace just tightened his lips.

Either Plunkett didn't notice the tepidness of his reception or he didn't care.

"Hey, Vern," Plunkett said. "Randall was looking for you."

Vern nodded and slipped out the door.

"So, remind me," Plunkett said to the rest of us. "What kind of car was it the dead guy drove?"

"The deceased drove a red Mazda MX-5," Horace said.

"Little bitty fire-engine red convertible, right?" Plunkett asked. "I think we found it. Want me to bring it in? I can get someone to hot wire it and—"

"No!" we all three shouted in unison.

"Suit yourself." Plunkett crossed his arms and leaned against the wall, beaming as if he'd done something to be proud of.

"You see," Horace said.

"Where is the car?" the chief asked.

"Over in the woods, other side of the Midway," Plunkett said. "There's an old access road hunters sometimes use. It's parked on that."

"Take Deputy Shiffley and Officer Hollingsworth there, if you please," the chief said.

"Sure thing." Plunkett levered himself off the wall, popped out the trailer door, and set off at a fast pace.

"Wait!" Horace called. Luckily his kit was nearby, but Plunkett already had a good lead on him. Horace was half running to catch up.

The chief and I followed them out.

"Vern!" The chief waved his arms and, when Vern saw him, pointed at Plunkett and Horace. Vern nodded, but he didn't immediately give chase.

The chief pulled out his cell phone.

"I have a bad feeling about this," I said. "I'm going with them. If Plunkett tries to pull anything before Vern gets there, I can always threaten him again with moving the Midway."

The chief hesitated for a few moments, and then probably came to the same conclusion I had reached about Horace's ability to control Plunkett.

"I'd appreciate it," he said. "I'd go myself, but some importunate attorney is demanding to see me. He won't say why. Did you recommend a lawyer named Twickenham to Ms. Riordan?"

"No, I gave her one of the usual locals. Never heard of a Twickenham."

"I'd better see what he wants, then. Thanks for helping us placate Horace."

He strode over toward Vern, looking cranky. Dealing with lawyers, importunate or otherwise, often had that effect on him. I scrambled to catch up with Horace and Plunkett.

Chapter 23

Both Horace and Plunkett were out of sight by the time I left the fair office, so I was on my own. Randall and I had spent a good deal of time tramping through the nearby woods while debating how much of the fairgrounds to fence in. I remembered the dirt access road Plunkett had mentioned—Randall and I had crossed it a number of times and had debated whether to use it for direct access to the Midway—an idea we'd abandoned, not just because of the expense of upgrading it. We were also afraid that if we used it, Clay County would want to set up a second entrance gate, and we didn't trust them to give us an accurate account of the take.

I headed through the woods and eventually struck the dirt road—not much more than a trail, really. I turned right, since that was more or less the direction in which Plunkett had gestured. I guessed correctly. After a few minutes' walk, I spotted a flash of metallic red through the trees.

The Mazda. It was parked in a place where the woods drew back from the road far enough that you could park. Though if the gleaming little convertible had been mine I would never have parked it there, where it was almost sure to be scratched if another car tried to squeeze by on the left. In fact, I would never have driven it down the road in the first place, and I was a great deal less obsessed with pretty cars than most men I knew.

Deputy Plunkett was sitting on the trunk of the car, smoking a cigarette. Horace was nowhere to be seen.

"Where's Horace?" I asked.

"On his way, I guess." Plunkett sounded annoyingly nonchalant. "He fell behind once we hit the woods. Not enough hustle."

Fell behind! More likely Plunkett had deliberately lost him. I was opening my mouth to tell him what I thought of his actions, when I realized, from the look on his face that he already knew what I thought. And he was enjoying himself. Why give him the satisfaction?

He flicked his cigarette butt onto some leaves and leaned back, crossing his arms and making himself comfortable, watching me.

I strode over and ground his cigarette butt out with a little more force than necessary, all the while imagining his head under my heel. Then I looked at the dense woods around us. Clay County was mostly woods and swamp, and if Horace took the wrong direction, he could wander for hours. Days.

I wanted to yell at Plunkett. In fact, I wanted to hit him, and I don't just mean a girly little slap. I fantasized, just for a few moments, how satisfying it would feel to land a good, solid punch on his nose. I'm taller than most women, strong for my size due to my blacksmithing, and thanks to a few years of martial arts training and a childhood of sparring with hordes of rowdy cousins, I was no slouch at self-defense. Plunkett might be surprised how good a punch I could land. And I was sorely tempted to surprise him.

Just then I heard a faint shout in the distance. It sounded like someone yelling for help.

"Guard the car," I said. "Don't touch it, don't drive it, and don't leave."

It took me half an hour to locate Horace and lead him back to the Mazda. When I found him, he was babbling anxiously on his cell phone, apparently begging Debbie Ann to send search parties. I took the phone away from him and assured Debbie Ann that I could probably find our way back to the car and from there to civilization. Then I calmed Horace down, mainly by pointing out how much Plunkett would enjoy seeing him angry or upset. By the time we arrived back at the Mazda, he was calm, if a little grim.

"Get off the damned car," was all he said to Plunkett.

Horace was still working on his examination of the car's exterior when Vern Shiffley showed up.

"Heard some of you folks got lost in the trackless forest," Vern said.

I winced.

"I wasn't lost," I said.

"Me neither," Plunkett said, smirking.

"You were supposed to be guiding Horace, and you misplaced him," Vern told Plunkett. "The way I see it that means you were as good as lost, too. I heard you were trying to hire yourself out as a hunting guide this fall. Anyone asks me for a recommendation, I'll steer them to Meg here instead."

Plunkett glowered. Vern sauntered over to the car.

"I'm good by myself," Horace said. "Thanks."

"Not butting in unless you want me to," Vern said. "Just watching. Always interesting, seeing an expert work."

He patted Horace's shoulder, and I thought I heard him mutter, "Sorry."

Horace nodded.

Plunkett ambled over so he could watch, too. I thought of heading back to the fair, but having successfully managed to find the car, and then Horace, and then the car again, I didn't want to risk spoiling my reputation as a fearless tracker, so I stayed put and after calling Michael to get an update on the boys, I found a vantage point from which I could watch the search.

Vern was pretty good at keeping out of Horace's way. Plunkett wasn't, but I had the feeling that annoying Horace—and the rest of us—was exactly what he wanted to accomplish. Horace wasn't rising to the bait, and I could tell that was spoiling Plunkett's good mood.

Horace was still working on the front seat and the two deputies were watching through the open back doors when suddenly—

"Ah-ah-choo!"

Deputy Plunkett sneezed vigorously all over the back-seat of the car, without even bothering to cover his nose and mouth.

"Watch it, will you?" Vern said.

"You're contaminating my crime scene," Horace complained. He was staring at the backseat of the car as if appalled at all the alien DNA that had just landed on it.

"Not to mention contaminating the rest of us," Vern said. He had pulled out his handkerchief and was mopping his face—apparently Plunkett had spattered him as well. "Keep your germs to yourself."

"It's not germs," Plunkett said. "It's these damned chicken feathers."

He held up one hand to display a couple of black-and-brown feathers, and then began shaking his hand as if trying to brush them off.

"Did those come from inside the car?" Vern asked.

Horace just closed his eyes and shook his head.

"Yup," Plunkett said. "Right here in the backseat."

"Vern, can you put them in this. Please." Horace's voice was shaking slightly. He held out an evidence collection bag. "Collect them all and put them very carefully in this bag."

"You think they have something to do with the murder?" Plunkett asked.

Horace made an untranslatable noise.

"Maybe the murder," Vern said. "Maybe the chicken theft. Which could be related to the murder, for all we know. Let's not get careless."

Plunkett shrugged. He tried to help with the feather gathering, but Vern shifted to put his body between Plunkett and the car. Plunkett shrugged and returned to leaning against the side of the car. Horace didn't take his eyes off what Vern was doing.

"Meg," Horace said. "What color were the missing chickens?"

"The Russian Orloffs?" I said. "Black and brown. The rooster had long black tail feathers."

Horace reached down with one gloved hand and picked up a long, curled black plume. We all stared at it for a few seconds.

"Do the Riordans raise chickens on that farm of theirs?" Vern asked.

"I know Molly doesn't," I said. "But Brett hasn't been living there lately. He's been over at Genette's farm. I have no idea what livestock she raises."

"Have the people who owned the missing chickens taken the cages home?" Horace asked.

"No, they've turned them into a shrine for the missing birds," I said.

"Vern," Horace said. "Can you hold down the fort here? Secure the car and arrange to have it towed back to town, to the impound lot? Or you could tow it as far as the fair gate and I'll get back here as soon as I can to finish up and go with it to the lot." Vern nodded. He was already pulling out his cell phone to call his cousin who ran the local towing service.

"I need to go to the poultry barn." Horace picked up the bag containing the feathers and trotted off down the road. I took off after him.

"What are you planning to do?" I asked when I caught up. Which I did fairly quickly—I had the longer stride and was in better shape.

"Identify these feathers."

"Okay, I guessed that much," I said. "Maybe I should have said 'Where are you going?' Because this is the long way, you know. We could save time cutting through the woods."

"I'd rather take the long way,"

"It'll take hours." Okay, I was exaggerating, but only a little. "Follow me."

He wasn't happy about it, but he didn't argue. After what Plunkett had done to him, I was flattered that Horace followed me into the woods, and didn't begrudge him his sigh of relief when we broke out of the trees again and spotted the pie and quilt barn dead ahead. Once inside the fairgrounds, he took the lead. We dived into the poultry tent and Horace almost danced with impatience as we shoved our way through the crowds until we reached the part of the tent where the Bonnevilles' chicken cages were.

"Here we are," I said.

Behind the cages, almost invisible behind the huge black bows, were the Bonnevilles.

"Are these the cages that your stolen chickens occupied?" Horace asked.

"We're leaving them here as a memorial," Mr. Bonneville said. Mrs. Bonneville just sniffled.

"There are feathers here," Horace said. "Have any other chickens been in these cages?"

"No," Mr. Bonneville said. "And no other chickens ever will. We plan to keep them as a shrine."

"Awesome," Horace said. He fished an evidence bag out of his pocket and reached for the door of the cage.

"What are you doing?" Mrs. Bonneville cried. "Those few forlorn feathers are all we have left of Anton Chekhov and Anna Karenina."

"Anton Chekhov?" Horace repeated. "Anna Karenina?"

"They're Russian Orloffs," I explained. "Hence the Russian names. Horace is our crime scene technician," I told the Bonnevilles. "If you want the feathers as keepsakes, Horace can return them after our investigation. But right now, he needs to collect them. Unless you have a problem with our borrowing the feathers to help our efforts to recover your missing chickens."

Putting it that way quelled their objections, and they cooperated enthusiastically with Horace's attempts to pick the cages clean.

"Now," Horace said, when he'd finished. "Do you recognize these feathers?"

He held up the evidence bag containing the feathers we'd collected in Brett's car.

"They're not the ones you just collected from Anton's cage?"

"We found these in another location," Horace said.

The Bonnevilles waxed sentimental over the feathers, particularly the long tail feather. "It could be Anton's," Mrs. Bonneville said. "It's just like his." But they ultimately admitted that the most they could say was that there was nothing about the feathers to prove that they weren't from their Orloffs.

"This other chicken," Horace said finally, pointing to the diminutive black-and-brown bird occupying the third cage.

"Agrippina Vaganova," Mrs. Bonneville said.

"Is she related to the stolen ones?"

A simple yes or no would have been sufficed. Instead, the Bonneville treated us to a lengthy discourse on their breeding program. I could see that Horace's eyes were glazing over.

"Let me make sure I have this straight," I said, finally, interrupting their explanations about chickens with strawberry-, cushion-, and walnut-shaped combs. "Agrippina is Anton's half-sister, and Anna Karenina is their aunt."

The Bonnevilles nodded, and Mrs. Bonneville choked back a few more sobs. Agrippina, by contrast, seemed to be taking her possible bereavement with admirable stoicism.

Further questioning revealed that while Anton's and Agrippina's sire had been eaten by a fox a few months ago, their mothers—Anna Karenina's sisters or half-sisters, all with polysyllabic Russian names—were still presumably clucking and foraging with the rest of their free-range flock back at the Bonnevilles' farm, and could be made available for DNA comparison testing. Mr. Bonneville took to the notion of DNA testing with such enthusiasm that we had a hard time preventing him from setting out immediately to fetch his entire flock.

"I wouldn't want you to upset them right now," Horace said. "After all, the DNA testing will only become necessary if there's any dispute over ownership of the missing birds after they're recovered."

The phrase "after they're recovered" was definitely to

the Bonnevilles' liking and we left them smiling for the first time since the fateful first night of the fair.

"Perhaps we should tell Mr. Twickenham to hold off for a bit," I overheard Mrs. Bonneville saying to her husband as Horace and I left. "It does seem as if the fair management is making a reasonable effort."

I made a mental note to ask the chief what Mr. Twickenham had wanted. Probably fodder for suing the Unfair. I hoped not, but then again, if they tried, I would have the pleasure of saying "I told you so" to Randall, who had protested about spending the time and money to have an attorney draft all the release forms we had exhibitors sign. Not that the forms would keep the Bonnevilles from suing us, but they might at least make it harder for them to prevail in court.

"Do you really think we have a chance of recovering them?" I asked, when we'd left the tent."

"No idea," Horace said. "Except that we have a much better chance of recovering them now than we did before. There's only so far we can afford to go to investigate a chicken theft. It's not even grand larceny unless the birds are worth a hundred dollars apiece."

"And even if they are, the DNA tests would probably cost several times that," I said.

"Precisely," Horace said. "It doesn't make sense to run DNA on a bunch of stolen chickens. But now that we found these Orloff feathers in the dead man's car, they're possible clues in a murder. That's a whole different ballgame."

"Can you really do DNA tests on chickens?" I asked.

"Absolutely!" Horace said. "Haven't you heard about the DNA testing on the Transylvanian Naked Neck chicken?"

I hadn't, but I'd have lied about that if I'd known he'd regale me with the details all the way back to the front gate. Apparently a breed of fowl with chickenlike bodies, red, naked necks, and small, turkeylike heads had appeared in Transylvania—it would be Transylvania—and was eventually imported to England and the United States. Genetic testing had eventually disproved the theory that the birds were a hybrid of chickens and turkeys—they were, in fact, simply mutant chickens.

By the time Horace had finished telling me about this, we had reached the gate. We spotted the Shiffley Towing Service truck with the sporty little red car attached just outside. And Vern Shiffley was standing nearby.

"You can take over the job of keeping Horace from strangling Plunkett," I told him. "My boys are showing the family dogs in the Open Dog Show, and I have exactly ten minutes to get over to the show ring. And for the record, for the next two hours, I am not available for anything short of an earthquake."

"We're cool," Vern said. "So what's this about mutant chickens?" he asked Horace.

I left them to it and tried to shove the chicken thefts and the murder out of my mind for a time. Which was a lot easier to do now that Horace seemed so optimistic about the new evidence.

Chapter 24

The Open Dog Show—also known colloquially as the "Cutest Dog Contest"—was open to any kid, twelve or under, who wanted to show a dog. A few of the entrants were pedigreed dogs who would also compete in the AKC show later in the fair, or sheepdogs who'd be competing in the herding trials. But most were just beloved family pets.

We'd been holding this at the county fair for decades, and it was proving just as popular with the Un-fair attendees. Unfortunately that created a considerable challenge for the judges. Although we didn't come right out and say it, the policy was that every dog who walked won a ribbon of some sort, and the vastly larger pool of entries was taxing the judges' imaginations.

I'd promised to help out with the category brainstorming—two pages in my notebook are already filled with ideas. Luckily I could beg off serving as an actual judge, since my own two sons were contestants.

I applauded wildly with the rest of the crowd when Michael and the boys stepped into the ring, starting off the parade. Jamie was being dragged along by Spike, our eight-and-a-half-pound furball. Spike clearly thought we had chosen wisely in putting him in charge of the parade. His demeanor showed that he had decided to be gracious to the other dogs in his kingdom and refrain from killing any of them, however deserving they might be, until after the parade. Josh was leading Tinkerbell, his uncle Rob's hundred-and-twenty-pound Irish Wolfhound, who got along splendidly with Spike, partly because she was too good-natured and laid back to fight with anyone, and partly because her coat was so thick that she didn't always notice when Spike was biting her.

More children streamed after them, leading, following, or carrying still more dogs. Most of the kids were also accompanied by parents, who could break up any fights that occurred—more often between overeager handlers than the dogs themselves—and deal with any other little crises, like kids suddenly getting stage fright and sitting down in the middle of the ring to cry.

Some of the dogs were wearing costumes. Quite a few four-legged Santas, reindeer, and Easter bunnies scampered by, but also dogs sporting more elaborate outfits, like the small black terrier with four extra furry legs attached to his harness, so he looked like an overlarge and very lively tarantula. The science-fiction community was well represented by a dog with a silvery gray coat and tin foil antennae and a surprising number of dogs in Star Fleet uniforms. Quite a few dogs wore jerseys proclaiming their owners' favorite sports and teams, local or national. A few small dogs wore obviously hand-knitted sweaters, and a few of the larger animals were fitted out with saddles with dolls or stuffed animals as riders.

A good thing I wasn't a judge, because midway through the procession one of the entries distracted me—a bloodhound, dragging behind him a tiny boy dressed as Sherlock Holmes, complete with Inverness cape, deerstalker hat, and pipe. I found myself wondering if we could use bloodhounds to track down the missing chickens. Would they be able to follow the scent of an individual chicken, as they could with humans? Or would they simply lead us to the nearest collection of chickens? I had no idea, but I jotted down the name of the bloodhound's owner, and was busily strategizing how to suggest the idea to the chief in a way he'd find helpful rather than annoying when the sight of Michael and the boys stepping back into the ring jolted me back to the here and now, just in time to begin applauding the first of the winners.

I didn't envy the judges' their job, but in the end, they came up with awards for all 143 dogs, and with the exception of a few children too young or too tired and cranky to care, most of the handlers went away beaming.

Tinkerbell had won the Most Enormous Dog ribbon hands down, and Spike's Fiercest Guard Dog award was certainly well deserved. We were celebrating back at the sheep barn with a round of chocolate ice creams and liver treats when my phone rang.

"Hey, Meg." It was Randall. "The boys have got Ms. Sedgewick's stuff all packed up. We know she's supposed to be over at the Caerphilly Inn, but she's not answering her cell phone and we're not quite sure what to do next."

"If you want to ship the stuff, you can look up her address in the exhibitor database," I said. "No, Jamie, don't eat the liver treat. It's yucky."

"Well, yes," Randall said.

"Not yucky," Jamie said.

"Whether or not it's yucky, it belongs to Spike. Sorry," I said to Randall. "Want me to come over and look it up for you?"

"Actually we're not sure we should do anything more until we have a signed contract," Randall said. "Preferably with a substantial deposit. The boys have been hearing a few things about Ms. Sedgewick. Not popular with her creditors, it seems."

"Interesting," I said.

But did it have anything to do with the murder? Probably not. Wasn't it usually the people who borrowed money killing off their creditors to avoid paying? And whether or not she owed money elsewhere, I was pretty sure Brett didn't have any to lend her.

"You think maybe she's not as rich as she lets on?" I asked aloud.

"Could be. More likely she's just one of those rich people who's careless with other people's money. The ones who say, 'What's the problem? You know I'm good for it,' and never think that other people might need the money to make their rent and car payments."

"So you want some of your money up front," I said. "That makes sense. What's the problem? Go over to the inn and let her know that her stuff's not going anywhere without a deposit."

"We were wondering if you could tackle her," Randall said. "Worked pretty well before."

"If she's not answering her phone for you, what makes you think she will for me?"

"But she's just over at the Caerphilly Inn. It's only a couple of miles down the road. You could pop over there, get the contract signed, and be back in a flash."

"Have you actually met Genette?" I asked. "Do you really think—"

"Okay, okay," Randall said. "It'll be a major pain, but you're the one person I can think of who might be able to pull it off, and it'll help the fair as well as the Shiffley Moving Company, and we'll all owe you. Big time."

It was the last part that sold me. The Shiffleys didn't quite have a monopoly on construction and repair work in Caerphilly, but damn near. And while being Randall's friend got us slightly better deals and noticeably faster service than most residents, I liked the idea of Randall feeling he owed me. The odds were high that something would need to be repaired or replaced in our Victorian-era farmhouse before his gratitude faded.

And there was always the chance that while I was there I could learn something that would help clear Molly. The chief could hardly object if I happened to learn something useful while performing a completely harmless fair-related task.

"Okay," I began. "I can go over there—"

"Not now!" Michael interrupted. "We have to get ready for the llama show."

"—immediately after the llama show," I finished.

"Awesome," Randall said. "I'll send Vern over to the show ring with the paperwork."

So much for any hope of a quiet afternoon.

Michael, meanwhile, had finished his ice cream and begun fussing over the llamas.

"Don't let Jamie drip chocolate on Harpo," he said. "I spent all morning shampooing and blow-drying him."

Harpo was a white llama—at least after a thorough bath. A couple of times a year, when we showed him, his coat actually gleamed impressively snow white, and the rest of the year he served as a reminder of why gray, brown, and black were more practical colors for farm animals.

"I helped, Daddy," Josh said.

"You did, indeed," Michael said. "You were both a big help."

I tried to imagine this and then decided not to.

"May I help, too?"

I glanced over to see Molly standing just outside the pen.

Chapter 25

I hurried over to give Molly a hug. She was wearing sunglasses. I wasn't sure whether she was trying to pass incognito, or hiding the signs that she'd been shedding tears over Brett's demise.

"How are you doing?" I asked, in an undertone.

"Lousy," she said, in an equally low tone. "I just want to not think about it all for a while. Looking for something to distract me."

"Distractions are us," I said. "If you want to keep an eye out to see that none of the four-legged occupants of the pen get anywhere near the ice cream, I'd appreciate it," I said. "Chocolate would be bad for the dogs, and we just washed the two llamas."

"Only the two?"

"Just Zeppo and Harpo," I said, pointing at them. "We're showing them off in the obedience trials in a few minutes. Groucho and Chico will be in the conformation trials tomorrow."

"And the fifth one? Gummo, I assume, in keeping with the Marx Brothers theme. Nice names."

"Of course the boys, who are a lot more familiar with *Snow White* than *Animal Crackers,* usually call them Grouchy, Zippy, Happy, Chicky, and Gummy. Gummo is old, and half blind," I added, pointing to where he was hanging over the fence, eyes focused on where my voice was coming from. "He's just here for the company. They're very social creatures, and he'd pine away if we left him home all alone."

"Poor old Gummy." She reached out and stroked his nose. I considered warning her that most llamas didn't like to be touched. But Gummo was a lot more touch tolerant than most llamas, and maybe she'd find patting his soft brown nose comforting.

"That's why we have the herd," I said aloud instead. "Michael got Groucho, and the poor thing was lonely. I held out a while, hoping Groucho would come to accept us as his herd, but I finally gave in and said yes to another llama. I'm still not quite sure how we got from two to five."

"That reminds me," Michael said. "I've narrowed the selection down to three chicken breeds. Let me show you." He began fumbling in his pocket for something, which would have been a lot easier if he wasn't still holding the llama brush in one hand and the hair dryer in the other.

"Narrowed what down?" Molly said. "Here, let me help with that."

She took over the brush and hair dryer and continued where Michael had left off, gently teasing Chico's soft brown fleece to maximum fluffiness. Michael watched for a few moments. Then, satisfied that Molly understood the job, he pulled out his cell phone and turned it on.

"Okay, I rejected these." He showed me a picture of the elegant black and white Yokohama rooster. "Apparently they require a lot of grooming to look anything like this one does. I think the Sumatrans are a better bet. The tail's not so extreme, and the black feathers wouldn't get dirty as fast. Although I am also rather taken with the Welsummer." He showed a picture of a black and reddish copper rooster whose tail, though smaller than the Sumatrans, was still full and arched.

"I like both," I said.

"I was rather tempted by the Rumpless Araucana." He showed me a picture of a chicken that was a bit nondescript except for peculiar tufts of feathers on either side of the head, looking rather like Victorian muttonchop sideburns. And unless he'd taken the picture at a particularly odd angle, the bird didn't have a tail at all.

"Yuck," I said. "Let's stick to either the Sumatrans or the Welsummers."

"The Araucanas lay pale blue eggs." Michael sounded rather wistful, as if suddenly realizing a long-felt yearning to own chickens that laid pastel eggs.

"The others just lay white eggs?" I asked.

"Well, no," he said. "The Sumatrans do. But the Welsummers lay bronze eggs. Sometimes speckled."

"Get both," Molly suggested. "Sumatrans and Welsummers. You can keep one kind at your place and the other at your parents' farm."

"I like her style," Michael said. "Speaking of style, I think Zeppo is ready, and just in time. Let's lead them over to the show ring."

"I should go." Molly sounded disappointed. Evidently she hadn't come entirely for distraction. She'd probably been hoping to talk to me when Michael and the twins and the llamas weren't underfoot.

"No, stay," I said. "You can lead one of the llamas. It's always an absolute goat rope when we try to travel with more than three children or animals. And we can find a quiet corner of the stands where the boys won't annoy anyone, and you and I can talk."

"Well, if I can help," she said.

Michael handed her Zeppo's lead.

We set out with Michael proudly escorting Harpo.

"Let me go in the middle," I said, when Molly was about to fall in line behind them. "It's never a good idea to let one llama follow another too closely. The one who isn't in front will try to goose the other."

"You're joking," Molly said.

"I wish," I said. "As a species, the llama has a very pronounced sense of humor, but unfortunately it's about as subtle and refined as that of the average second-grade boy. If you could wave a magic wand and make them human, they'd look elegant, but they'd drive you crazy holding burping contests and telling fart jokes. Come on, boys; let's follow Daddy."

We marched in stately procession toward the show ring. Harpo and Zeppo seemed to know that they were about to have their moment in the spotlight and stepped even more proudly and elegantly than usual. Michael basked in all the attention Harpo was getting. The boys waved at everyone we passed. Molly hid her face behind Zeppo's now dramatically fluffy wool but seemed to be enjoying herself. And around us, threading through the crowds singly or in well-spaced pairs, other llamas were also making their way to the show ring.

"We're going to kill them." Michael gave me a quick peck on the cheek before taking Zeppo's lead from Molly and leading the two into the backstage area. I glanced quickly at Molly, but she didn't seem upset by the phrase.

We found a seat in the front row. The llama trials, I noted with disapproval, were not nearly as well attended as some of the livestock events—one of the things Michael and his fellow llama fanciers were hoping to change. And the front rows were empty, possibly because many of the spectators were afraid of being spat upon. Which

I could have told them wasn't likely to happen. A well-socialized llama never spat except at other llamas, and very few people wasted their time entering badly socialized llamas in the obedience trials.

"So what's this contest about, anyway?" Molly asked. It had taken a few minutes to get Josh and Jamie properly penned in between us, and I gathered she'd only just now caught a glimpse of the obstacle course the llamas would be tackling.

"Apart from their wool, llamas are also pack animals," I said. "And getting more popular all the time for wilderness trekking. The obedience trial challenges them with obstacles that are similar to things they'd encounter in a typical hike. Oh, look, there are Michael and Harpo. They must have drawn number one."

"Happy!" both boys shouted. "Go, Happy, go!"

We all watched as Michael brought Harpo up to the first obstacle—a tangled pile of branches that both handler and llama had to walk across. Michael stomped vigorously as if to show Harpo there was nothing to fear underfoot. Harpo picked his way as delicately as a cat, but without hesitation. Scattered applause greeted their success.

Next they approached a series of white-painted rails, four to six inches off the ground.

"Llamas aren't high jumpers, I gather," Molly said.

"Actually, they aren't bad," I said. "But they're supposed to step over this obstacle, not jump. When you're trekking through the wilderness, you really don't want a four-hundred-pound llama carrying a hundred pounds of gear to be bouncing up and down like a jackrabbit."

Harpo handled the rails beautifully—he strolled over

them as if on flat ground, without touching a single rail, without the slightest hint of a hop, and without appearing to look down.

Next was the fence gate, where Harpo had to stand while Michael opened it, walk through without balking, and then stand again while Michael closed it. The slalom, where they wove in and out between half a dozen artificial Christmas trees without knocking any of them over. Harpo walked delicately over a layout of old car tires, through a series of large hoops, and then through a child's wading pool filled with stuffed animals. He followed Michael up a ramp and then down a series of rather high steps. He only flicked his ears a bit when Michael picked up and checked a front foot, and then a back foot. He allowed Michael to lead him down a path between two narrow rails and then, on command, backed up the whole length of the path. And finally he stood as if at attention while Michael tied his lead to the fence and unloaded his packs.

Toward the end of their routine, I was holding my breath, and I could tell half of the onlookers were, too. The llama-owning half. When the judge nodded for Michael to lead Harpo out of the ring, the audience broke into thunderous applause.

"I'm impressed," Molly said. "But I guess I wasn't cut out to be a llama owner. I can't quite fathom the level of enthusiasm."

"That's because you just saw pretty darn close to a perfect performance," I said. "It gets a lot more interesting when things don't go as planned."

And for the next dozen or so llamas, things definitely got interesting. Llamas refused to step on the sticks and tires, or stubbornly detoured around them. Llamas shuffled their feet into the rails, or leaped over them like steeplechasers. Llamas dug in their heels and refused to go through the gates. Llamas fell off the ramp, jumped off of it to walk beside it, or stood immobile at the top surveying their surroundings with lordly stares. The occasional llama completely ignored the course and trotted over to the stands to study interesting spectators, dragging his hapless owner behind him. One llama tried to eat the artificial Christmas trees. Another jumped over the fence rather than wait for his owner to open the gate. One very young llama became fascinated with the stuffed animals in the wading pool and refused to stop sniffing them. He finally had to be led off the course by dangling a grungy teddy bear in front of him. Even the llamas that didn't completely blow one or more obstacles failed to execute them as quickly, cleanly, and calmly as Harpo had.

"Okay, I see what you mean," Molly said. We were watching the volunteers trying to deal with a llama who got fed up midway through the obstacle course and was lying down just outside the tunnel, humming to himself with his eyes closed. "Harpo is a llama genius, but imperfection is a lot funnier."

"Let's just hope Zeppo doesn't completely destroy Michael's reputation as a brilliant llama trainer," I said. "It would be fabulous to have them come in as first and second."

"Zeppo's not as well trained as Harpo?"

"He's just as well trained, but more eccentric," I said. "Some days he'll sail through the course perfectly, but all too often on competition days his mind is elsewhere. I'm hoping he's focused today."

"Well, at least if he doesn't place second, we'll have a

few more laughs." Molly's face suddenly grew serious. "Thank you," she said.

"No need to thank me," I said. "That's one of our missions at the fair—to proclaim the joy of llamas. Michael won't be content until every farmer has a few."

"Not sure they'd get along with my goats and cows," Molly said. "No, I mean thank you for everything. For recommending the lawyer. Both the lawyers, actually. I like them both a lot. And I understand that if it wasn't for you, I'd be languishing in a jail cell in Clay County instead of out on bail in Caerphilly. Which I gather that would be a very bad thing, unless all the stories I'm hearing are just gossip."

"Some are and some aren't," I said. "It's more like Dogpatch than *Deliverance,* but still—you don't want to be in jail anywhere."

"I just wish I'd thought to ask you to recommend a divorce lawyer sooner." She sighed. "But I guess I've been in denial. Apparently I should have closed all the joint accounts as soon as Brett moved out, rather than waiting till he spent all the cash and maxed out the credit cards. I'd be a lot less broke, and look a lot less suspicious to your chief. But I didn't even get around to changing the locks until I came home one day last week and found our stereo was gone."

I wasn't sure what to say to that, so I just shook my head. Molly didn't seem to expect an answer. We watched in silence until, to my relief, she broke out in giggles again at the sight of a black-and-white pinto llama standing, proud and dignified, basking in what he no doubt assumed was the approval of the crowd, while his owner tugged in vain on his lead.

"Actually, according to my attorney—my defense

attorney—I may owe a debt of gratitude to Clay County as well," Molly said. "She seems to think she'll be able to get a lot of the evidence thrown out in court because the Clay County police are careless about processing it."

"Yes, Deputy Plunkett is pretty careless," I said. "I think they're doing all they can to keep him from touching anything from now on."

"Damn," she said, with a wry laugh. "There goes my defense."

"Not necessarily. After all, if they find any evidence that would clear you, you don't want that getting thrown out, right? Look, do you have any idea how the gun got in your van?"

"No." She shook her head slowly. "I've been racking my brains. Did I leave one of the doors open? Maybe. The van's old, and the back hatch sticks sometimes. Maybe it was open."

I nodded. Of course, this begged the question of why the killer would make a beeline from the crime scene to her van in the hope that it would be open and he could deposit the gun there. Maybe he'd just planned to leave it in or near her campsite, noticed the imperfectly closed van door, and seized the opportunity. Or maybe the killer was someone who knew her well enough to know about the tricky latch.

Or someone who knew that Brett might still have had a key to Molly's van. Vern had said his key ring was missing. If Molly hadn't changed the house locks until last week, had she even begun to think about the van locks? Probably not; or even if she had, it probably hadn't seemed a high priority for spending some of her meager cash on.

"Of course, someone could have jimmied the van doors," she was saying. "It's not that hard—Brett knew how. He was always losing his keys. Or having them taken away from him at bars and parties."

She smiled sadly.

"You don't sound very mad at him," I said.

She considered that for a moment.

"Actually, I'm not." She looked around as if to make sure no one was eavesdropping. "To tell the truth, when he actually left, all I could feel was an enormous sense of relief. As if I'd been carrying around a huge weight but I was so used to it that I never realized how much it was dragging me down until suddenly poof! It was gone. I was almost dizzy with relief. Okay, I was terrified about the possibility of losing the farm, but didn't blame Brett for that. I knew perfectly well it was her idea."

"Genette's?"

She nodded.

"I gather you don't like Genette," I said. "Understandable."

"It wasn't just me," she said. "No one liked her. If you ask me, I think the killer wanted to hurt her. Or maybe was trying to kill her and got Brett instead. I can't think of any reason why someone would want to kill Brett. Most people found him either annoying or likable. Or both. But you don't kill people because they're annoying. And no one hated him."

"Interesting," I said.

"Which is what your mother always taught you to say when you can't say anything nice." Molly's laugh sounded bitter. "You think my theory's stupid."

"No, this time I meant it," I said. "It's an interesting theory, especially since Genette seems to share it."

"Genette?" She sounded startled. And then she frowned. "How do you know she . . ."

"Mother spotted Genette packing up her booth and presumably planning to skip town, so I got the job of stalling her until the chief could get there," I explained. "She was completely panic-stricken, saying the killer had been after her and gotten Brett by mistake. She was about to leave all her stuff behind, thinking the fair had bellhops to pack it for her."

"Bellhops." Molly actually smiled. "Yeah, that's Genette. But she could be right. About the killer mistaking Brett for her. Or even more likely, killing Brett to get back at her. I can see that. She has enemies. Not just me. She's hurt a lot of people."

"Such as?" I wondered if she would name Paul Morot, the former winemaker.

Just then I saw Vern Shiffley step up to the fence around the ring, a little to our left. He seemed to be scanning the crowd. I suspected he might be looking for me.

"Hey, Meg!" Vern spotted me and waved.

Just then Deputy Plunkett appeared at his side. Vern headed for the stairs to the bleachers, followed by Plunkett.

"Oh, dear," Molly stood up. "I hate to desert you, but— you understand."

She began picking her way across the bleachers to the other side, where there was another set of steps. By the time Vern and Plunkett reached me, she was gone. Along with my best chance of finding out if she knew anything that would help solve Brett's murder.

Chapter 26

"Hey, Meg," Vern said, when he reached us.

"Hey," Josh said.

"Hey, junior." Vern patted Josh on the head. "Meg, got some papers for you."

"Was that who I think it was?" Plunkett asked.

"That was Molly Riordan, yes," I said. "The papers for Genette to sign?"

"Right," Vern handed me a manila folder containing a thick wad of paper. "You can leave if you like, Plunkett. Like I told you, this is Shiffley Moving Company business, not law-enforcement business."

"I'm in no rush." Plunkett sat down and began studying the llamas with puzzled eyes. Vern shook his head and went on.

"Randall says get her to sign on the last page and initial all the places where he put those little 'sign here' sticky things. The total amount and the deposit are by the signature line, and get a credit card number if you can't get a check."

"Or cash," I said. "I assume cash would also be acceptable to your cousins at the moving company."

"Cash would be the best," Vern agreed. "But most people don't carry a grand or two on them, so we'll settle for what we can get. Don't forget the date of expiration—"

"And the security code, yes," I said. "I do a lot of credit card sales when I'm at craft fairs. I can handle it."

"So what did the black widow lady want?" Plunkett asked. He had parked both arms on the bleacher behind him and was leaning back, making himself comfortable.

"Ms. Riordan wanted to thank me for finding her an attorney," I said. Which was true—it just wasn't all of the truth.

"Her lawyer should work on getting as many women as he can on the jury," Plunkett said. "Older women. And fat ones. A jury full of dumpy wrinklies would understand why she shot the cheating dog. And maybe she won't fry."

"Plunkett, that's—" Vern began.

"Actually, I think most Virginia executions are by lethal injection these days," I said. "But if Molly actually goes on trial, I'll give her lawyer your thoughts on the jury-selection process."

Plunkett looked disappointed, as if he'd have enjoyed seeing me leap to Molly's defense or revile him for his sexist thinking. I smiled blandly at him, and he looked downright annoyed.

Vern caught on and stifled a grin. And changed the subject.

"So do I hear you're buying some fancy chickens?" he asked.

"Thinking about it," I said. "After all, we've got the space. We've even got at least one shed that started life as a chicken coop. Why not?"

"Get yourself some Rhode Island Reds," Plunkett suggested. "Decent layers, and they're mighty fine meat birds."

"Actually we're looking more for ornamental birds who'll produce a few eggs," I said, wincing a little. "Michael thinks either Sumatrans or Welsummers."

"So Michael's in favor of it, too?" Vern asked.

"It was my idea," I said. "But I think he's encouraging it

so he won't feel as guilty when he asks if he can buy another llama. Which I suspect he's working up to. He's been paying a lot of attention to crias here at the fair."

"To what?" Vern asked.

"Crias. Baby llamas."

Plunkett snorted as if he found the whole thing ridiculous. We ignored him.

"Don't worry," Vern said. "Michael's probably only checking out the crias on account of our project to get the chief a llama for Christmas."

"Are you serious?" I said. "And do you really think the chief wants a llama?"

"Absolutely," Vern winked at me when he said it, and glanced over at Plunkett. Who couldn't exactly swivel his ears like Jim Bob the donkey, but was definitely paying attention. "And Minerva won't let him spend the money. Says it's an extravagance. But she can't exactly object if his loyal staff give him one, can she?"

I had a sudden vision of how the chief would react if anyone actually gave him a llama and had trouble fighting back an attack of the giggles.

"There's Michael now," Vern said.

"Daddy!" Josh cried.

"Zippy!" Jamie shouted.

While the twins waved and shrieked, the rest of us watched in breathless silence as Michael led Zeppo over the course Harpo had completed so brilliantly. To my astonishment, Zeppo was alert and focused. He breezed through the obstacles as well as Harpo had—maybe better.

"This one's not as funny as some of the others," Plunkett remarked.

"That's because this one is doing it right," I said.

Maybe I jinxed things by saying that. Michael and Zeppo had reached the point where Zeppo was supposed to stand in the little circle while Michael picked up one of his hooves. Zeppo stood. Michael bent down and carefully picked up the hoof.

Zeppo squealed and fell over as if pole-axed. Then, he began flailing around, scratching his back on the ground, raising great clouds of dust and waving all four legs in the air in his delight. It took Michael a good five minutes to get him on his feet again.

"So much for our hopes of a one-two victory in the obedience trials," I said, shaking my head.

"Funniest things I've ever seen," Plunkett said. "Maybe I should get me some llamas. They good for anything apart from the entertainment value? Can't say as I've ever eaten roast llama, but I'd be willing to give it a try. What's it taste like?"

"We've never eaten any of our pet llamas," I said in my coldest voice. "So I have no idea what they would taste like. We don't grill the dogs, either."

"Llamas look as if they'd be tough and stringy anyway," Vern said.

I was opening my mouth to say that while older llamas probably were tough and stringy, the young ones were considered quite a delicacy in the Andes. But then I realized that Vern was probably feeling as protective about the llamas as I was.

"They expensive, these llamas?" Plunkett asked.

"I have no idea," I said. "Michael buys them. I just say, 'Oh, goody, another llama.'"

I was relieved when Plunkett left. Until I saw him at the other end of the stands, chatting with one of the county board members. Looking for allies in his job campaign, most likely. I found him obnoxious, but he could probably turn on a smarmy kind of good ol' boy charm when he wanted. He and the board member seemed to be getting along just fine. Not something I could do anything about now, so I did my best to shove it out of my mind.

"He's job hunting, all right." Vern was also frowning at Plunkett and the board member.

"And what if he really tries to butter up the chief by giving him a llama?" I asked.

"No idea," Vern said. "But it should be fun to watch. Meanwhile, I need to run."

I stayed through the award ceremony. Harpo, to no one's surprise, won first place. Zeppo actually came in fifth, which shows how unruly most of the other llamas had been. We led Happy and Zippy, as the boys insisted on calling them, back to the sheep barn in triumph.

"I have to run over to the Caerphilly Inn," I told Michael. "Fair business."

"Can you stop off at the chicken tent on your way?" he asked. "To see the Sumatrans and Welsummers in person?"

He seemed so keen that I agreed. So we all four trooped over to the chicken tent. Some of the farmers had set up an incubator, and we arrived just in time for the boys to watch some Leghorn chicks hatching.

"Mommy, can we have them?" Josh asked.

"No, I want big chickens," Jamie said, pointing at an enormous Brahma rooster.

Michael disappeared while the boys and I were watching the chicks, and then reappeared with two farmers, each carrying a chicken. One was a soft, fluffy black-and-copper Welsummer hen, the other a glossy black Sumatran rooster.

"Mine," Jamie said, pointing to the Sumatran.

"Good taste," the Sumatran's owner said, with a laugh.

"Want that one," Josh said. For once, they weren't fighting for the same thing—he was pointing to the Welsummer.

"Either one's a pretty good choice for a hobby farmer," the Welsummer's owner said.

"What do you think?" Michael asked.

What did I think? I thought these guys would have a lot more luck selling chicks to people like Michael and me if they could learn not to use the phrase "hobby farmer." Couldn't he have said "small-scale farmer" or "backyard farmer" or something?

I stared back and forth between the two birds, as if pondering our choices, while I sorted through my negative reactions to the hobby farmer thing. Michael and I had five llamas, a vegetable garden fortified behind eight-foot deer fencing, and a fifty-tree semi-organic orchard. We weren't trying to grow everything we ate. We weren't selling anything. We just wanted to raise a little fresh produce, and maybe let the boys enjoy a life that was more connected than most to nature and history. Michael was a tenured professor at Caerphilly College, in line to become head of the drama department when the current chair retired. I had a career as a blacksmith that was not only lucrative and satisfying but allowed me the flexibility I needed now that we had a family. We didn't have time to run a real farm. The orchard and the vegetable garden were an overgrown version of a typical suburban backyard garden patch, and the llamas were just for fun. We were the very definition of hobby farmers.

So why did the term sting so badly?

Probably something I should get used to. Since moving to our converted farmhouse, I'd come to realize how embattled traditional family farms were. The giant agricultural corporations drove prices down to a level small farmers couldn't match, and developers were always waiting to snatch up choice tracts of land. Maybe hobby farmers were the least offensive alternative. People who bought a few acres—or even a whole lot of acres—not to farm but so they could live in an idyllic rural setting, and then began planting a few fruit trees, and raising a few sheep or cows. Or llamas. I'd never had the feeling that any of the nearby farmers resented Michael and me for buying our house with its few acres. Or Mother and Dad, who had bought the much larger farm next door. In fact, since my parents had bought the farm to save it from developers and rented much of the land to a nearby working farmer at a very low rate, most of the county's farmers heartily approved of Dad. And at least we weren't the kind of incomers who moved into a farm community and then began complaining about the smell of manure and honking furiously whenever we had to slow down behind a tractor.

Maybe I should work on thinking of "hobby farmer" as a badge of honor.

"I like them both," I finally said aloud. "And I'm a little frazzled right now for decision making. Can I mull it over for a little while and let you know later?"

Both farmers nodded. They didn't seem disappointed.

"It's a responsibility," one said. "Raising any of God's creatures. Best not to take in on lightly."

They went back to their booths, and Michael and I strolled out of the tent.

"If you prefer one, let me know which," he said. "I'll take the heat—tell them you left the decision to me and it was my choice."

"I might do that," I said. "Although right now I don't

know which one I like better. Right now, I covet them both."

"Let's get some of each then."

"If we get both, we'll need to keep them separate," I said. "Or we won't have Welsummers and Sumatrans, we'll have Welmatrans and Sumsummers."

"I figured we could keep the Sumatrans in our barn yard, and the Welsummers at the far end of our yard, right across the fence from Rose Noire's herb garden. She's keen on the idea—apparently they would eat up bugs and serve as a kind of organic pest control for her crops. And she also likes the idea of organic eggs, and organic chicken manure for the herbs."

Clearly he'd been thinking about this.

"Want chickens, Mommy," Josh said.

"Want black chickens," Jamie said.

"Brown chickens," Josh countered.

Michael and I simultaneously recognized the signs of impending physical combat and each grabbed a twin.

"Apparently we're getting chickens," I said. "Black chickens *and* brown chickens."

The boys cheered loudly.

"But don't tell anyone yet."

"Okay," Jamie said.

"Why not?" Josh asked.

"Because if we tell people which chickens we want, someone else might buy the ones we want before we can."

They both got that, and nodded solemnly.

"I'll start negotiating on price and quantity and delivery date and whatever," Michael said.

I left him to it and set out for my car. On my way, I ran into the Bonnevilles, sitting on one of the hay bales that lined the wide walkways, both to provide impromptu seating and to help steer the flow of traffic. Mrs. Bonneville was picking at a small salad. Mr. Bonneville was eating a chili dog. Apparently sorrow hadn't taken away his appetite. He tried to frown after every bite and wait a decent interval between bites, but clearly he was counting the seconds until he could take his next bite.

"How are you?" I said as I passed them. I meant it as a greeting, not a question.

"Doing the best we can to bear up," Mr. Bonneville said. Mrs. Bonneville burst into tears.

"I'm so sorry." I tried to sound sympathetic, but my sympathy for them was definitely wearing thin.

"We heard you were in the chicken tent." Mrs. Bonneville's voice had the nasal, stopped-up sound of someone who had been crying recently. "Looking at—*chickens*!"

"Yes, I was." I couldn't quite understand her frown at hearing that. Did she think that no one else should be buying or selling chickens while theirs were still missing? Or was she simply miffed that we were looking at other people's chickens?

"People were looking at our chickens when we first got here," she said.

Nostalgia? Or was she suddenly suspicious of everyone who showed an interest in acquiring heirloom chickens—including Michael and me, who weren't even interested in Russian Orloffs?

"Yes," I said. "The chief is taking a very keen interest in everyone who showed an interest in your chickens."

That didn't seem to mollify them.

"In fact—" I looked around as if making sure no one was near, and took a step closer. "I'm on my way to the Caerphilly Inn to see one of the suspects now."

"Do you mean—that woman?"

"Genette Sedgewick," I said. "On fair business, of course, not police. But while I'm there, I intend to keep a sharp lookout for any signs that she might be hiding any chickens there."

Where did that come from, I wondered? I tried to imagine anyone sneaking live chickens past the inn's overzealous staff. The first—and last—time I'd taken Spike there we were followed around the whole time by a staff member carrying a whisk broom, a dustpan, and a little spray can of something called Pee-Off! I took the hint and the Small Evil One never returned. The inn's entire staff would probably have a collective conniption fit at the very idea of someone bringing in a live chicken.

But the Bonnevilles seemed to like the idea of my proposed search. When I left them, they were both wearing little conspiratorial smiles, and Mrs. Bonneville was attacking her salad with a zest that permitted Mr. Bonneville to finish off his chili dog.

As I drove to the inn, I shoved them out of my mind. I was making happier plans. We could move one of the sheds from our backyard out to the pasture where Rose Noire grew her herbs. The yard was already fenced in to keep Spike from roaming—did we need to subdivide it to protect the chickens from Spike? Or maybe to protect Spike from the chickens—the Sumatran rooster looked pretty fierce. And how soon would we be getting our chickens?

Our chickens. I found I liked the sound of that.

I got almost the whole way to the inn without thinking about why I was going there, which made for a much more pleasant ride than if I'd fretted the whole way about having to deal with Genette.

Chapter 27

As I trudged from my car to the front door of the inn, my good mood vanished and I began to feel put upon. Dealing with Genette was bad enough, but there was also the always difficult staff of the Caerphilly Inn. The doorman wasn't bad—it was his job to open the door and bow deeply to anyone who showed up, even unprepossessing people in blue jeans and a Caerphilly College t-shirt with chocolate ice cream stains on it. And he'd been there a while and knew me, so his welcome was almost cordial.

"May we help you, madam?" the desk clerk said. Unlike the doorman, he was new. And not local. Desk clerks never were, here at the inn. Apparently management had decided that they had to import staff to achieve the right blend of elegance and chilly hauteur. I had to fight the urge to look myself over to see if I had suddenly sprouted a crop of facial warts, or if maybe I was trailing a long piece of toilet paper from one shoe.

"I'm here to see Genette Sedgewick," I said.

The change in the desk clerk's expression was almost imperceptible, but I could tell her name had not improved his opinion of me.

"On official Un-fair business," I added. "Ms. Sedgewick is leaving the fair early, and I'm here representing fair management, to arrange for the removal and transportation of her booth and its contents."

"So Mrs. Sedgewick will be leaving us?" He sounded

eager. "Of course, we're always sorry to see our guests leave," he added, though I suspected Genette came as close to an exception as anyone ever could. His tone was considerably warmer. Was it because he realized I was a representative of the fair, which was currently paying for half a dozen out-of-town dignitaries to stay here at the inn? Or was it Genette's departure that made him so cheerful?

"You'd have to ask Chief Burke that," I said. "No one connected with the murder is being allowed to leave just yet."

"Ah." He hid his disappointment reasonably well. "So unfortunate about poor Mr. Riordan."

"Was he staying here, too?" Not that I had been planning to pry, but he had opened the subject.

"He wasn't a registered guest," the desk clerk said. He stopped just short of saying, "Thank goodness!"

"But as a friend of Ms. Sedgewick, he might have come to visit her."

"Yes," the desk clerk said. "Although we would have no real way of knowing," he added, as if afraid I'd start questioning him on Brett's movements. "Ms. Sedgewick is staying in one of the cottages. Very secluded. Guests in the cottages often find it more convenient to go straight from the parking lot to the cottage, without coming through the lobby. Particularly those who are . . . less accustomed to the amenities of valet parking."

So much for finding useful evidence from the desk clerk. Although he'd probably gone farther than he should in saying Genette was in one of the cottages. There were only three, each named after a Virginia-born president— Washington, Jefferson, and Madison. Presumably if the inn ever expanded, Monroe, Harrison, Tyler, Taylor, and Wilson could expect their own cottages, too, but for now finding Genette would only require knocking on three doors.

"I'm sure the chief understood why you can't give him any information about Mr. Riordan," I continued. Actually, from the look on his face, I suspected the chief hadn't been all that understanding. "I'll go see Ms. Sedgewick. You said the Jefferson Cottage, right? I know the way."

"The Madison," the desk clerk said quickly. "But Ms. Sedgewick is not in her cottage at the moment. Madam will find her in the restaurant."

His voice dripped disapproval. I'd heard rumors that occasionally, when guests did not meet their standards, the inn banned them from the restaurant and ordered them to confine themselves to room service. Was Genette about to suffer this humiliation?

I thanked him and crossed the lobby to the entrance of the restaurant. On those few occasions when Michael and I had splurged to eat at the inn's restaurant, the maître d' invariably kept us waiting well past our reservation time. And eyed our best clothes as if they only just barely met his standards. Luckily he wasn't there at the moment, so I could invade his domain uninvited.

I threaded my way through the tables in the cavernous and dimly lit room. My feet sank into the thick, soft carpet and seemed to make little swishing noises as they emerged. Thanks to the heavy drapes, lush upholstery, and fabric-covered walls, those little swishes were the only noise I heard until I drew near the table where an elegant gray-haired waiter was murmuring the specials into the waiting ears of the three wine judges.

I paused by the table to exchange muted greetings with the judges, and then continued on. Three tables farther down, at the very back of the restaurant, in a corner almost completely lost in the shadows, I found Genette.

She was dressed in black, or at least dark colors. It was hard to tell in the near blackness. And she was wearing oversized dark glasses.

"Ms. Sedgewick?"

She lifted her head, peered up at me, then removed the sunglasses and peered some more. Her face looked tear streaked, and she was squinting as if she ought to be wearing corrective lenses.

"Meg Langslow," I explained. "From the fair."

"Yeah. Siddown." Her voice was overloud and startling in the dim hush. As I took a seat opposite her I could see the waiter and the wine judges casting curious glances our way.

Genette fumbled blindly among the various items on the table until she found a highball glass. She picked it up with a shaky hand, gulped down the remaining inch or so of whatever liquid it contained, and set it down carelessly on the table, clinking against the silverware.

Genette was soused.

"Waiter," she called in the overloud voice of the very, very inebriated. The waiter arrived at our table with surprising speed, as if eager not to have her call again.

" 'Nother Scotch," she said. "Nosso many rocks."

The waiter frowned and glanced at me.

"Nothing, thanks," I said.

He blinked disapprovingly, as if he'd really been expecting me to say, "No, I think she's had enough." I smiled back, declining to do his dirty work for him. He murmured something and slid noiselessly away.

"Ms. Sedgewick, it's about your booth," I said.

"I tol' you," she said. "Pack it all up."

"We did."

"Break much?"

"I arranged to have it packed by a reputable professional moving company," I said. "In the unlikely event that they break anything, their fee includes insurance. I came to ask what to do with it all."

She stared back, uncomprehending.

"Do you have a truck into which they should load your stuff?" I spoke as slowly and distinctly as I could. "Or would you like for me to arrange to have it all delivered to your farm?"

"Who cares?" she said. "Not the truck. No one to drive it. Send it all. Whatever."

It took forever, but I got her signature on the paperwork from the Shiffley Moving Company, and then on a very large check. The waiter was nowhere to be found, which was probably just as well. I suspected another whiskey would send Genette into oblivion, and I was grateful to the waiter for postponing his arrival until I'd finished with the signatures. Of course, since she was drunk as the proverbial skunk, I wasn't sure any of the paperwork would hold up to legal challenge. I'd let Randall figure out how to deal with that.

I tucked the check and the contract into my purse and pondered what to do next. Common sense suggested that I should hurry back to the fair. But it might be a lot easier to get information out of her in her current inebriated condition. I was trying to figure out how to ask a few leading questions—something slightly more subtle than "Did you have an argument with Paul Morot? Or maybe with Brett himself?"—when a figure loomed up beside us.

"'Bout time," Genette said. But it wasn't the waiter

returning with her refill. It was a young woman—not much more than a girl, really—in jeans and a t-shirt. Clearly the maître d' wasn't guarding the entrance to his cave very well today—normally denim was a sure way to get turned away at the door.

"Hussy!" the young woman shouted. "Murderer!"

Genette just stared back at her.

"You couldn't stand that he was leaving you for me," the young woman said. "You had to get rid of him."

Genette put down her drink, took off her sunglasses, and blinked, clearly startled.

"Wha'?" she asked.

"He wanted to be with me and the baby!" the young woman shrieked. "He was going to marry me as soon as he was free! And you couldn't stand it, could you?"

The young woman pulled something out of her purse and was shaking it in Genette's face. Genette was visibly having trouble focusing on it, so I leaned around to see what it was. A photograph of a baby, probably a newborn, wearing one of the little yellow knit hats they put on them in the delivery room. "Cranky bishop hats," Michael and I had called them. I had pictures of Josh and Jamie at that age in identical hats.

"You're a killer!" the young woman wailed. "Brett said he was going to tell you yesterday, and look what happened!"

I glanced around to see two sleek, gray-haired waiters frozen in shock, while the wine judges had all turned around to stare with unabashed fascination.

"Who the hell are you?" Genette sounded puzzled.

The young woman burst into tears, turned, and began running away.

"Madam!" One of the waiters took a few futile steps in pursuit of the young woman, who increased her speed and escaped into the lobby. The other waiter came over to our table.

"Who was she?" Genette asked. She still sounded more puzzled than upset or angry.

The waiter frowned at us as if he really wanted to ask the same question.

"Does madam require any assistance in returning to her room?" he said aloud.

"I think they're cutting you off," I told Genette. "Let me help you."

"Bastards." Genette didn't sound surprised though. More resigned. "Who was that woman?"

She asked the same question at least a dozen times in the time it took me to help her out of the restaurant, through the lobby, out the back door, and down a short walkway to her cottage. By the time I dumped her on her bed, the young woman's words appeared to have finally sunk in. When I reached to pull her shoe off, she kicked me.

"Why didn't you tell me he was cheating on me?" she wailed. "After all I did for him!"

She began spitting out a stream of bitter and increasingly obscene invective against Brett and the unknown young woman, all the while kicking viciously in my general direction. After a few sentences, I realized she was starting to confuse me with the young woman, so I decided to get out while the getting was good.

"Sleep in your shoes, then," I said.

Before leaving, I checked the bathroom, the closet, and the armoire. No chickens, and no telltale signs of recent chicken occupancy. Not that I expected any, but you never knew, and at least I could honestly tell the Bonnevilles I'd tried. I turned the bedside light out, then went to the door. I paused and listened for a few minutes, in case she said anything of interest, like, "Now I'm really glad I killed you, you jerk!" or "And after I stole those bantam chickens you wanted!" But her rant was repetitive and uninteresting, except for the couple of times that she shrieked "I'll kill him when I get my hands on him!" As if she'd forgotten Brett was already dead.

I stepped out into the hallway, pulled the door closed, took a deep breath, and called the chief.

"I have another suspect for you," I said.

Chapter 28

The chief sent out an APB on the unwed mother, and suggested that he would appreciate talking to me when I got back to the fair. Within half an hour I was in the fair office, seated in one of our uncomfortable folding chairs.

"We'd have a lot better chance of locating this young woman if we had a more specific description," the chief was saying. "Young and wearing blue jeans and a t-shirt doesn't help much."

I winced.

"I can't really tell you much more," I said.

"Try," the chief said.

"I am trying. But I didn't really get a good look at her."

"You were able to recall a fairly lengthy conversation," he said. "Are you telling me you weren't looking at her all that time?"

"I was looking at her," I said. "But we were in the very back of the restaurant at the Caerphilly Inn. The part where they put guests when they approve of your wallet but not your wardrobe. The part where the menus ought to be printed in braille. The part—"

"Understood," the chief said. "You can't give me the kind of precise description I could normally count on you for. But any details you can remember would help."

I closed my eyes and took several deep breaths. I pretended I was walking into the Caerphilly Inn again. I replayed my conversation with Genette. And then we heard the cry of "Hussy!" and we'd both looked up and saw her. I tried to remember if there was anything memorable about her hair, her eyes, the shape of her face, her mouth, her nose—

"A ski jump," I said.

"I beg your pardon?"

"She had a nose like a ski jump," I said. "Long and sloping and with a little upward swoop at the end. It was very distinctive."

"Ski jump," I heard the chief mutter, as his pen scratched in his notebook. "Anything else?"

"Shorter than me."

Which wasn't much help, because at five ten, I was taller than most women. The chief refrained from saying so.

"You were sitting, she was standing," he said instead. "Can you show me about how far above you her head was?"

I held up my hand. But then I wobbled it a bit to emphasize that I wasn't sure how accurate I was being.

"I'd make that about five foot five inches, give or take. What do you remember about her shape."

"Average," I said.

He waited in silence while I continued to replay the scene in my head.

"Hair's brown, I think. Medium color, medium length, a little on the poufy side. She might have acne."

"You don't know whether you saw acne or not?" His voice held a trace of exasperation.

"I might not have spotted leprosy in that light, but she wore her hair pulled over her face. She was just peering out from this tangled cave of hair. Some girls do that to hide acne. Then again, some just think it's cool."

I heard the faint skitter of his pen.

"And she's probably from Virginia," I added. "Not that far from here, at a guess."

"You could see that?"

"I could hear it." I opened my eyes. "Her accent. Not a Tidewater accent. Could be from the mountains. Or a country accent from the Piedmont. Probably not from Caerphilly; it's a little too heavy. But not that far away."

"Would you recognize her if you saw her again?"

"Maybe," I said. "Probably, if I could hear her talk."

"Keep your eyes and ears open, then," he said. "And if you do recognize her, call me. Don't confront her."

I nodded.

"I'd like you to work with Horace on doing a composite sketch," the chief said.

"Horace is a sketch artist now?" I said. "Cool."

"No, but he's got some kind of software he'd been nagging me for months now to let him try." This time the exasperation was more than faint. "And this is the first time in months we've wanted to find someone and didn't just have a photograph we could circulate."

He stood up and turned to Vern.

"I'll be over at the Caerphilly Inn," he said.

"The lobby's better lit," I said. "Maybe the doorman or the desk clerk got a better look at her."

"Find Horace," the chief told Vern. "And tell him to bring his laptop. We want him to use that crime scene sketch artist program to do a likeness we can use in that APB."

"You think she's a suspect?" Vern asked.

"For now we're just considering her a potential witness," the chief said. "But when Horace finishes his sketch, I want you to take a look at it and have Plunkett do the same. If she's from around here, odds are one of you will recognize her."

But an hour later, after Horace and I had produced our masterpiece, both Vern and Plunkett shook their heads.

"Looks vaguely familiar," Vern said. "But I can't place her."

"I think you got the nose wrong." Plunkett frowned and shook his head at our drawing. "Nobody really has a nose like that."

But I stood my ground on the nose. I could see it so clearly, emerging from the tangle of hair.

Or did I only want to believe I could see it because it was really the only distinctive thing about the drawing Horace and I had labored so hard to produce?

I even called in Rob to take a look at it, on the theory that if a young woman was even moderately attractive— and the unwed mother was, in spite of the odd nose— Rob would have noticed her.

"Sorry," he said. "I don't remember seeing her. But I'll keep my eyes peeled."

"Well, so much for the drawing," I said to Vern. "On a happier note, I have the signed contract and a check for your cousins."

"Fantastic. We owe you one. Want me to take it to them?"

"That'd be great." I handed him the manila folder. "You might want to warn them to hold off a little about actually delivering her stuff."

"They're just hauling it back to the office for storage," he said. "We're sure as heck going to wait until her check clears before we let any of it out of our hands."

"Yes, you said that," I said. "But that wasn't what I was thinking of." I relayed what had just happened at the Caerphilly Inn, though not in as much detail as I'd given the chief.

"So maybe the contents of Genette's booth might just have become a lot more interesting to you and the chief," I suggested. "Maybe she wasn't as drunk as I thought, and was only pretending not to recognize Brett's new girlfriend. That would make her a suspect, wouldn't it?"

"Genette's always been a suspect," Vern said. "Someone gets knocked off, we look first at the significant others—legal or otherwise. So the contents of her booth were already very interesting to us, which is why I closely supervised every single bit of the packing. Me and my digital video camera. Didn't find anything that seemed relevant to the murder, but the movies will still be useful if she tries to claim we broke anything. And she looks like the type who might."

"Agreed," I said. "And there's also the fact that she was drunk as a skunk when she signed the contract and the check. I have no idea if that matters."

"Could invalidate the contract," Rob said.

"Oh, great." Vern held up the manila folder and shook it. "Does that mean we have to get her to sign this thing all over again?"

"I'm not a contract specialist," Rob said. He had, in fact, never actually practiced law, in spite of graduating from the University of Virginia's prestigious law school and passing the bar exam on his first try. "But I think it'll be fine if you get her to initial an amended contract tomorrow. If you decided it wasn't quite as involved as you expected and knocked a couple of hundred off the price, she'd probably sign in a heartbeat. You might want to run that by your own attorney, just to be sure."

"Great idea," Vern said. "Thanks."

"Just when I think you didn't learn anything in law school, you surprise me," I said.

"Is that like an apology for telling people I flunked the bar exam?" Rob asked.

I winced.

"I never told anyone you flunked the bar exam," I said. "I probably did tell a few people I wasn't sure you ever bothered to show up for it, but that's completely different. And for the record, you have my apology."

"But I told you I passed it." Rob didn't look angry. More puzzled.

"Yes, but I thought you only said that to stop all of us from nagging you about when you were going to take it," I explained. "That's what I'd have done if I'd finished law school and decided I was never going to practice and taking the bar exam would be a waste of time."

"Wow. When you put it that way, it almost sounds like a compliment." Rob ambled off, looking mollified.

I sat at my desk in the temporarily empty trailer and pondered what I'd heard from Vern. To my surprise, I realized that I wasn't disappointed to hear that they hadn't found incriminating evidence in Genette's booth.

Much as I wanted the chief to find some evidence that would clear Molly, I didn't want them to arrest Genette instead.

"She didn't do it," I muttered to myself.

I was glad no one heard me and expected me to justify the statement, because I couldn't have—not in any logical way.

I pulled out my notebook and was looking to see if there were any urgent tasks that had fallen by the wayside while I was at the inn when my cell phone rang.

It was Randall.

"Meg, could you come over to the chicken tent?" he said. "We've had another theft."

Chapter 29

Back at the chicken tent, I found Randall introducing the chief to a familiar-looking farmer.

"Mr. Beamish here tells me his chickens were stolen this afternoon," Randall said, by way of introduction to me and the chief.

"This afternoon?" I echoed. "But weren't there— Oh, no!" I suddenly realized who Mr. Beamish was. "Not the Sumatrans!"

Mr. Beamish nodded sadly.

I realized I was feeling this a lot more personally than the theft of the Bonnevilles' bantams. Perhaps because I didn't remember actually seeing the missing Orloffs. But I'd seen the Sumatrans. I'd admired the proud elegance of the rooster's long tail feathers. I'd stroked the hen's soft feathers. I'd wondered if they would be the parents of the chicks Michael was arranging to buy. The Sumatrans were a lot more real to me.

"Sumatrans?" the chief said.

"Black Sumatran chickens," Mr. Beamish said. "The ones I was showing Meg and her husband earlier today."

"Showing you why?" the chief asked me.

"Michael and I were thinking of raising a few chickens," I said. "And what better place than the fair to see all the available breeds and talk to the owners to find out what kind would suit us."

Which sounded a lot more grown-up than "I had a

sudden crazy impulse to own some chickens, and since Michael was feeling guilty about all his serial llama purchases, he seized my impulse and ran with it."

"So someone stole the chickens you were thinking of buying?" the chief asked. I had to admit, if it was a coincidence it was a long one.

"Not the actual chickens," the farmer said.

"We were going to buy some chicks," I added. "From Mr. Beamish's flock."

I suddenly wondered how big a flock he had. They were ornamental chickens, bred for show—would he have that many more at home to make new chicks? Even if he did, he'd almost certainly brought his best chickens to the fair.

"I'm so sorry," I said.

Mr. Beamish nodded sadly.

"But how did they get stolen in the middle of the afternoon?" the chief asked. "Didn't anyone notice someone walking out with a pair of chickens under his arm?"

"People walk out of here with chickens all the time," Mr. Beamish said. "Every time there's a chicken judging over at the show ring. Weren't many people here when it happened, so maybe no one noticed the thief was walking out with someone else's chickens. Most everyone was over at the show ring watching the competition. Youth division. All the FFV and 4-H kids showing the poultry they've raised. Our kids are grown, but I remember how proud they were when they showed their animals, so the wife and I went over to swell the crowd. Most of the other chicken people did the same. Thief must have known that."

Mr. Beamish was staring at the empty cage that had so recently held his beautiful Sumatrans. Around us, I could see that just about all the other people in the tent were either watching us out of the corner of their eyes or flat out staring. Just then Vern showed up. He glanced at the chief's face and didn't say anything.

I could guess why the chief looked so thunderous. He always took it personally when any crime occurred in Caerphilly. And it was more than likely that whoever stole the chickens was hoping that the chief wouldn't have the resources to mount a full investigation on top of the already ongoing murder case. And that would anger the chief even more, because it was partly true. Investigating the thefts on top of the murder was going to be a stretch. And if you added in the possibility that the killer had also committed the chicken theft, in a deliberate attempt to distract the chief's forces from the main goal . . .

It probably didn't help the chief's mood that the black-clad Bonnevilles were lurking nearby like crows hovering over a choice new bit of roadkill, with smug looks on their face as if it didn't exactly displease them to see someone else suffering as they had.

"I'll get Horace over here to do a thorough workup of the crime scene," the chief said finally. "And we'll start taking statements from the other occupants of the tent. All of them," he said, glancing up at Vern.

"You got it, Chief." Vern was looking a little stern himself as he gazed around at the dozens of people he was about to interrogate. A few of the nearby chicken owners looked anxious. Vern was giving an excellent impression of a man who had too much prime jail space sitting vacant. He pulled out his cell phone and began calling other deputies to help.

"Meg," the chief said. "Can I speak to you a minute?"

I nodded and followed him out of the tent.

"Who else knew that you and Michael were taking an interest in these particular chickens?" he asked.

"Just about anyone in the tent could have known we were taking an interest in chickens in general," I said. "We weren't making a big secret of it. Michael spent quite a bit of time interrogating various chicken owners about their birds, to help us figure out what kind to get. And he'd narrowed it down to two birds—the Sumatrans and another breed called Welsummers. You might want to see if anyone is missing any of those. I have no idea how many people knew we had narrowed it down to those two breeds. I suspect Michael didn't want to make it too obvious in front of all the other chicken owners which breed we were favoring. You think the thief picked the Sumatrans because we were interested in them?"

"There must be a couple hundred chickens in that tent," he said. "And the thief picked one of a handful you and Michael were interested in? That's a devil of a coincidence. And I don't like coincidences."

"Maybe not such a coincidence," I said. "The thief was after unusual birds. Rare or heritage birds. And I get that—I wasn't having Michael look at plain old reliable Leghorns or Rhode Island Reds that would produce more eggs than we could use. I was coveting fancy ones. So it might be just a coincidence that the thief stole one of the same fancy breeds that caught my eye."

"Or it might be a deliberate attempt on the part of someone to muddy the waters," the chief said. "You and Michael found the body. Now some chickens from a breed you were interested in are stolen."

"You think someone's trying to frame us?"

"If they are, they're doing a pretty lousy job of it. Maybe

someone who has a grudge against you, taking advantage of the situation."

"Or maybe someone trying to put pressure on you to take the chicken thefts more seriously," I suggested.

"You're thinking of the Bonnevilles?" the chief asked. "Are you suggesting they might be capable of stealing someone else's poultry to draw greater attention to the chicken theft aspect of this case?

I thought about it for a moment and then responded with the sort of elaborate shrug that said, "I wouldn't out it past them."

He sighed.

"I already noticed that they didn't seem particularly sympathetic to their colleague's plight," he said.

"And doesn't a daring daylight theft sound rather like an inside job?"

"Just keep your eyes open," he said. "But don't confront anyone."

I nodded.

"By the way," I asked. "Have you located Paul Morot?"

"The winemaker you mentioned as having a grudge against Genette? You think he might have had something to do with this chicken theft?" The chief"s tone was clipped, as if he was very close to telling me to mind my own business.

"I have no idea," I said. "But he spent much of yesterday hanging around there."

I pointed to the trash cans where I'd first spotted Morot.

"I thought you said he was lurking outside the wine tent." I saw that he was flipping back through the pages of his notebook.

"He was watching the wine tent," I said. "But from a distance. He was actually lurking there, by the trash cans."

"A lot closer to the chicken tent than the wine tent."

I nodded.

The chief stared at the trash cans for a few moments. Then he scribbled in his notebook, nodded to me, and ducked back into the tent.

I stood there for a few moments, thinking. Did I really suspect Morot? Or did I only want to find that someone— anyone—other than Molly was guilty?

I realized that I was probably blocking traffic. I stepped back and sat down on a hay bale. I pulled out my notebook and flipped through the pages, looking for something to do. Actually, I could see plenty of things that needed doing, but none that was urgent. None that I cared about enough to get up and do them.

Clearly I needed cheering up. I got up, put my notebook away, and headed for the llama exhibit.

As I'd hoped, Michael was there, showing off the llamas. In fact, the llama pen was crowded with not only Harpo, Zeppo, Chico, and Gummo but also the third-, fourth-, and sixth-place llamas from the morning's judging. There were also a few alpacas in the pen, and beneath the JOY OF LLAMAS! sign someone had hung a smaller, hand-lettered sign that read AND ALPACAS!

"What about the vicuñas and guanacos?" I asked. "Don't the other camelids deserve a mention?"

"We don't have any vicuñas or guanacos at the fair," Michael said. "Thank goodness. I spent all morning making peace between the llama people and the alpaca people. Don't stir them up again."

"Okay, on a more practical note, where's Groucho?" I asked. "And where are Josh and Jamie? And what happened to the second-place llama—sulking because Harpo beat him?"

"Groucho is back in the pen—the boys are helping Rob groom him for the costume contest tonight," Michael said. "And the second place winner is female, so we don't want her here with all the guys."

I nodded my agreement. The male llamas all got along together famously as long as you didn't introduce any females. Apparently having a female in the same pen or pasture—or even within sight—set the male llamas' hormones racing, and they would spend all of their time fighting with each other and hovering over the female. Before we'd found this out, Michael was planning to buy a female llama, and we'd had long debates over whether to name her Minnie Marx, Margaret Dumont, or Mary Livingstone, after the Marx Brothers' cousin who married Jack Benny. But now we'd put off adding any lady llamas until we could set up a separate barn and pasture for them. The longer that project stayed on Michael's to-do list, the happier I'd be.

"You look down," Michael said.

"We've had another chicken theft," I said. "Someone stole Mr. Beamish's Sumatrans."

"Oh, no."

"I feel like going over and apologizing to the Bonne-villes," I said. "I'm depressed, and the Sumatrans weren't even our chickens."

"Well, maybe it's for the best," Michael said. "Maybe we're rushing into this. We can take a little time, do a little more research, make sure we really want chickens, and that Sumatrans really are a good option. And then—"

"I know you're trying to make me feel better, but it's not working," I said. "I'm still depressed. It's not just the chickens, you know."

"Yes, there's also the whole experience of finding a

dead guy at our fair and having one of your friends accused of his murder."

"Yes," I said. "And the chickens were the last straw. I feel so bad for Mr. Beamish. And also guilty, that I'm selfishly worrying if he will have any Sumatran chicks left to sell us. This must be why they warn you not to count your chickens before they're hatched. Or in our case, bought."

"You need something to raise your spirits," Michael said. "I have an idea—let's take the boys to the Midway."

If he expected me to cheer at the idea, he was doomed to disappointment. I probably scowled instead.

"Oh, come on," he said. "It'll take your mind off everything."

"You think the boys are up for it?" I asked.

"They've been dying to go since they first saw it," he said. "And it's gotten worse since we moved the llama exhibit here, right next to the Midway and they've been seeing it all day."

"I know they want to go," I said. "But will it scare them? All the blaring noise and blinking lights? And are there any rides they can ride?"

"If we go now, while it's still light, it won't be as overwhelming. And the Midway has a merry-go-round, and kiddie bumper cars, and a couple of those rides where they can drive toy fire trucks or boats or whatever that don't even leave the ground."

"They'll want cotton candy and every other kind of junk food."

"Yes, but they've just had snacks. They will want junk food, but they won't be able to eat much of it."

I suddenly realized that I was feeling a strong and arguably illogical aversion to the Midway. Was my brain associating it with Brett's murder?

"If you'd rather not go," Michael said. "I can probably recruit your brother to help me take them some other time. He loves the Midway."

"He would," I said. "Okay, you're on. I'll go. Although I think we probably should take Rob with us anyway."

"To provide additional adult supervision, or another playmate for the boys?"

Always a good question with Rob.

"A little of both," I said. "And he can help eat up any surplus junk food."

So we collected the boys and their uncle Rob and set out for the Midway.

Chapter 30

I realized when we walked into the Midway that, quite apart from its proximity to the scene of the murder, I had a slightly jaundiced view of the place because of what a pain it had been to set up. Many of the members of the fair organizing committee had been against the whole idea of a Midway—in fact, they'd reacted to the idea as if Randall and I were suggesting that we stage a reenactment of the fall of Sodom and Gomorrah. Clearly they had seen way too many movies in which carnival people were depicted as either psychopathic, homicidal geeks or sinister, irresistible Svengalis. I had to admit, when I started interviewing vendors to find one to run our Midway, I encountered a few outfits that gave me the creeps— but they were outnumbered by the companies that promised a family-friendly carnival experience. Of course, a few of the self-proclaimed family-friendly companies turned out to be a little creepy, too. I didn't take my recommendation to the committee until I had three bids from firms whose events I'd personally inspected—firms that regularly did church fund-raising events and could provide wads of testimonials from satisfied priests and ministers. Even then, some of the committee members had balked until Randall pointed out that the Midway would be in Clay County, not Caerphilly. Strangely, the committee didn't seem reluctant to inflict geeks and barkers on our unloved neighbors.

After all that time driving around the state and inspecting other people's midways, I'd had my fill of carnival life. Not to mention all the time I'd spent on our setup day, meeting, greeting, and surreptitiously vetting the Midway barkers and vendors. I assumed even the most family-friendly outfit occasionally hired some bad apples, and I wanted to make sure none of them ended up at our fair. A few of the barkers and ride operators were a bit rough around the edges, but they seemed honest enough. And Randall and I hoped that between my vetting of the personnel and his safety inspection of the rides, we could defuse any complaints by those anxious committee members.

"I just won a hundred dollars," I told Michael, about two minutes after we walked through the new gate.

"Where?" Michael said. "I didn't see you stop at a booth."

"There," I said. "And there."

I pointed to a refreshment stand where one of the members of our fair organizing committee was buying giant balls of pink and blue cotton candy for her grandchildren, and then to a nearby booth where another committee member was attempting to shoot revolving targets with a toy gun.

"Cotton candy!" Jamie was tugging on my hand and pointing.

"I want a teddy bear," Josh was saying, tugging Michael's hand in the opposite direction, toward the target booth.

"Nice to see the committee members out supporting the fair," Michael said. "But where's the hundred dollars coming from?"

"Randall," I said. "Cotton candy first, then we'll see if Daddy can win a teddy bear," I added to the boys. "Those are two of the three committee members who tried so hard to veto the idea of a midway in the first place." I told

Michael. "I made Randall a bet that before the fair was out, we'd catch at least one of them over here."

"Cool." Rob pulled out his cell phone. "I'll get a few photos of them in case Randall doesn't believe you. Can you get me some cotton candy, too?"

"I'm just getting some for the boys right now," I said. "Chances are there will be leftovers."

"Leftover cotton candy?" Rob sounded incredulous.

"They have small stomachs," Michael said. "And they're easily distracted."

"At least I hope they will be," I muttered, as I handed each boy a mountain of blue cotton candy

"Okay, I've e-mailed the photos to Randall," Rob said.

"Teddy bears now?" Josh said through sticky blue lips.

"Teddy bears now," Michael said.

To the boys' astonishment, it was Mommy rather than Daddy or Uncle Rob who proved good enough with the toy guns to win teddy bears. The men redeemed themselves at the ball toss, winning a brace of garishly colored plush snakes.

And there was enough leftover cotton candy for Rob. Also leftover funnel cake, corn dogs, snow cones, kettle corn, soft pretzels, buttered popcorn, caramel apples, and lemonade. On average, the boys would have about two bites of each new food before getting distracted by something else and handing over their treasures to one of their entourage. Even Rob looked relieved when Michael suggested that we take a rain check on ice creams.

In between snacks, the boys slid down the inflatable slides, bounced on the Moon Bounce, careened around the bumper car rink, and rode on the Pirate Ship, the Kids' Scrambler, the Kiddy Swing, the Tubs of Fun, the Whip-o-Whirl, the Flying Elephants (purple, no less), and the

Lady Bugs. But their favorite—and mine—was the merry-go-round. I rode a couple of times, but mostly I stood, camera in hand, waving as they all flashed by and trying for the perfect greeting card moment.

At some point I realized that Michael had been wiser than me—seeing the Midway through the boys' eyes was cheering me up. I loved watching them absorb all the new sights, sounds, and smells.

We finally gave in to Josh's pleas to go on the Ferris wheel—Jamie sensibly wanted nothing to do with it. And neither did Josh once the car swung up about six feet into the air to load the car after ours. In his defense, he was rather overdue for a nap. To avoid a major meltdown, I handed him down from the car to Michael. It was probably against the safety rules, but given the volume of his shrieks, the Ferris wheel operator didn't object to this quick solution to the crisis. Then, while Michael and Rob whisked the boys back to the sheep barn for milk and naps, I took a solo ride on the Ferris wheel. I told Michael that I didn't want to disrupt everyone else's ride any further by making the operator let me off, but I was also eager for a little peace and quiet. I hoped I wouldn't change my mind when the Ferris wheel actually began moving at full speed, but the first slow, jerky revolution, with the operator stopping to unload and reload each car, was surprisingly peaceful.

Especially as I neared the top of the wheel, where I could get a panoramic view of the whole fair, teeming with ant-sized people. I could see mosquito-sized cows being led around the show ring by ant-sized farmers in overalls. On the distant stage an aphid-sized kilted bagpiper was marching up and down. The John Deere and Kubota equipment exhibits looked like a collection of child's toys, with a flock of overall-clad termites swarming around them. Closer at hand, in the Midway, people didn't quite look like ants, of course. More like Barbie and Ken dolls. And all of them, ants, aphids, termites, and dolls, were swarming busily but peacefully.

Well, with the possible exception of a booth almost at my feet, where a Ken-sized Deputy Plunkett and the G.I. Joe–sized operator of a ringtoss were having some sort of altercation. Not a shouting match—I saw the ringtoss operator look around as if for eavesdroppers, and then lean closer before saying something to Plunkett.

And just then the Ferris wheel swooped into motion. I lost sight of Plunkett and the barker. For the first couple of revolutions, I tried to find them again, but I realized the effort was making me uncomfortably dizzy. So I leaned back and tried to push Plunkett out of my mind to enjoy the ride.

And I did enjoy it, but as soon as the Ferris wheel operator released me from my car, I threaded my way through the Midway to the ringtoss. Plunkett wasn't there, and the operator was doing a lively business, so I decided not to interrupt him. But I spotted Plunkett approaching a food concession a few booths down the row. I watched for a few moments as Plunkett stared up at the menu and then spoke to the man behind the counter. The man called something over his shoulder, then handed Plunkett a can of Pepsi. Plunkett leaned against the booth, popped the can open, and took a long swallow.

Curiously, I hadn't seen any money change hands.

I strolled up to the booth and ordered a fresh-squeezed lemonade and slid two dollar bills across the counter to pay for it.

"Lemonade, Sam," the man said.

A high school kid plucked a lemon out of a nearby bin, deftly sliced it, and began rotating the first half on a juicer. The fry cook lifted an Italian sausage from his grill, laid it on a bun, and then slathered on layers of green pepper strips and translucent onion slices. One of my favorites. My mouth began to water, and I made a mental note to call Michael and ask if I should bring dinner back from the Midway.

But not just yet. I turned to Plunkett.

"Afternoon," I said. "Nothing much happening with the murder investigation?"

Plunkett, who had just taken an enormous bite of his sausage, shook his head.

"Suspect's out on bail," he said, when he'd chewed and swallowed his first bite. "And we get some time off. Only for the weekend. Monday, the crime lab in Richmond should get back to us about the evidence we sent down there."

"That's good," I said.

"Good? You really think anything they find down in Richmond is going to get your friend off?"

"I just meant it's good that you're all getting a break," I said.

It could be true. I hoped that Horace and Vern and the chief were getting a little time off to enjoy themselves. At least if they were still putting in long hours, they'd been able to rid themselves of Plunkett for a while by pretending to be taking some time off. They'd probably find that as relaxing as actual time off.

"Yeah, 'bout time we got a break," Plunkett said. "Of course, not all of us are slacking off," he added. "I'm still working on the case. Got an angle of my own I want to follow up."

"An angle you're not telling Chief Burke about?" I asked.

He frowned and took a bite of his sausage—a little hastily, as if to give himself time to think. As he chewed, I could see him studying me. I had the feeling he was trying to sort out how well the chief and I knew each other, and whether I was one of the people he needed to win over to get hired in Caerphilly.

"I said an angle," he said, when he'd finished chewing and swallowed. "If I had any kind of evidence, of course I'd take it to the chief. But right now, for all I know it could only be a wild idea. Lot of people bothering him with wild ideas, so I'm looking for some evidence before I tell him mine."

"That makes sense," I said. "The chief appreciates both initiative and thoughtfulness." I didn't add that he hated sneakiness. Plunkett would find that out soon enough. In the meantime, he looked very pleased with himself.

"Have a good day," he told me. Then he took another large bite, nodded to the vendor, and strolled off.

"Here's your lemonade," the man behind the counter said.

As he handed it to me, I noticed that my two dollar bills were still on the counter. In fact, they were closer to me than they had been when I put them down. I ignored them, sipped my lemonade, and nodded appreciatively. After a long few moments, the counter man picked up the bills and put them in his cash register.

"I didn't see any money change hands when Deputy Plunkett was here," I said. "He's running a tab with you?"

"You could say that," the vendor said.

"Is that all he's asking for?"

The man snorted as if I'd said something ludicrous.

"Anything you want the fair management to do about it?" I asked.

"Best not." He shook his head. "No need to antagonize the local law enforcement. Especially if the whole fair's moving over here to Clay County next year."

I choked slightly on my lemonade.

"Just where did you hear that?" I asked.

"From him." The vendor nodded in the direction Plunkett had taken. "You mean it's not true?"

"It may be true that Clay County will be having a fair next year," I said. "But if they do, it won't be the Un-fair, and they'll have to organize it all by themselves. There's considerable sentiment in Caerphilly County for having the whole Un-fair in our own county next year. Midway and all."

"That's good to hear," he said. "I'd come back for that. I'd have to be pretty hard up for business to come back to Clay County again."

"You think that's a general sentiment?"

He nodded.

"A lot of us were disappointed when we got here," he said. "We knew you'd checked us out pretty thoroughly before going with our outfit, and that's usually a sign of a well-run event that treats the vendors fairly. Plunkett and his bully boys were a nasty shock."

So it wasn't just Plunkett. I filed away the information.

"Imagine how our chief of police feels," I said aloud. "Having to deal him into our murder investigation."

He laughed and shook his head.

"Yeah," he said. "Hard enough to catch whoever did it without somebody trying to undermine you while you're doing it."

I was startled—not at the idea, which had occurred to

me, but that someone with no inside knowledge of the investigation had come up with it.

"You think Plunkett is deliberately trying to undermine the investigation?" I asked. "I assumed he was just incompetent."

"Who knows?" He shrugged. "He keeps bragging to us about how he'd have solved it by now. Making fun of what your chief of police is doing. Claiming he'll never solve the case. Maybe Plunkett is just gloating. But do you really think he's above doing everything he can to keep your chief from solving it?"

"No," I said. "It sounds just like him. He probably resents our taking charge of the case, so it makes sense he'd cause trouble." Or maybe he was counting on solving the case to boost his chances of getting hired on in Caerphilly.

"Besides," the man said. "He keeps bragging about how low the Clay County crime rate is, and how they hardly ever have any unsolved crimes."

"So I've heard," I said. "Of course, I've also heard that that when they can't find the real crook, they can always find someone to frame. Someone who's been stupid enough to tick off Sheriff Dingle, for example."

"Or a carny," the man said. "We make great scapegoats. We've all been pretty impressed that your police chief hasn't taken the easy way out and arrested one of us."

"He won't," I said. "Unless he finds good evidence that one of you did it."

"I can't be a hundred percent sure no one from the Midway did it," he said. "But if I had to put money on it, I'd say it was someone from your side of the fence. No offense meant."

"None taken," I said. "I agree with you."

I thanked him for the lemonade and strolled off. I decided I didn't need to talk to the ringtoss operator. I had a pretty good idea what was going on.

As I made my way back to the gate, I realized, a little sadly, that I was seeing the Midway with my own eyes again, rather than the boys'. The booths and rides might be brightly painted, but the colors were harsh and garish and the paint was getting a little chipped and faded. The games of skill weren't completely rigged, but the odds always seemed to be with the house and when you came down to it the prizes were a little tawdry. And the fairgoers might be happy, but the barkers and concession operators had a pinched, anxious look. And they might have good reason to feel anxious. The counterman hadn't said anything, but it was obvious that Plunkett's free meal was only the tip of the iceberg.

I waited until I was back on the Caerphilly side of the gate before stepping away from the path and pulling out my cell phone to call the chief.

Chapter 31

"Is there anything you can do about officers extorting money from fair vendors?" I asked.

"If you have any evidence that any of my officers are—"

"Clay County officers," I added.

"Oh." His tone changed from indignant to rather melancholy.

I relayed what I'd heard from the counterman—including his suggestion that Plunkett was trying to sabotage the murder investigation.

"I've already had my suspicions about the wisdom of including Deputy Plunkett in our investigation," the chief said. "But it shouldn't be a problem now that the sheriff—our sheriff—has announced that he's taking personal charge of the investigation."

"He is?" The sheriff of Caerphilly was over ninety, and had won his last few elections largely by proclaiming that he was going to keep delegating everything to Chief Burke, who in addition to being the police chief of the town of Caerphilly was also deputy sheriff of the county. I suspected a ruse.

"He's conducting the investigation from his farm," the chief said. "So if Plunkett wants to stay involved, he's welcome to go out there. Might have to slop a few hogs while he's there. On the sheriff's orders, I've put all my officers back on general patrol here at the fair."

"Where if they happen to run into any information that seems relevant to the murder—"

"They can bring it to me, and I will assess whether it's something the sheriff will want to hear about. Getting back to those allegations of extortion over in Clay County— we'd need to get the state police involved. I can contact them if there's someone willing to stand up and make a charge. If no one's willing—well, accusing another county's law enforcement of corruption's like taking a stick and whacking at a hornet's nest."

"I'll see if I can find at least one victim willing to complain before we let the hornets know we're coming," I said. "It'll be a lot easier if we wait till the end of the fair, when they'll be less afraid of retaliation. And if Randall and I can talk the rest of the fair committee into dumping Clay County from next year's fair."

"That last idea has my vote," the chief said. "And I'll see if our sheriff has any suggestions about how to handle the situation. He's been jousting with Sheriff Dingle a darn sight longer than I have. Might have some good insights."

"As long as they're not old buddies."

"They most definitely are not," he said. "In fact, the only times I can recollect our sheriff using intemperate language were a few occasions when he had to deal with his Clay County counterpart. Keep me posted if you find a witness willing to talk."

With that we hung up, and I headed back to the sheep barn.

I found Michael and Rob trying to swaddle Groucho with what seemed like several acres of hot-pink polyester fabric festooned with matching feathers. Groucho wasn't spitting at them, which I'd have been tempted to do if I were a llama in his situation, but he wasn't cooperating one bit.

"What on earth are you trying to do to the poor beast?" I asked.

"Get his costume on," Rob said. "We're going as pink flamingos."

"Both of you?"

"From what I've seen, the judges really go for it when the llama and his handler have coordinated costumes," Rob said.

Michael held up what appeared to be a jumpsuit made of the same garish pink polyester and feathers—presumably Rob's costume. His mouth was twitching as if he were having a hard time not bursting out laughing.

"Awesome." I resorted to Rob's favorite word. I probably giggled a little as I said it.

"It's not awesome yet," Rob said. "It's a mess. And we only have forty-five minutes till show time"

"Let me try."

It took nearly all of the forty-five minutes, but Michael and I got both Groucho and Rob into their flamingo suits. Then we glued on all the feathers that had come off in the struggle. Groucho made a rather odd-shaped four-legged flamingo, so I improvised a second flamingo head out of surplus polyester and feathers, and attached it to the middle of his back. It bobbed and nodded as he walked, an effect I hoped the judges would find as comical as Michael and I did.

"Cool!" Rob said. "Now there are three of us!"

I'd have felt completely ridiculous doing all of this if not for the fact that throughout the barn, other llama and alpaca owners were stuffing their darlings into equally ridiculous costumes.

When we finally had the flamingos ready, Michael and I collected the boys from the nearby pen where they'd been napping, and we all set off for the show ring.

There were more llamas competing in the costume contest than there had been in the obedience trials. Did people really enjoy dressing up their llamas—and themselves? Or was it merely easier than obedience training?

There were several llamas dressed in brightly colored serapes and sombreros, to pay homage to their South American roots. One golden-brown one was rigged out as a bumblebee, completed with black stripes on his body and huge gossamer wings. One exhibitor dressed each of his four llamas and one alpaca in the uniform of a different branch of the armed forces. I hoped no one in the audience took offense at the fact that he chose the diminutive alpaca to wear the Marine dress blues—although from what I could see, the alpaca was certainly the feistiest of the five. And there were the bride and groom llamas. A dragon llama being led by a helmeted Viking. A llama dressed as Santa, pulling a small, present-filled sleigh. A headless horseman llama. A *QE2* llama led by his tugboat owner. A llama dressed in a black-and-white–striped prison suit, dragging a Styrofoam ball and chain behind him. A llama dressed as a bunch of grapes, featuring dozens of purple balloons.

Michael and the boys and I cheered Rob on to a third-place ribbon, behind the bumblebee and the bunch of grapes. I decided not to depress Rob by saying that they probably wouldn't have placed at all without the third head bobbing maniacally on Groucho's back.

"Silly judges," Josh said, when we met Rob outside the ring. "Groucho is the best llama."

"Yeah, but your uncle Rob isn't the best costume designer," Rob said. "Meg, you think next time you could help me plan it? Your head totally won us the yellow. Maybe if we'd enlisted you earlier, we'd have scored a first."

"I have some ideas," I said. "Let's talk after the fair is over."

"Awesome!" Rob turned to the boys. "Come on, junior llama wranglers. Let's go back to the barn and celebrate. But you've got to help me hold on to Groucho."

He waved and strolled off with both boys clinging fiercely to the lead rope.

"Do you really have time to take up llama costuming?" Michael asked.

"No, but if I play my cards right, I can get Mother interested in it," I said. "And if she balks, I can probably enlist Rose Noire."

"Good plan," he said. "Incidentally, Rob agreed to baby-sit for a few hours if I helped him with Groucho's costume, so now we have some time off. Want to go someplace nice for dinner?"

I didn't even have to think about it.

"No," I said, with a sigh. "We'd have to clean up and drive somewhere and mind our manners while we wait for our food. I don't have the energy for that. I just want to go over to the Midway and have an Italian sausage topped with a mountain of onions and green peppers and then skulk around for a while to see if I can catch any of the Clay County deputies in the act of extorting from the Midway vendors."

Michael blinked.

"Okay," he said. "I like those Italian sausages, too, and I have to admit it will be easier. But do you seriously suspect the Clay County deputies of committing extortion, or have they just been getting on your nerves lately?"

"Both, actually. I'll fill you in on the way there."

By the time we reached the Italian sausage booth, Michael was just as outraged at Deputy Plunkett as I was. Just as outraged, but a lot less sanguine about our chances of bringing him to justice.

"You can't solve everyone's problems, you know," he said, as we strolled along, trying not to wolf down our sausages.

"Right now, it feels as if I can't solve anyone's problems."

"You've helped Molly."

"I've helped her find a divorce attorney and a defense attorney," I said. "I wish I could find a way to help her that wasn't going to cost her a lot of money. I can't track down the missing chickens. Chief Burke would have my head if I tried to barge into his murder investigation. But this I might be able to do something about."

So we strolled up and down, chatting up the vendors as we bought food and played games. Michael won a stuffed penguin. We spent way too much money trying to win a matching one before giving up and deciding to give it to Rose Noire, who was fond of penguins.

We didn't find any carnies ready to give evidence against Plunkett and the other rogue Clay County deputies, but we did find a few people who said they'd think about it. We got a lesson from a friendly barker on which games were least stacked against the customer, and a tutorial on running the Ferris wheel from the carny in charge of it. I took dozens of dramatic shots of the nighttime Midway—especially the Ferris wheel and the merry-go-round—for possible use on the fair Web site. At about eleven or so, we both hit the wall.

"I think that's as far as we'll get tonight," Michael said.

"And I just had a horrible thought—are we going on patrol after this?"

"No," I said. "I gave us the night off. After all, we were up most of last night."

"Not to mention how you've been running yourself ragged all day." Michael stifled a yawn. "But who's going to supervise the patrols?"

"Vern," I said. "Who is also off duty tonight, but doesn't mind having an excuse for hanging around."

"Good man. Want to split a funnel cake before we head back to the barn?"

"You're on," I said. "But you're going the wrong way— funnel cake's this way."

"Are you sure?"

I was. And I was right. By now, I had a pretty good mental map of the Midway in my mind. It was actually pretty small: three rough lanes lined with booths and rides, anchored at one end by the merry-go-round and on the other—the end farthest from the fence—by the Ferris wheel. Either by accident or design, the lanes were crooked enough that you couldn't see all the way up or down any of them. The little zigs and zags meant you were constantly turning the corner to see new vistas, and gave the impression the place was a lot bigger.

Michael was impressed that I led him unerringly to the funnel cake concession. I thought it was a lot more impressive that I could, if asked, tell you exactly what, if anything, we'd learned from every carny we'd talked to and where they stood on the question of testifying against Plunkett. Ringtoss? Played dumb. Taco stand? Mad as hell but afraid of talking. Funnel cake? Thinking about it.

I'd figured out that some of the booths were owned by the company we'd hired and staffed by their employees, while others were independent contractors. The independents seemed more willing to consider speaking up—probably because they could choose not to come back to an event in Clay County, while the employees might have no way to refuse an assignment if they wanted to keep their jobs. Would it help if I contacted the company and let them know what I suspected? I decided to talk it over with Randall first.

Michael and I saved a small bit of funnel cake in case the boys spotted the telltale splashes of powdered sugar and demanded their share. When we arrived back at the barn, we found that Rob had already tucked them in bed in our stall. We let them nibble their bits of funnel cake as a bedtime snack, and after a quick toothbrushing, they drifted off to sleep, with Spike and Tinkerbell curled up beside them and the llamas leaning over the fence to watch.

Then we tried to settle down ourselves. As usual, Michael dropped off to sleep almost immediately. I lay there, listening to his not-quite-snores and the quiet breathing of the boys, the dogs, the llamas, and the countless sheep in the stalls surrounding us. My eyelids were so heavy I couldn't keep them up. My body ached with tiredness. My brain was foggy from lack of sleep.

Why couldn't I sleep?

I tried to toss and turn quietly, to avoid waking all the sleepers around me. I lay there, thinking about the events of the day. No, not thinking: fretting.

"This isn't going to work," I told myself.

I got up and tore a page out of my notebook. I scribbled "Checking on the patrols," on it and put it on my pillow, so Michael would see it if he woke and not worry. Then I set out to walk the fair.

Chapter 32

I ran into some of my patrol volunteers almost immediately, just outside the pig barn. I turned on my flashlight and saw that three of them had arranged folding lawn chairs in a semicircle around a large cooler. They all had beers in their hands and their feet propped up on the cooler.

"I thought you guys were on the early patrol," I said.

Two of them shifted uneasily, but the third just shook his head.

"We're going to keep watch from here," he said. "No sense prowling up and down the whole fair. From what I hear, chicken thief's got his comeuppance."

"You think he deserved to die for stealing a few bantams?" one of the others asked.

"No," the first one said. "But sounds like that wasn't the only thing he got up to."

"He's getting a bum rap, if you ask me," the third one said. "She's the one who stole the chickens."

"His wife?"

"No, the girlfriend. And she tucked her tail between her legs and ran home, so we don't need to worry about her."

"She was the one who wanted the chickens," the first one said. "And maybe she egged him on to do it. But if you think she did it herself, you're crazy. No way she'd pull it off."

"She prefers to delegate," I put in.

"That's it," the first one said, nodding. "She doesn't do what she can delegate. And she doesn't have anyone around here to delegate to anymore, so the birds are safe."

"And our pigs," the third one added.

"And we aim to keep them that way," said the second.

"You did hear that there was another theft in the chicken tent late this afternoon, didn't you?" I asked.

They paused to consider that for a few moments.

"Could be an inside job," one said. "You might want to see if they have the birds insured."

"Or maybe it was a friend of that Riordan guy," another said. "Someone who didn't want to see him blamed for the thefts. What better way than to stage another theft that his dead friend couldn't possibly have pulled off?"

"Yeah, death's the ultimate alibi," the first one said.

"It was another chicken theft, right?" the third asked. "Seems pretty clear to me the thief's after chickens."

"They're a lot easier to steal than pigs or cows," the first said.

The other two nodded and mumbled agreement.

I was annoyed but after talking with them for a few minutes, I could tell that they'd been working on the contents of the cooler for a while. Better to have a few sober patrols than a whole herd of drunks careening around the fair. So I bit back both the recriminations I wanted to hurl at them and the pep talk I'd considered administering. I turned off my flashlight, wished them a good evening, and moved on.

I ran into another group of volunteers taking an extended coffee break in one of the vacant tents by the food stands. Another bunch were playing poker near the front gate. It was bridge at the back entrance to the chicken tent, and a tape of *A Prairie Home Companion* show at the front entrance. More beer drinkers and a Monopoly game outside the duck and goose tent.

I had to admit, things seemed peaceful. Of course, things had seemed that way last night, up to the point when Brett had been murdered. And this had been my original idea. Instead of having the patrols wander around, station them at every entrance to every building we wanted to protect and couldn't lock up tight. Maybe I should have stuck to it. The pig farmers weren't going anywhere, and they weren't going to let any unknown person pass.

I felt a little better.

But no sleepier than before.

So I continued to prowl. We'd chained and padlocked the arts and crafts barn and the farmers' market barn, so I tested all the padlocks. And then I continued making the rounds, checking to see that there was at least one wide-awake volunteer at the front and back doors of each barn and tent.

It suddenly occurred to me that while the barns were solidly built, with no windows and only the two doors, the tents were . . . well, tents. Wouldn't it be possible for someone to slip into a tent by ducking under the side, or maybe even cutting a slit in the canvas?

I was passing the chicken tent when this thought occurred to me. I nodded to the volunteers, who were singing along with Garrison Keillor, and turned down the narrow space between the chicken tent and the duck and goose tent.

Of course, maybe the chicken tent wasn't the best place to test, because the volunteers here should logically be on high alert. The pig farmers might be complacent, but the chicken owners had just had a graphic demonstration that their birds were highly vulnerable. Maybe I should test someplace else.

But I was here already. So I stopped at the middle of the tent side, or as close to it as I could calculate. As far as possible from the volunteer guards on either end. I tested the canvas.

It wasn't fastened down, and it was loose. Loose enough to crawl under?

I got down and tried. It was a tight fit, but I made it.

I stood up inside the tent, fully expecting to be pounced on by volunteers from one or both entrances.

Nothing happened.

I could hear an occasional cluck or squawk, and one soft human snore, over to my right.

So much for relying on the guards at the tent entrances. The tents were vulnerable, unless some of the owners had decided to set up an ambush for potential thieves. I had to stifle a giggle at the thought of the Bonnevilles, still wearing their elaborate mourning, crouching in the dark behind the bantam cages in hopes of pouncing on the returning chicken thief.

I stepped a little farther into the tent, still expecting—or at least hoping—that someone would tackle me or shine a flashlight beam into my eyes.

Nothing. The tent was—well, not empty, but there was, as the saying goes, nobody here but us chickens. And, judging from the snores, maybe one tired chicken farmer who'd been trying to keep watch inside and fallen asleep.

Or was there someone else here? I thought I saw movement out of the corner of my eye. I stepped carefully into the nearest area of deep shadow and stood, breathing as quietly as I could, listening.

Was I only imagining soft footfalls at the other end of

the tent, barely more than a rustling on the straw that covered the ground?

Then I saw a brief flash of light—probably the beam of a flashlight, turned on so the holder could get his bearings and then off again as fast as possible. It was on my left, near the back entrance of the tent.

I held my breath and began slipping down the right-hand aisle, which I thought would let me reach the place where the flash had been with the least chance of being seen. As I passed their cages, a few of the chickens roused slightly and clucked or squawked. Rose Noire would probably have advised me to calm them by beaming comforting thoughts about plentiful feed and warm nests. I just tried to walk as softly as I could.

I had reached the end of the tent where the bantam fowl were kept. I could see well enough now to make out a shadowy form in one corner. A tall form. And oddly shaped. Was the midnight chicken thief a hunchback?

I heard a slight metallic noise. Someone opening the latch on a cage? And then a faint squawk, soon muffled.

I stopped, aimed my flashlight at where the noise was coming from, and turned it on.

Genette. She had frozen when the beam hit her, with a startled look on her face. She was wearing all black— formfitting black leggings, black suede ankle boots, a hooded black jacket, and gauntlet-style black gloves. She even had a snazzy little black suede purse slung over one shoulder. About the only sour note in her outfit was the black plastic trash bag slung over the other shoulder—a bag that was writhing and squawking slightly. In one hand she held a small, copper-colored chicken—probably a Nankin, according to the part of my brain that had been studying chicken breeds so assiduously. She was holding the chicken's beak closed with her fingers to keep her from making noise, and the poor creature seemed too sleep-befuddled to put up much resistance when Genette moved again and stuffed her into the mouth of the bag.

"Unhand that chicken," I said. "And drop the bag."

I wasn't really expecting cooperation, so I wasn't taken by surprise when Genette turned and fled down the far aisle. I gave chase. I had the flashlight, and kept the beam down low, so it helped me more than it did her. I could hear her bumping into cages as she ran. About halfway down the aisle, she whirled and threw the garbage bag at me. It missed, but I had to swerve to avoid trampling the chickens in it.

Near the tent entrance, I finally caught up with Genette and brought her down with a clumsy but effective tackle.

I tried to pin her to the ground, but she wriggled onto her back and slashed at my face with her nails.

I punched her in the jaw. Oddly, she screamed before the blow landed.

"Owwwwww!"

She curled up into a fetal position. I scrambled to my feet and took a step back, so I was close enough to do something if she made another break for it, but not close enough for her to reach me easily.

I could feel blood running down my face. I reached up to see how bad the scratches were, and encountered a foreign object stuck into my cheek. I held it up to the light from my flashlight. A fake nail. At least part of it was fake. Maybe there was some real nail stuck to the long clawlike bit of acrylic. I dropped it in distaste.

"You broke my nail!" Genette keened. "Do you know how much that hurts?"

At least I think she said hurts. Her voice was muffled,

so it could just as easily have been "Do you know how much that costs?"

"A broken nail can't possibly hurt you as much as it would have hurt me if you succeeded in scratching my eyes out." I had pulled out my cell phone. It was hard to dial with the hand that was still holding the flashlight, but I managed. After all, 911 is a pretty short dial.

"I'm in the chicken tent," I said when Debbie Ann answered. "I've caught the thief."

"I'm not the thief!" Genette wailed.

Just then one of the Nankins who'd apparently escaped from the bag popped into the pool of light from the flashlight, took one look at Genette, and left, squawking.

"I rest my case," I said.

"What's going on here?"

A man holding a fistful of Monopoly money in one hand and a flashlight in the other was standing in the aisles.

"I caught her stealing chickens," I said.

"I wasn't stealing," Genette said. "I was going to leave some cash to pay for them."

"Yeah, right," the man said. Two more people loomed up behind him.

"What are they doing here?" one asked.

"Meg caught the chicken thief," someone answered.

"Chicken purchaser," Genette insisted.

"'Chicken purchaser'?" I echoed. "Was there a reason you couldn't come by in the daytime to discuss the terms of the sale with the owners?"

"They were so stubborn," she said.

"Then I guess they don't want to sell."

"Damn straight we don't," one of the volunteers said.

"Not to her," another volunteer added.

"It was idiotic—I was offering them three times what

the silly birds were worth. I can't believe they turned it down."

I could, easily.

"That's their right," I said. "Where did you put the Orloffs and the Sumatrans?"

"I didn't take any of them," she said. "I just figured if everyone else was stealing chickens, why not?"

I was opening my mouth to say how ridiculous that was when Vern Shiffley strode into the tent.

"What's going on here?" he asked.

"Chicken thief," I said. "She's all yours."

Chapter 33

It was a great exit line. Too bad I didn't actually get to exit after it. I had to explain to Vern how I came to be in the tent and what I'd seen Genette doing. I wouldn't have minded if I hadn't known I'd have to explain it all over again when the chief arrived.

"So what's your side of the story?" Vern asked Genette.

"I wasn't stealing anything," she said.

"Then what were you doing here?"

"I left something here in my booth, and I had to come back to get it." She was batting her eyes and trying to look helpless. "Silly me! I guess in the dark I must have wandered into the wrong tent."

"Looks more like you cut a slit in the wrong tent and crawled in," Vern said.

"I didn't want to run into any of the other winemakers," she said. "They all hate me."

"Not surprising," Vern said. "Have you been slicing up the sides of their tent?"

They went back and forth about that for a few minutes before she changed her angle.

"You see, I heard a noise in here," she said. "And I was sneaking in to see if I could catch whoever was in here red-handed. And when I came in here, she was here—stuffing chickens into that bag!"

She pointed to me with a triumphant look on her face. Vern and I looked at each other.

"She gets points for gall," I said. "None for brains."

"It's my word against hers," Genette said.

"No, it's not," came a hollow voice from behind us. We all started—even Vern—and I think he clapped his hand to his gun when he saw that one of the trash barrels lined up against the other side of the tent had begun to rise straight up into the air.

Then I realized that the trash can had legs. Short, stubby, black-clad legs.

Mr. Bonneville heaved the trash can off his head and turned to lift the trash can next to him, revealing Mrs. Bonneville. They were both wearing new-looking black tracksuits.

"We were staking out the tent," Mrs. Bonneville said.

"We had a feeling the thief would come back," her husband added. "And we saw the whole thing."

"From your trash cans?" Genette said. "How could you see anything?"

Mr. Bonneville picked up one of the trash cans, stuck his hand into it, and wiggled two fingers out of a couple of conveniently cut peepholes.

"Well?" Vern was looking at Genette.

Her mouth hung open for a few minutes.

"Well they weren't the only ones who were suspicious," she finally said. "The guy who owns these chickens—he had a quarrel with Brett. And I think he's the one who killed him. So I came in to kidnap his chickens. I was going to hold them for ransom until he came forward and confessed."

She smiled, crossed her arms, and looked very pleased with herself.

"Of all the—" Vern began.

"What in blue blazes is going on here?"

The chief had arrived, accompanied by another deputy.

"Chicken thief." Vern knew how the chief appreciated brevity in his officer's reports. "Caught red-handed by a reliable witness," he added, indicating me.

"But I just told you—" Genette began.

"Yes, I heard your assertions," the chief said. "Very interesting. I'd like to discuss them in more detail."

Genette wilted slightly.

"Aida, you secure things here," he said to the deputy at his side. "Take initial statements from Mr. and Mrs. Bonneville and then bring them over to the fair office in half an hour or so. Ms. Langslow, can you come along with us now?"

So Genette, Vern, the chief, and I trudged over to the fair office. I unlocked it, and we all took seats around my desk. Once we were all in the close quarters of the trailer I realized that Genette had been drinking again. Something with gin in it, by the smell.

"So, Ms. Sedgewick," the chief began. "Would you like to tell me how you came to find yourself in the chicken tent at midnight?"

She looked back at him, frowning slightly, as if puzzled.

"Maybe I should talk to my attorney first," she said.

"That's your right." The chief very deliberately put his notebook down on the table, placed his pen on the table beside it, and folded his hands atop the notebook. "If you're refusing to talk without an attorney present, I can let you call now, and then we'll take you down to the jail to await his or her arrival."

"Jail? I'm not refusing to talk to you," she said. "I just want to talk to him before I talk to you. Where's my cell phone?"

She patted several pants and jacket pockets and then,

when the cell phone didn't appear, she unslung the chic little purse and began pawing through it and dumping the contents on my desk.

The chief watched her over his glasses with a tight-lipped expression. He was drumming his fingers on the table, ever so softly. He probably thought he was concealing his impatience pretty well. Maybe he was to someone who didn't know him.

Then his expression changed.

"Ms. Sedgewick." Something about his tone made her look up and freeze.

He reached out with his pen and snagged something from the litter of things that had landed on the desk.

"What is this?" He was holding a key ring on the end of the pen.

"My keys." She sounded puzzled.

We all stared for a few moments at the small tangle of metal dangling from the chief's pen. Half a dozen keys, and a miniature beer can.

The chief dropped the key ring back on the table.

"Then what is this?" He fished into the litter with the pen and picked up a second key ring.

"Also my keys," Genette said. "The first one was Brett's key chain. That's mine."

"Then why did you say they were your keys?"

"It was Brett's key chain, but most of the keys were to my stuff," she said. "My house, my boat house, my car, my truck."

"Why is Mr. Riordan's key ring in your purse?" the chief asked.

"I keep it there for Brett sometimes," she said. "He loses things."

"What make is your truck?" the chief asked.

She frowned slightly as if puzzled by the question.

"Ms. Sedgewick," the chief began.

"A Ford," she said. "I don't see what that has to do with anything."

"And your car?"

"A Mercedes."

"This Mazda key would be for Mr. Riordan's car, then?" He was holding up Brett's key ring.

"I assume it is," she said. "That's his key ring."

"And the Dodge key?"

"How should I know?" She rolled her eyes and sighed in exasperation. "It's *his* key ring."

"A Dodge Caravan, maybe?" I asked.

Genette shrugged. Either she didn't know that the murder weapon had been found in Molly's Dodge Caravan or she was pretending not to.

"Keep looking for your cell phone," the chief said. "You'll be needing that lawyer."

Chapter 34

After the discovery of the two key rings, Genette decided maybe she'd rather wait for her lawyer after all and Vern hauled her off to the jail. The chief thanked me for my cooperation and announced that he was heading over to the chicken tent to talk to the Bonnevilles before following Vern.

"This is going to help Molly, isn't it?" I asked the chief. "The fact that someone with a real reason to dislike her had access to the van where the murder weapon was found."

He frowned, and I realized I'd probably stuck my nose in too far. Then the frown vanished.

"It certainly doesn't hurt," he said. "Now get some sleep."

Easier said than done. I didn't feel one bit sleepy. Exhausted, yes, but too wired to sleep. If I went back to the barn, I'd toss and turn and keep everyone up. Even Seth Early's sheep, who needed their beauty sleep for tomorrow's competition.

I flipped off the harsh overhead fluorescent light, which was almost as glaring as a bare lightbulb would have been. I waited a moment for my eyes to adjust, then walked back to my desk and turned on the table lamp there. The warm circle of light was strangely comforting.

I sat down in the swivel chair and leaned back. Maybe if I stayed here for a little while and did my yoga deep breathing, I would start to feel sleepy.

I gave up after a few breaths. I was too wired. I kept wondering if the chief was interrogating Genette. More likely he was standing by until Genette's attorney arrived. No doubt some highly paid defense attorney was even now being roused from slumber, or perhaps already speeding toward Caerphilly. I couldn't see the chief waking one of the local judges at this hour to preside over a bail hearing, so Genette was probably spending the night in a cell. She was lucky Caerphilly had finally regained possession of its police station and jail. Last year this time, the police had been temporarily quartered in Dad's barn, and Genette would have spent her night in a padlocked box stall. We'd actually had one upscale prisoner who found the experience quaint and charming, but I didn't think Genette would feel that way.

To my surprise, I found I felt just a little bit sorry for Genette. Not because she'd probably have to spend a few hours in jail. She deserved that. But she'd probably be spending most of the day being interrogated by the chief, and odds were he'd spend a whole lot more time trying to find information to prove that she'd murdered Brett than talking about chickens.

And I had the sinking feeling he was wasting his time. I didn't really think Genette had murdered Brett.

Which made no sense. I didn't like the woman. I didn't trust her an inch. She was a home wrecker, a bully, and a chicken thief. She had reason to know what Molly's van looked like, and access to it to plant the gun. And I didn't have any trouble imagining her as a killer.

I just had a hard time imagining her killing Brett. He was too useful to her. And from what I could see, her surprise and dismay at learning he'd fathered a child with another woman seemed too genuine. Maybe I was deluding myself, but I had a hard time believing Genette was that good an actor.

"She didn't kill him," I muttered.

Of course, my believing in her innocence wouldn't count for much if I couldn't prove it. And I couldn't do that any more than I could prove Molly's innocence. As things stood, both women were still under suspicion, and even if the chief could gather enough untainted evidence to take one of them to trial, either woman could probably get off on reasonable doubt as long as the other hadn't been definitively proven innocent. Of course, getting off didn't mean that either of them would have her reputation restored. They'd both live under a cloud of suspicion for the rest of their lives.

Unless someone found out who had really killed Brett.

I tried to tell myself that that was the chief's job. That mine was to help run the fair, and that I'd probably handle that job a heck of a lot better if I got at least a little sleep. That maybe if I dozed off while thinking about the murder my brain would keep working while I slept and I'd wake up with important new insights about the case.

I closed my eyes and tried to concentrate.

It wasn't working.

I gave up and turned on my laptop. For want of anything else useful to do, I opened up my database of exhibitors and reread everything I had on file about Genette. And then my record on Molly. Nothing jumped out at me as useful. I didn't have a record on Paul Morot, but I did an Internet search for the Fickle Wind Winery and found where it had been located.

I called up my map of where the exhibitors had come from. Molly's dot was off by itself but the now-defunct Fickle Wind Winery was in the midst of a fairly dense cluster of other exhibitors. Other winemakers. Including Genette, of course.

I wasn't sure why I was focused on Morot so much. He certainly wasn't the only winemaker who had a reason to hate Genette. Just the one I knew about.

If I were the chief, I'd look very closely at all the winemakers. They all knew each other. And all hated Genette. And probably, by extension, Brett. Would they cover for each other if they thought one of their own had killed him?

And it wasn't just the winemakers here at the fair. There could be others who weren't exhibiting. Or others like Morot who weren't technically winemakers anymore but were still part of the close-knit community.

And what should I make of the fact that even one of the winemakers was suspicious of Morot?

Mother would know. She'd become a part of that close-knit community. She might know who else had been hurt by Genette, or even driven out of business. I should talk to her. Correction: Suggest that the chief talk to her.

Tomorrow. In the meantime, I opened my browser and did an Internet search on Genette. I wasn't sure what I was looking for. Maybe that was a good thing. If I'd had a definite goal in mind, I'd have gotten frustrated pretty quickly. Most of the articles I found were puff pieces published in her local weekly paper. Either she and the publisher were buddies or she was a major advertiser.

I wasn't finding anything, but I kept going, because the search was so dull it was bringing me closer to sleep than I'd been for hours. I stared at picture after picture of Genette. Genette hosting wine tastings. Genette hosting concerts. Genette winning ribbons at her county fair, although a visit to the fair's Web site proved they were fourth place and honorable mention ribbons. Pictures of Genette with various dignitaries. She had a habit of striking the same pose and smiling the same overwide toothy smile, so consistent that you could have cut her out of any picture and pasted her into any other and barely notice the difference.

It was almost interesting when I came across a June article in a Richmond paper about the upcoming fair being held on Genette's land. The fair Brett was supposed to be organizing, although there was no mention of him in the article. Maybe my suspicions were right, and Genette had involved him in a futile attempt to avoid tainting the event with her unpopularity. If I'd been trying to do that, I'd have found a front man who was well known and above reproach, or at least someone not known to be committing adultery with me. Genette had to use what she had, and what she had was Brett.

I narrowed my search by adding the words "agricultural exposition" to Genette's name, just to see if I could figure out when she'd started using Brett as a figurehead.

The second article I came across had only a minor mention of Genette—it was mostly about Clay County's attempt to put on its own fair, with a roundup at the end about other contending fairs, like ours and Genette's. I had to laugh because the article featured a picture of a group of Clay County notables at what the article claimed was the breaking ground ceremony for the construction of the Clay County Fairgrounds. I remembered hearing about it at the time—they'd staged the whole thing in what was still a swampy field on Sheriff Dingle's hog farm.

I studied the photo. Sheriff Dingle was there standing behind his brother-in-law, the county board chairman, who was pretending to dig up the first shovelful of earth. I didn't recognize most of the others, but their faces looked familiar. Probably other Dingles along with a few Plunketts, Peebleses, and Whickers. Those four names accounted for at least two-thirds of the Clay County phone book. Deputy Plunkett was there, smiling broadly.

And right beside him was a familiar sharp-nosed face.

I zoomed in on that part of the picture. It was her—the self-proclaimed mother of Brett Riordan's out-of-wedlock child. She had blond hair pulled back into a ponytail—evidently the unruly mop of brown hair had been a wig. But I recognized her. And Horace and I had gotten the ski-jump nose right. So there, Deputy Plunkett.

Of course, he probably knew that. He had to have met her before. In the picture, she was smiling, and had one arm around him and the other around a man whose shape and features suggested he was either a Dingle or a Plunkett.

And so was she. I checked the caption and counted over the list of names until I figured out which one she was. Aurelia Plunkett Dingle. A Dingle *and* a Plunkett.

I searched for her name and came up with a two-year-old account of her wedding, from the *Clay County Advertiser,* their local weekly. She and her husband—also her third cousin, and one of the sheriff's nephews—had moved after the wedding to West Virginia, where the groom was studying agriculture at Pineville College. That probably accounted for the fact that I hadn't seen her around before. But not the fact that Plunkett hadn't recognized my description of her, or the sketches Horace and I had come up with. The ski-jump nose wasn't unattractive—in fact, in the posed wedding photo, it looked curiously elegant. But it was absolutely distinctive. And the sketches we'd made with Horace's software program were dead on. Plunkett had lied.

"It's a setup," I muttered. I'd bet anything the woman hadn't had an affair with Brett. I suddenly realized something that should have occurred to me when I'd witnessed her scene with Genette. The supposed unwed mother mentioned "the baby"—but she hadn't given the offstage child a name. A mother would name her child. And she hadn't even brought the baby along. Why not? A cooing or howling infant would be much more effective in shaming Genette and enlisting the sympathy of the onlookers. But I was willing to bet there was no baby. She'd simply gone to the Caerphilly Inn to stage a scene—a totally fake scene that would shift suspicion in the murder case onto Genette. But why?

Possibly to make sure the rival fair Genette was organizing would fail. I suspected from my snooping over in the Midway that the Clay County powers-that-be were only pretending to be content with the tax revenue from the Midway. If they were planning to revive their plans for a Clay County fair, Brett's murder gave them a golden opportunity to throw a wrench in the plans of one of their main rivals. Or maybe two of their rivals—having a murder happen on our grounds wasn't going to do the Un-fair any good.

Was it an opportunity they'd seized or one they'd created?

"Ridiculous," I said aloud. Surely no one would really commit murder over the fair.

But it wasn't the fair. It was all about the money. Caerphilly was moving past its financial crisis, but Clay County was still mired deep. They'd never been prosperous, thanks in no small part to nepotism and incompetence, so the downturn had been that much harder for them. And everyone in Caerphilly knew it. It was why we included them in the Un-fair—so they'd have a chance to share in whatever prosperity the event might bring. And maybe I shouldn't have been surprised that a lot of people in Clay County seemed to feel resentment rather than gratitude.

What if that hadn't been enough for them? Plunkett had told at least one Midway barker that the fair would be in Clay County next year. What if they thought the way to make that happen was to get rid of some of the competition? And had knocked off Brett because they thought he really was the organizer of the Virginia Agricultural Exposition? Or maybe they meant to kill Genette and got Brett by mistake. Either way, they could have sent the supposed unwed mother to make a scene that would draw suspicion back onto Genette—not because they had something against Genette, but because framing her would be a lot more useful to their cause than framing Molly. And Genette's attempt at chicken theft had tightened the noose around her own neck, playing right into their hands.

They. I was starting to sound like a conspiracy theorist. And even if there was a conspiracy, somebody's hand had to have been holding the gun. To convict anybody, the chief would have to put a name to that hand.

The chief would also have to find a way around all the problems with the evidence. And if someone from Clay County was involved, maybe Deputy Plunkett wasn't quite the idiot we all thought he was. What if he was deliberately tainting as much of the evidence as he could—literally— get his hands on? It made sense if he knew that someone from Clay County was involved.

And even more sense if it had been his own hand holding the gun.

He'd appeared at the crime scene awfully quickly. He could have gone away long enough to conceal the murder weapon, and then come back to make his attempt to control the crime scene. Had he been alarmed when Caerphilly had succeeded in asserting jurisdiction? Or had he been secretly gloating, because he thought with us in charge his cover-up would be all the more believable?

Maybe he hadn't even hidden the gun. Maybe he'd had it with him all the time, ready to dispose of when he got a chance. And by allowing him to help with the search of Molly's van, Vern had unwittingly handed him a perfect opportunity not just to dispose of it but to plant it where it would divert suspicion from him. He hadn't failed to lift the floor mats—he'd lifted them all right—to put the gun there. And then he'd wandered off, pretending to need a smoke, leaving it for Vern to find.

And the bantam feathers in Brett's car. Plunkett actually found those. He could have collected them by skulking around the chicken tent, but I would have bet anything that he'd taken the Russian Orloffs and hidden them somewhere. Although it might take some doing to search all the Dingle, Plunkett, Peebles, and Whicker farms in Clay County to find them.

Suddenly I felt curiously anxious and exposed in the brightly lit trailer, so close to the scene of the murder. I whirled to look out the window behind my desk, but all I saw was my own reflection. I turned off the desk lamp and felt a little better with just the glow of the monitor lighting the room. And better still when I checked both that window and the other and saw nothing but the empty field around me and the barns in the distance.

But it was still a little creepy here, and past time for me to get back to the barns.

I hit my printer's on button and printed out the two articles—the one with the groundbreaking ceremony, and Aurelia's wedding piece. I waited impatiently while the pages chugged out of the printer. Then I folded them and stuffed them into the back pocket of my jeans. I turned off the printer and the computer and stepped out of the stuffy little trailer.

And out into the night, which was dark and velvety and pleasantly mild after the heat of the day. I could hear a stray cow mooing over in the barns. I suddenly felt calmer. I pulled out my cell phone to call the chief.

The chief, or 911? Debbie Ann would probably turn right around and call the chief. I could save hassle by calling him directly. Then again, if he had gone home to get some sleep, better to let Debbie Ann do the waking. Besides—

Something struck my hand, hard, and the cell phone flew out of my grasp and landed somewhere with a barely audible thump. And I could feel something metallic pressed against the back of my neck.

Chapter 35

"What are you—" I began.

"Sssshhh. You don't want to make a fuss." Plunkett. "You'd be surprised how many vital body parts run through the neck. Almost impossible not to hit at least one of them if this gun should go off, accidental-like."

I thought of telling him how much I hated mealy-mouthed people, and how much I'd rather he just came right out and said, "Shut up or I'll shoot." But I could think of only one thing stupider than ticking off a man holding a loaded gun to my spine, and that was provoking him to hearty laughter.

"I want you to know I'm not trying to get fresh," he said. "But I need to see what you stuck in your pocket."

I felt his finger reaching into my back pocket, and pulling out the folded printouts. Then I heard the faint crackle as he unfolded them.

He sighed.

"Dammit," he said. "I told Reely to be careful. To pick a dark spot and put on enough makeup so that she couldn't be recognized. She should have listened."

Actually, she should have explained to him that nothing short of plastic surgery could hide her very distinctive nose.

I heard another bit of crackling, presumably as he stuffed the crumpled sheets of paper into his own pocket.

"Get moving," he said. "Slow and sure, now. You don't want this thing to go off prematurely."

He chuckled as if he'd said something hilarious. Maybe he had. I wasn't in the best frame of mind to judge. All I knew was that I could really learn to dislike the sound of his chuckle. The pressure on the back of my neck increased, and I took a step forward, then another. He steered me with a gentle nudge against the left or right side of my neck. We were heading for the Midway. Away from the populated part of the fair.

My brain was racing frantically, although so far it hadn't come up with anything more useful than a graphic picture of what the bullet would do if he fired the gun. He was holding it at an upward angle, so if it missed the spinal cord it'd head for the brain. I didn't like the odds.

"And how do you plan to explain away my death?" I asked. "Genette's in custody. And if you were planning on framing Molly again—well, never mind."

I was trying to give the impression that I knew Molly was alibied. I probably just gave the impression that I was getting frantic.

"I figure I'll just wait and see who your chief seems to be suspecting and plant the gun in some useful place," Plunkett said. "Worked just fine with Riordan."

"Is that the way you do things over in Clay County?" I asked.

"Pretty much."

"I have to give you credit for nerves of steel." I tried to make my tone sound like grudging admiration. "You had the murder weapon in your pocket the whole time, didn't you? At the crime scene, I mean."

"Yup." There was that annoying chuckle again. "And straight-arrow Vern never even suspected I planted it."

So now I knew, just in case I had any doubts, that I was right about who killed Brett. Of course, now I also knew he had no intention of letting me stay alive to share that information.

Every step took us farther away from the barns, the most likely source of help. And I figured that once we got through the gate into the Midway, my odds of successfully getting away from him got much worse.

But he realized that, too. The closer we got to the gate, the more alert he seemed to every bit of rough ground, every misstep.

Was he just a little on edge at passing so close to the place where he'd killed Brett?

No, I decided. He was on edge because we were getting close to the gate. He thought he was home free once we were through the gate, and he was expecting me to make a break for it on the Caerphilly side. I could use that. I hoped.

"Is it just because of the fair?" I asked.

"'*Just* because of the fair,'" he echoed. "You people have no idea what you've done, have you? You killed our chances of putting on our own fair, and then threw us the Midway as a bone."

"The sales tax revenue from the Midway—" I began.

"Yeah, the sales tax money's nice. Helps a bit with the county budget. It'd help a lot more if we got the lion's share of the revenue."

"You *are* getting the lion's share of the revenue."

"Yeah, right," he said. "I've seen the attendance numbers. And I know what a ticket costs. You're taking in a pretty penny at the gate. Not to mention the competition entry fees."

"Yeah, Caerphilly's getting the admission fees," I said. "But we're still paying for the construction. We have water bills. Power bills. Portapotty bills. And maybe even huge legal fees if those people whose chickens you stole decide to sue us. Take me back to the fair office and I can show you the figures. We might not even break even."

"On paper," he said. "We all know the big money's in the kickbacks."

"Kickbacks?"

"Keep it down." He prodded me with the gun. "Yeah, kickbacks. I know how these things work."

"In Clay County, maybe," I said.

"You have no idea how things work over in Clay County." Plunkett suddenly sounded furious, and the gun was digging into my back. "We're dying by inches over there. Did you know they're laying off almost our whole sheriff's department at the end of the month? All except Sheriff Dingle's son and two of the mayor's nephews. They're only gonna patrol from eight to five. The rest of us are out on our ears, and I'm betting we never see our final paychecks. They're already six weeks behind. I'm already driving a piece of junk since the bank repo'd my pickup, and the mortgage company is breathing down my neck something fierce. So I decided to do something."

"I'm not sure how killing Brett Riordan solves the Clay County budget problem," I said.

"Maybe it doesn't." To my relief, he sounded calmer. "But I figure it brought down two rival fairs with one bullet. Gives us a much better chance at floating our event again. And even if that doesn't work out, it should solve my personal budget problem. Like I said, I haven't decided who should take the heat for killing you, but when I figure out and bring him in, I figure I'm a shoo-in for a job as a Caerphilly County deputy."

Either the chief was much better at hiding his feelings than even I imagined, or Plunkett was terrible at reading people's reactions to him. Possibly both.

"Hey, maybe I should frame Vern Shiffley," Plunkett said. "Create a vacancy in the ranks and prove myself the best man to fill it, with the same bullet. Pretty efficient, don't you think?"

There was that annoying psycho chuckle again. We were through the gate now, and he seemed more relaxed now that he was back on home ground. The end of the gun barrel wobbled a little as he laughed.

I ducked my head and stomped on his foot, hard, while turning to grab for the gun. I succeeded in getting loose without being shot, and I even managed to knock the gun out of his hand, but it skittered off to his left. I was on his right. I didn't fancy my chances of beating him to it. In fact, his hand was already on it.

So I kicked him in the face to distract him and slow him down, and then I took off at a run. I managed to put a row of Midway booths between me and him. I hid in the shadows of a booth until my breathing slowed. Then I started out again, keeping my footsteps as quiet as possible and slipping from one set of shadows to another, trying to put as much distance as I could between us.

I heard him swearing quietly as he tried to figure out which way I'd gone. For now, I'd eluded him. Should I scream for help?

No. If I screamed, he could find me. And then he could just shoot me, and claim he'd spotted a suspicious person prowling around the Midway.

I decided my first instinct was right. I should keep going farther into the Midway. Maybe I could make him think I was going to take off through the woods and then circle back to the barns.

Or maybe I should take off through the woods for real?

No. Plunkett would know these woods. He'd found Brett's car in them. Maybe he'd even parked it there.

Of course, he knew the Midway, too. But at least thanks to my wandering around this afternoon and evening, so did I.

I called up my mental map of the Midway. And took a few moments to push away all the irrelevant information I'd stored there about which vendors seemed willing to talk about Plunkett's extortion so I could focus on the bare geography. I was in the first of the three lanes of booths that led in a rough diagonal from the merry-go-round, near the gate, to the Ferris wheel at the far end. I was about a third to a half of the way along toward the Ferris wheel. To get back to safety, or at least to the Caerphilly side of the fence, I needed to go to my left, past the merry-go-round to the gate.

But Plunkett knew that. He'd be watching for me. So maybe the safest thing would be to go the long way round. Turn right and keep going down the lanes until I reached the Ferris wheel, then sneak back around on the far side.

I tried to flatten myself against the booth beside me to keep as low a profile as possible while I peered out. I nearly fell into the booth. I realized that it was made of canvas—a canvas skirt around the bottom half, and canvas flaps that rolled down to close off the top. Could I squeeze under the canvas skirt?

It worked. Inside, I breathed a little more easily. Plunkett couldn't spot me for the moment.

I tiptoed over to peer through a slit in the canvas on the gate side of the booth. I couldn't see anything at first. Then I spotted movement. A flashlight flicked on, and I could see that Plunkett was peering into another canvas-sided booth a couple of doors down. Not just peering in, but poking into every corner of the booth with something. A stick. No, from the clang it made when it hit something metal, a crowbar.

"Nowhere to hide, little lady." His voice was low—designed to reach me if I was still nearby, but not to carry beyond the deserted Midway.

The flashlight flicked off.

Okay, it wasn't as if I'd planned to stay in the booth forever. I waited until his flashlight flicked on again, now one booth closer. Then I slipped out the other side of the booth I was in and under the canvas into the next booth.

I managed to traverse three booths this way, but as I was about to duck under the third one, my head met solid wood. Luckily I managed to stop myself with only a muffled thud. I slipped back into the shadow of the next to last booth and peered out.

Thank goodness for the slightly curving layout of the lanes. I could only see about three booths down. Unless Plunkett was doing only the most cursory searches of the booths he came to, I would have gained on him. Had I gained enough to slip across the lane?

No answer to that unless I tried. I took a deep breath and dashed. Could he hear my footsteps? They sounded like thunder to me. As did my breathing. I reached what I hoped was the safety of a booth on the other side of the lane and hid in the shadows.

"It's no use, little lady."

I had to stifle a gasp—he sounded so close. But when I peered out, I saw that he was still several booths away, starting to search another booth—the first booth I'd hidden in.

I waited till he began thrashing about with his crowbar

then slipped toward the rear of the booth beside me. Another booth backed up to it. I kept on past that, and then across the second lane. I didn't stop to get my bearings until I was in the farthest lane, between the last row of booths and the lesser rides that lay on the outskirts of the Midway. The rides didn't offer as much cover, so I stuck to the inner, booth side of that lane.

I ducked under the canvas of a ringtoss booth and tried to come up with a plan. "Escape from Plunkett" had brought me this far, but it wasn't really what you'd call a full-fledged plan. More like an aspiration. And I had a feeling "keep dodging around from booth to booth until dawn arrives or someone comes along to rescue me" wasn't going to work too well. I could get tired. I could get unlucky. Or Plunkett could call in some of his less savory cousins to help him.

I decided to work my way to the Ferris wheel and see if I could do something to make Plunkett think I'd taken off beyond it toward the woods. Plant something, maybe, pretending I'd lost it. Although the only thing I could think of that I might plausibly lose was a shoe. Not a good idea.

I set out toward the Ferris wheel anyway. A pity you could only run it from the ground. I fantasized, for a moment, about having a remote control for the wheel, and whisking myself up to the top, where I could hide behind the iron walls of the passenger cars and laugh down at Plunkett.

Although come to think of it, the cars were probably made of wood, not bulletproof steel.

Then I realized there was something else I could use the Ferris wheel for. A distraction for Plunkett—and maybe a beacon to call for help. If the Ferris wheel started running in the middle of the night, someone would come to check on it, wouldn't they?

First I had to get there. I kept going, slipping from shadow to shadow, flattening myself against the nearest booth if I heard a sound. Once, when I was passing through a gap in the lane, I flattened myself against the ground, and realized, too late, that I'd landed in a sticky puddle of something. Melted snow cone, I hoped.

I finally reached the Ferris wheel and took shelter behind the controls. I took a few deep breaths, then reached over to pull the switch that would set the wheel in motion.

Nothing happened.

Probably because the operator had turned off the power when he left. And padlocked the controls.

Fortunately, I'd been around when my father had decided to learn how to pick locks—just for the fun of it, because he'd been reading too many Donald Westlake caper novels. Since he'd never been particularly good at opening locks even when he had the proper keys, the project would have been a complete failure if he hadn't realized that I was succeeding where he'd failed. Not the sort of thing you want to put on your résumé—"Ability to pick simple locks if given unlimited time"—but it sometimes came in handy.

After what seemed like a small eternity but was probably only five minutes, I heard a satisfying click from the padlock.

By this time, I had no idea how close Plunkett was. Time for decisive action. I flipped the big switch on the wheel's power grid.

A motor chugged into life, and the Ferris wheel lit up the sky.

Also the immediate surroundings. I couldn't see Plunkett nearby, but I knew this would bring him running.

I flipped the switch that turned on the music, and then

the one that set the wheel into motion. Then I sprinted to the shadows of the nearest booth.

I didn't have to worry about my footsteps, or my breathing—they were drowned out by the strident, over-amplified opening chords of Bruce Springsteen's "Born in the U.S.A."

I started working my way along the far side of the last row, keeping careful watch through the gaps between the booths, until I spotted Plunkett running toward the Ferris wheel, gun in hand. Not running very fast, I was pleased to note. He was panting, and clutching slightly at his side. Probably lucky for me that Sheriff Dingle apparently didn't make his officers pass the kind of annual physical fitness qualifications Chief Burke required of the Caerphilly deputies.

I set off jogging in the opposite direction, toward the merry-go-round. I kept hoping someone from the main part of the fair would come over to investigate the Ferris wheel suddenly coming to life.

"Patience," I muttered to myself. "It's only been on a minute or two."

And then suddenly the Ferris wheel was off. No light, no motion, no deafening guitar riffs. Damn.

Would someone still come to investigate? Or would they turn over and go back to sleep, planning to investigate in the morning?

I was nearing the merry-go-round. Should I keep sprinting toward the gate? Or would Plunkett figure out that was my destination?

Maybe I should send up another beacon.

The merry-go-round, I found, wasn't even locked. Again I flipped all the switches. Power, lights, music at full volume, and then the merry-go-round spinning into motion. I nodded with pleasure when "The Carousel Waltz" boomed out.

Much more satisfactory than the Ferris wheel. And a lot closer to the barns. Though I'd feel a lot better if I were even closer to the barns. But I didn't head for the gate—Plunkett would be expecting that. I jogged toward the fence, aiming for somewhere between the new gate and the old.

I was halfway there when I heard Plunkett's footsteps closing in behind me. The idea that at any second a bullet might come whizzing toward me did wonders for my speed.

But Plunkett didn't want to shoot me here. He might hope to get away with it by claiming he'd fired at a prowler, but he'd much rather avoid that. The real danger wasn't a bullet in the back of my head—it was being tackled, knocked unconscious, and dragged out into the woods, where even if anyone heard the shot they'd just think someone was shooting at a squirrel or a grouse or what-ever was in season in September. So the longer I could keep running—

I hit the fence before Plunkett, but he caught up while I was trying to scramble over. He tried to pull me back, but I lunged over the fence and managed to bring the top rail crashing down. We landed in a heap on the other side.

I was opening my mouth to scream when I felt a huge hand clapped over it.

"Shut up," he hissed. "Or I'll— AAAAHHHHH!"

He suddenly let me go and began scuttling away from me. I looked up and saw a set of enormous yellow teeth emerging from a huge, hairy mouth.

"HEEEEEEEEEEE-HAW!"

"Jim-Bob!" I shouted. "Good donkey!"

Jim-Bob trotted past me and began kicking Plunkett

and trying to bite him in between loud heehaws. I wasn't sure whether Jim-Bob was on my side or whether he was avenging some past cruelty Plunkett had performed on him. And I had no idea if he was capable of killing Plunkett or if it was safe to try to intervene or if I even wanted to intervene. I was tired of making decisions.

I jogged to the other end of Jim-Bob's pen, scrambled over the fence, and headed for the nearest barn.

Halfway there I ran into Vern and my brother, Rob.

"What the dickens is going on over in the Midway?" Vern asked.

"Deputy Plunkett is the killer," I said. "And he tried to kill me."

"Where is he now?" Vern asked.

"Over there in the donkey pen." I pointed. "Be careful. Jim-Bob's trying to kick him to death."

"Awesome!" Rob said.

He began trotting toward Jim Bob's pen.

"Who's Jim-Bob?" Vern asked.

"Rob, he has a gun," I called.

"Jim-Bob?" Vern asked.

"Jim-Bob's a donkey," I said. "A four-legged donkey. Plunkett has the gun."

"Roger," he said. I saw him draw his own weapon as he loped after Rob.

Luckily, by the time Rob and Vern got to the pen, Jim-Bob had stopped kicking and was merely standing over Plunkett, heehawing whenever the deputy twitched a muscle. Plunkett was curled up in a ball, whimpering, and his gun had landed safely in a heap of donkey dung at the other side of the pen.

The merry-go-round had moved on to "The Blue Danube."

"Can we get someone to turn that damned thing off?" Apparently Vern wasn't a fan of the waltz.

"I'll do it," I said. "In just a minute. Does either of you have a flashlight?"

Rob handed me his. I jogged over to the fair office and searched around outside the door till I found my cell phone. Then I returned to the donkey pen and took several pictures of Plunkett cowering away from Jim-Bob.

"For the fair Web site," I said aloud, to anyone who cared.

Then I strolled over and shut off the merry-go-round.

"The Blue Danube" disappeared in mid-bar, leaving behind blissful silence.

Well, not quite silence. I could hear sirens in the distance. And shouts from over toward the barns. I could see quite a few lights over in the barns as well.

I realized, suddenly, that my legs had started shaking, and I wasn't sure I trusted them to get me back to the donkey pen.

No reason I had to go back there right now. It was going to be a long night. Or maybe a long morning would be more accurate.

I sat down on the edge of the merry-go-round, against a pole that held a curveting Palomino.

I pulled out my phone and texted Michael. "I'm fine. Back soon. Love you." Just in case he woke and got worried. I turned my phone off and then back on again, so I could look at the screen saver—a laughing photo of Michael and the boys. Then I sat back on the edge of the merry-go-round and took deep breaths and waited for my legs to settle down.

Chapter 36

"I'm fine," I said. "Really."

I tried not to sound cranky, but I'd been telling people I was fine on and off for hours now. Even the chief, although intent on having me tell him every detail of my encounter with Plunkett, had interrupted his interrogation a time or two to ask if I was sure I was all right.

Maybe he didn't believe me. Maybe he was letting me sit here in the fair office, eavesdropping as he wrapped up his investigation, because he thought my knees would buckle again if I tried to leave. Or maybe he approved of my desire to avoid talking to any reporters.

"Are you sure you're all right, dear?" Mother actually touched her hand to my forehead, as if concerned that my frantic middle-of-the-night struggle with a cold-blooded killer might have given me a temperature.

"Dad thinks so," I said. "He gave me a clean bill of health hours ago. About the only thing wrong with me is lack of sleep, but I'm running on adrenaline now, and I don't want to go home until this whole thing is wrapped up."

"You mean it's not wrapped up?" Mother turned to the chief with a slight frown. "I thought you'd already apprehended the perpetrator."

"We have," the chief said. "Perpetrators, actually. It appears likely that in addition to Plunkett, who pulled the trigger, Sheriff Dingle will be charged with conspiracy to commit murder, and Plunkett's cousin, the one who pretended to be the mother of Brett Riordan's child, will be an accessory after the fact."

" 'Appears likely'? You have yet to arrest them?" Mother asked.

"I think the state police will have done that by now," the chief said. "Given the jurisdictional complexities of the case, they're assuming primary responsibility. We're just tying up a few loose ends to assist them. Meg is free to leave any time she wants."

"And I don't want to just yet," I said. "I want to be the first to see those loose ends tied up, not the last."

"As long as you don't overtax yourself." Mother patted my shoulder. "And when you're free, the entire population of the wine pavilion wants you to know that we have some sparkling wine on ice, ready to toast your service to the industry. We'll be standing by to pop the corks whenever you're ready. If you don't feel up to it till tomorrow, that's also fine."

"Tell them thanks," I said. "And I'll see how it goes."

Mother nodded, and sailed out.

"Thank you," I heard her say outside, presumably to someone who was holding the door for her.

The someone came in—Stanley Denton, our Caerphilly-based private investigator.

"Good morning, all," he said. "I came to make my report."

"Report?" I echoed.

"I assumed you were serious when you asked me to check up on Ms. Sedgewick."

"I was," I said. "But—"

"If you were investigating her in connection with the murder—" the chief began.

"I asked him to do it before the murder even took place," I said.

"Day before yesterday, as a matter of fact," Denton added.

"And it was about chicken thefts she was alleged to have committed before she came to Caerphilly," I added. "In someone else's county. I needed to know if she was a danger to the fair."

"All right, all right," the chief said. I was relieved to see that he seemed more amused than annoyed. He indicated one of the folding metal chairs.

Denton sat down and pulled out his notebook.

"Meg called me to ask if I could find out whether Ms. Sedgewick owned any property other than her winery," he said. "Apparently some of the exhibitors suspected that she was stealing their valuable birds and stashing them someplace where no one would think to look for them."

He paused there as if waiting for a reaction. Apparently the chief and I were both equally impatient.

"So, did you find anything?" we asked, almost in unison.

"I did indeed," he said. "Ms. Sedgewick owns a farm outside of Ashville, North Carolina, under her maiden name of Janet Hickenlooper. We found livestock there. And a very disgruntled caretaker. People who have secrets to keep shouldn't treat their staff like dirt."

"Did he spill the beans about the stolen chickens?" I asked.

"The caretaker didn't know anything about stolen chickens," Denton said. "He doesn't like chickens, so he resents that she keeps bringing new batches down to the farm and ordering him to build coops and pens for them. What he really had a lot to say about was Genette's winemaking

operations. Apparently she's not doing too well at growing grapes on her farm."

"I hear everyone had a bad year or two lately," I said.

"She hasn't had a good year since she bought her place,"
Denton said. "She's been regularly buying up grapes and
tanks of grape juice from out of state and having them
shipped to the Ashville farm. Then the caretaker has to
paint over anything that would identify where they really
came from and deliver them to her Virginia farm in the
middle of the night. He says he's pretty sure about ninety
percent of the grapes she used to make her wine came
from out of state. He also hints that her wine's so bad
when she wants to enter a contest, she fills up one of her
bottles with somebody else's wine."

"We need to tell someone about this," I said.

"I already did." Denton smiled as if he'd enjoyed doing
it. "The Virginia Alcoholic Beverage Control Board, whose
rule about what kind of grapes you can use in a Virginia
wine she seems to have completely ignored."

"And that is not an agency you want to trifle with," the
chief said, with satisfaction.

"I also dropped by the wine pavilion here at the fair
just now and had a few words with a couple of people who
are active in the Virginia Winemakers Association. I figured they'd have a vested interest in notifying anyone
who gave her a medal that it might not have been fairly
won."

"I suspect it won't take them too long to do the notifying," I said. "Even with pirated wines she hasn't been doing
too well in wine competitions."

"So I gathered," Denton said. "And she's not too popular with her colleagues, is she? Before I'd even finished

telling them the news, they all started popping corks, pouring me glasses of wine, and toasting me. And you, incidentally, for siccing me on the case."

"Well, that solves one mystery," I said.

"They were also toasting to the return of Fickle Wind—any idea what that is."

"A winery Genette put out of business," I said. "It's coming back?"

"The other winemakers seem to have a plan for that," Denton said. "As far as I could tell, it seems to involve several dozen of them agreeing not to sue her for millions if she sells the vineyard back to its rightful owner for peanuts."

"Mother will be delighted." And I made a silent promise that once Morot got on his feet again, I'd buy a case of Fickle Wind's most expensive wine, as a silent apology for suspecting him. "But getting back to your mission—you didn't find any sign of the stolen chickens?"

"If you mean the Russian Orloffs, no," Denton said. "Nor the Sumatrans."

"Are you sure?" I asked. "I don't mean to be insulting—before I started working with the fair, I couldn't have told one breed of chicken from another."

"I still can't," Denton admitted. "So since I knew sooner or later someone would be asking me that very question, I took the precaution of bringing along a poultry expert when I checked the Ashville property out. Friend of mine who judges chickens at the North Carolina state fair."

"Well done," the chief said.

Denton flipped to a new page in his notebook.

"We didn't find any of the chickens stolen here at the fair," he said. "But according to my friend we found

Minorcas, Cochins, Ko Shamos, Silkies, Malays, Frizzles, Burmese, Lemon Millefleur Sablepoots, Rumpless Tufted Araucanas, and Transylvanian Naked Neck chickens."

"Oh, Horace will be so excited, I said. "About the naked chickens, I mean. He's been reading about them."

"Whatever floats your boat." Denton looked up from his notebook and shook his head. "Not a one of them I'd want to give barnyard space to. Most peculiar collection of poultry I've ever seen in my life. Peculiar and in some cases downright ugly. But it got my friend real excited. And then real mad—seems he figured out some of the birds belonged to a friend of his."

"He recognized the chickens?" The chief sounded skeptical.

"No, he recognized some kind of distinctive leg band the friend puts on his chickens," Denton said. "Guess Genette figured she'd hidden the stolen ones well enough— out of state and all—that she didn't need to worry about prying the ID bands off. Or maybe she didn't notice they were there. According to the caretaker, she doesn't actually go near the chickens—just drops by every week or two to survey her domain and gloat a bit. And the telltale ID bands were on a bunch of chickens with big, fluffy tufts of feathers all over their feet."

"The Sablepoots," I said. "I know someone who had some Lemon Millefleur Sablepoots stolen—by Genette, he thought, although he couldn't prove it. Mr. Stapleton," I added, seeing the chief's frown. "I gave you his card, re-member?"

"Yes, that's his name," Denton said. "The guy with the distinctive ID bands."

"And you can find him in the wine tent," I added.

The chief nodded.

"I'll check with him," the chief said. "And we should let the Virginia State Police know as soon as possible about her other property—they'll need to liaise with their counterparts in North Carolina."

"And while all this is fascinating," I said. "And we're grateful to you for uncovering it, we still don't know what Genette did with the Orloffs and Sumatrans."

"Genette didn't do anything with them," said a new voice.

We all looked up to see Vern Shiffley standing in the doorway.

"Do you know who did?" the chief asked.

Instead of answering, Vern turned to someone outside.

"Bring those on in here," he said.

Two more deputies came in, each carrying a small cage with a pair of chickens in it.

"That's them!" I said. "The Sumatrans and the Orloffs."

"Where did you find them?" the chief asked.

"I went along when the state police searched Plunkett's farm," Vern said. "Found these in his barn. I studied up on what the missing chickens looked like, so I was pretty sure these were the ones. We also found a sledgehammer splattered with pumpkin juice nearby, and a pair of pumpkin-stained overalls dumped in his laundry room. I think we caught us a pumpkin-smashing, quilt-spoiling chicken thief!"

"The state police okay with you bringing these back to the owners?" the chief asked. "They don't need them as evidence?"

"They're okay with returning the chickens after their owners have identified them," Vern said. "A trooper just went over to fetch the owners. We thought we'd do the official ID in your office. And here they come."

Vern stepped aside, making way for Mr. Beamish and the black-clad Bonnevilles. A tall, stern-looking state trooper brought up the rear.

"It's Anton! And Anna!" Mrs. Bonneville threw her arms around the cage containing the Orloffs.

"I never thought I'd see this day," Mr. Bonneville said. He put one arm around his wife and, with the other hand, fumbled for his pocket handkerchief.

Anna and Anton clucked excitedly. I couldn't really tell if they were happy to see their owners again or just over-excited by having someone throw her arms around their cage, but at least they didn't sound upset.

"Yes." Mr. Beamish's manner was more quiet, but in his own way he seemed just as moved. "Those are my Suma-trans. I can't thank you enough."

He was looking at me.

"Vern found them," I said.

"Me and the state police," Vern said. "But we never would have known where to look if Meg hadn't collared that lowlife Plunkett."

The door opened again and Randall stepped in.

"I've found her," he said into his phone. "Meg, I need a minute of your time."

"We're a little busy here," the chief said. "Is it important?"

"Very." Randall turned to me. "Are you in favor of terminating our agreement with Clay County and hosting the entire Un-fair in Caerphilly County?"

"For next year?" I asked. "Absolutely."

"And the rest of this year, too," Randall said. "I've been on the phone with all the other Un-fair board members already, and if you're in favor, it's unanimous. I've got people standing by to start the move as soon as you cast your vote and the chief gives the okay."

"Sounds great to me," I said.

"Provided you leave the area around the murder scene untouched, I see no reason to delay the move," the chief said.

"It's a go," Randall said into the phone and hung up. "Between the Shiffley Construction Company and the Shiffley Moving Company, we've got a pretty good crew. And all the Midway people are up for it. And we've got a lot of exhibitor volunteers. Especially the chicken farmers and winemakers. But it's a big job. Chief, can you release Meg to handle a few little things for me? I'd like to get over and supervise."

"Also fine with me," the chief said.

"What kind of things?" I was always suspicious when Randall tried to delegate "a few little things."

"Well, for one thing, we need to organize a shuttle service from our overflow parking areas," Randall said.

"Overflow parking areas?" I echoed. "We've never even filled the parking areas we've got."

"We will today," Randall said. "People started lining up outside the ticket office hours ago, and that online ticket sale thing you had us set up went wild this morning. Parking lot's close to full already, so I've arranged overflow at a couple of farms along the road from town. And you know my cousin Norbert—the one who runs all those charter busses to Atlantic City? I've got him bringing over every bus and van he can round up. But someone needs to pull it all together."

"Roger." I was already scribbling in my notebook. "I guess this answers my question about whether the murders and chicken thefts are going to ruin the fair."

"They might have if you hadn't solved them all so quickly and dramatically," Randall said. "Which reminds me—I thought you might like to represent the fair management at a couple of ribbon presentations. Biggest pumpkin, for example. After all the time I spent convincing the judges to declare that poor kid's smashed pumpkin eligible, I want someone from management there to make sure they don't change their minds at the last minute."

"How'd the kid do, anyway?" I asked.

"Came in fifth," Randall said. "He thinks he might have made it as high as third if Plunkett hadn't smashed his pumpkin. And he's determined to come back even stronger next year."

"Good," I said. "We want him going home energized and determined, not demoralized. I'll be there."

"Oh, and someone from the Guinness Book of Records might be calling you," Randall went on. "There's no shame losing to this year's first-place winner. It's well over a ton and might be a contender for the new world record. They're going to try to send someone by to verify it today or tomorrow."

"Awesome." I scribbled more notes. "Any word on the quilt cleanup?"

"I hear Daphne worked her usual magic," Randall said. "The judging's this afternoon, so we'll find out soon enough if it did the trick. We might want to have someone show up there as well."

"Speaking of judging, we need to get Anton and Anna ready, now that they're back." Mr. Bonneville picked up the cage containing the Orloffs. "The bantam event is at ten."

Mrs. Bonneville walked over and took both my hands in hers.

"Thank you," she said. "You have no idea how much this means to us."

With that, they left.

"But you can start getting an idea whenever you want," Mr. Beamish said. "Just tell me when you want your Sumatrans delivered. Eggs, chicks, young birds—you name it."

With that he left.

"You're going into the chicken business?" the chief asked.

"Business, no," I said. "We're going to expand our hobby farming to include a few chickens."

He nodded.

"Dangerous, having this fair in our backyard," he said. "Minerva's got her heart set on some chickens. She likes the idea of having fresh eggs for the grandkids."

"We can build you a coop if you want, Chief," Randall said. "Or a pen for the llama, if you're going ahead with that."

"Llama?" The chief sounded puzzled.

"Meg." Randall turned to me. "I'll send a few men over next week to make sure the coops and pens you already have are ready for your chickens. It's the least we can do after all you've done for the fair. I'm off to supervise—I'll let you know if I think of anything else that needs doing."

He strolled out.

"We should get back to it," Vern said. "We have a lead on a possible witness to the theft of the Sumatrans."

"And we've put a rush on processing the evidence you've already delivered to the crime lab," the state trooper added to the chief.

"Keep me posted," the chief said.

Vern and the trooper headed for the door.

As they left, they let someone else in.

"Grand Central Station," the chief muttered.

I was starting to agree, but then realized I was glad to see this new arrival.

"Molly!" I said. "Did you hear the news?"

"I'm so glad you're all right," she said, giving me a fierce hug.

"And that we found out who really killed Brett," I said.

Molly looked over at the chief.

"Yes," he said. "We're satisfied that you had nothing to do with your late husband's murder. I'm sorry for any additional stress our investigation caused at what I'm sure was already a difficult time."

"You were doing your job," she said. "And I can understand why you suspected me."

"So what's the prognosis with your farm?" I asked.

"I think one way or another I'll manage to keep it," she said. "Thanks in no small part to you and your family."

"Not sure what help I was," I said. "It's not as if you need a divorce lawyer anymore."

"No, but the guy your mother recommended also does family property law, and he can represent me if anyone tries to claim a part of the farm."

"Like Brett's family," I suggested.

"Precisely," she said. "And I bet they will. And my lawyer says they won't have a leg to stand on."

"Of course, paying the lawyer to get rid of them will take money," I said.

"And paying the attorney I had to hire when I was arrested," she said. "Not to mention settling Brett's debts. Most of which were incurred while he was living the high life with Genette, so it doesn't seem quite fair that I should be the one to pay them, but trying to fight it would take more money than just paying them. Between one thing and another, I'm going to have a lot of expenses in the near future, so thank goodness your brother came up with such a good idea."

"Rob had a good idea?" I said. "I mean, he has lots of them, but most of them involve shooting aliens or driving race cars through lava, or whatever else people do in his company's video games."

"Apparently he's been learning a lot about the financial world while running his company," Molly said.

I nodded, and tried not to look alarmed. The last time Rob had taken an interest in the financial side of Mutant Wizards, his computer gaming company, his treasurer had nearly had a nervous breakdown trying to undo his meddling.

"It all started because your cousin Rose Noire sold all the cheese I'd brought," she said. "So I had nothing left to sell—what a great problem to have! And she said some people were asking if they could place an order to be shipped later, which sounded good to me, but we didn't want to take more orders than I could fill in the next few weeks. So while I was figuring out how much cheese I had at home and how much I could have ready within the next month or so, your brother was there, and that was when he had his idea."

"And what was the idea?" I asked. I was hoping it wouldn't be something so stupid that I had to try talking her out of it.

"He suggested I sell cheese futures," Molly said. "People pay up front to have cheese mailed to them over the next several years. If someone pays a hundred dollars up front, for example, they are entitled to get fifty dollars' worth of cheese each year for the next three years."

"That actually sounds rather practical," the chief said.

I nodded agreement.

"It's better than practical," Molly said. "It's brilliant! I get the money I need to pay all my bills—and probably enough to make some improvements to the farm that will let me produce more cheese at a lower unit cost, so fulfilling all those orders will be a breeze. Everybody wins."

"It does sound like a win-win," I said.

"And speaking of winning," Molly said. "Wish me luck—the cheese judging is this morning. At ten, in fact, so I should run."

"Is it almost ten?" I started flipping through my notebook for my schedule. "I think there's someplace I should be at ten."

The door opened.

"Mommy!" It was Jamie. "Daddy says come help Grouchy and Chicky win their ribbons."

Outside, I could see Michael and Josh, each holding a llama halter. Groucho and Chico had been washed and brushed and were holding their heads high as if well aware that they were the two handsomest llamas at the fair.

"I knew there was something I should be doing," I said. "The llama conformation contest is also at ten. Chief, if that guy shows up here with the buses before it's over, give Randall a call. I'm going to go watch our llamas win their ribbons."